MOCK APPLE ALIBI

MOCK APPLE ALIBI

AUNTIE CLEM'S BAKERY COZY MYSTERIES
BOOK TWENTY-FIVE

P.D. WORKMAN

ISBN: 9781774688762 (KDP Paperback)
ISBN: 9781774688779 (KDP Hardcover)
ISBN: 9781774688793 (Lulu Paperback)
ISBN: 9781774688786 (Large Print)
ISBN: 9781774688809 (Digital)
ISBN: 9781774688816 (Auto-narrated audiobook)

ALSO BY P.D. WORKMAN

FIND MORE BOOKS AT PDWORKMAN.COM

Auntie Clem's Bakery

Culinary & Pet Cozy Mysteries

Gluten-Free Murder

Dairy-Free Death

Allergen-Free Assignation

Witch-Free Halloween (Halloween Short)

Canine-Free Christmas Caper (Christmas Short)

Stirring Up Murder

Brewing Death

Coup de Glace

Sour Cherry Turnover

Apple-achian Treasure

Vegan Baked Alaska

Muffins Masks Murder

Tai Chi and Chai Tea

Santa Shortbread

Cold as Ice Cream

Changing Fortune Cookies

Hot on the Trail Mix

Fateful Plateful

Cut Out Cookie

On the Slab Pie

Wedding Cake Crush

A Waffle Death

Murder Meringue Pie

A Fowl Play on Christmas Day (Christmas crossover story)

Cinn-Full Secrets

Muffin to Lose

Custard Cream Conspiracy

Mock Apple Alibi

Chocolate Eclairvoyant (Coming Soon)

Quiche Me Goodbye (Coming Soon)

Recipes from Auntie Clem's Bakery

Kenzie Kirsch Medical Thrillers

Unlawful Harvest

Doctored Death

Dosed to Death

Gentle Angel

Rushin' Death

Posed for Death

Death of a Corpse

Endowed with Death

Shattered to Death

Captured in Death

Currying Death

Healed to Death

Death's Charm

Bleeding Hearts Valley Thrillers

An Abrupt Departure

AND MORE AT PDWORKMAN.COM

In the memory of those who are absent

CHAPTER 1

*E*verything was quiet in Bald Eagle Falls. Erin stood at the front window of Auntie Clem's Bakery, looking out at Main Street. Trees and flowers bloomed along the road. A gentle breeze carried the light scent of dogwood into the bakery.

It was too quiet.

The town looked just as it had the first time she had rolled into town to claim her inheritance from Clementine after an absence of twenty years. When her mother had taken her away from Bald Eagle Falls that fateful night, Erin had not had any idea that it was the last time she would see the town until she was an adult. Driving by the charming storefronts with their colorful sunshade canopies, she had thought that it was just a trip like any other. They were going into the city. Maybe for shopping or visiting a friend; she hadn't really had any idea then. Her parents were not in the habit of consulting with her about their plans.

Returning to Bald Eagle Falls had been like coming home, even though it had never been her permanent home. Just where they visited Aunt Clementine and crashed at her place for a while. Much like they had crashed with many other friends and relatives during Erin's short lifetime, living a somewhat nomadic existence as her parents moved from one short-term job to another.

Erin had loved staying with Clementine and going with her to work in what had then been a tea shop. Erin had been a mature child and enjoyed helping Clementine with the tea orders and baking cookies, but she must have gotten underfoot sometimes. She couldn't imagine having a seven-year-old working alongside her at Auntie Clem's Bakery. But Clementine had always been kind and patient with her and Erin couldn't remember her ever getting angry or impatient about her mistakes or clumsiness.

Main Street seemed to be frozen in time. The cars and clothing styles had changed. Some of the storefronts had changed. Auntie Clem's was now across the street from the storefront she had inherited from Clementine. But in other ways, it looked and felt just the way it had when Erin had been there twenty years before.

"Is everything okay?" Harold asked. He leaned on the top of the display case, his lanky teenage body relaxed, acne-pocked face curious.

"It's too quiet," Erin said, looking up and down the street again. "I don't like it."

"You're worried about not getting enough business?" Harold asked.

"No…" There was a momentary lull in the arrival of customers, but Erin knew it would pick up again as people left work and started to think about what they wanted to make for supper, or for breakfast or lunch the next day. "It isn't customers I am worried about. It's… I was expecting everything to change. I thought that with Willie claiming leadership of the Dyson clan, there would be a lot of… unrest."

"You're worried that there *isn't* a gang war going on in front of the store?" Vic asked as she came out of the kitchen with a tray of muffins. "You were hoping for gunplay?" As usual, her long blond hair was neatly tucked away in a baker's hat, and Erin's shorter dark hair was forever escaping bobby pins and getting in her face.

"No!" Erin's cheeks got hot. If anyone should be worried, it was Vic. She was the one who had belonged to the opposing clan, born into the Jackson family, and whose romantic partner had just claimed leadership of the Dysons.

Maybe because Vic had already been disowned by the Jackson family for being transgender, she thought she was safe from anyone targeting her for her choice of partner. Or maybe she felt that because Willie was now the leader of the Dysons, no one would dare lay a finger on her.

But she was the one who had the most to worry about. The Jacksons could easily target her because she was important to Willie. Or because she had turned traitor and joined the Dysons— even though she hadn't. Vic didn't want anything to do with either clan. Raised to hate and fear the Dysons, she had been pretty upset when she had first found out that Willie had neglected to mention his history with the clan to her. It had nearly broken them up for good. But Vic had eventually accepted that Willie had done his time as a Dyson soldier and wasn't involved in clan business anymore.

Until now. Erin had expected her young employee to blow up when Willie accepted leadership of the clan, even though the only reason he had done it was to prevent Erin and her sweetheart, Officer Terry Piper, from being killed. But Vic hadn't had much to say about Willie's claim on the leadership of the Dyson family as a direct descendant of Hannah Dyson.

"Why aren't you worried?" Erin asked Vic. "Aren't you concerned about Dyson members gunning for Willie because they don't like someone who has previously turned his back on the clan suddenly taking over? Or about someone coming after *you* to hurt him?"

Vic was silent as she arranged muffins in the display case with practiced ease. She looked back over her shoulder at Harold. "Shouldn't you be doing the washing up back there?"

Harold straightened up and nodded, agreeing that he should get back to his duties.

"Yes, Miss Victoria." He walked through the door into the kitchen to do as he was told.

"Of course I'm worried," Vic admitted. "I know that sooner or later, something is going to happen." She looked out the front window, scanning up and down the street to reassure herself, as

Erin had, that it was still quiet. "But I don't think there is any point in scaring Harold about it. Or saying anything to any of the customers. For now, just… wait…"

"Pretend there is nothing to be worried about?"

"What good is it going to do to fuss about it?" Vic challenged. "Is that going to stop it from happening? Is it going to make you feel better? Make you better prepared?"

"Well, no," Erin admitted. Vic was barely out of her teens, but she had been raised with clan warfare and politics, and had wisdom beyond her years as a result. "Although, if there is something I can do to be better prepared for what's coming… I would like to do it."

Vic nodded her agreement and understanding. "We'll talk about that later. For now, since there are no customers, why don't we take the opportunity to talk about your mock apple pie?"

She said it as she turned around and walked back into the kitchen, raising her voice so that Erin could still hear her with her back turned.

Erin left her place at the window. Vic was right, of course. Standing around looking out the window, worrying when something terrible was going to happen, wouldn't do anything but give her an ulcer and keep her from her work. The actual running of the bakery was her life's work. A clan war wasn't going to change that. No matter what happened, people would still need to buy bread. The clans didn't have any reason to target the bakery. It would stay open and keep running no matter which clan had the upper hand in their ongoing, generations-long feud.

"What exactly *is* a mock apple pie?" Harold was asking as Erin followed Vic into the kitchen.

"It is an apple pie made without apples," Vic told him. She took a binder out of the niche under the upper cabinets where they stored several binders of information on procedures, ingredients, and vendors. The slim binder contained copies of the recipes that had been in the vintage recipe book published by the Bald Eagle Falls Women's League, the original of which was no longer in Erin's possession.

Vic flipped through the binder to find the recipe for mock apple pie.

"It doesn't have apples in it," Harold repeated doubtfully.

"Nope. No apples."

"Why would anyone make apple pie without apples?"

"Because sometimes, historically, apples were very expensive to ship across the country and spoiled faster than something like crackers, which could sit on the shelf for months."

"Crackers?"

"Ritz crackers. There was even a recipe on the back of the cracker box."

Harold looked at Vic, his brows furrowed, then turned to Erin, waiting for her to tell him it was all just a joke.

"It's true," Erin said. "During the depression and wartime, women made apple pie with Ritz crackers."

"And no apples," he said.

"And no apples."

Harold shook his head like it was the most bizarre thing he had ever heard, and Erin had to agree with him. When she had first heard of mock apple pie, she hadn't believed it either. But she had talked to several women who had eaten it and assured her it was a fairly convincing fake.

"It has to do with the spices," she told Harold, "and lemon juice for tartness. Apparently, the way you prepare the crackers in the filling gives them a texture that is like cooked apples."

Harold shook his head slowly. "Ain't that something!" he declared. "And how are you going to make gluten-free mock apple pie? Ritz crackers are not gluten-free, and if you get the gluten-free crackers, won't they just dissolve without any gluten to hold them together?"

Vic turned and looked at Erin, raising her brows. They'd already had this discussion, and Erin had been researching different approaches to the problem. Make her own gluten-free crackers that would stay together better? She was sure that the texture still wouldn't be right.

"Okay," Erin got closer to Harold and Vic so that it was easier to hold the conversation without raised voices and the possibility of anyone who came into the bakery overhearing them. "I've been working on it, and I have a few ideas about the direction to go…"

CHAPTER 2

The bells over the door jingled and Erin hurried out to the front to greet her customer. It was a face that she didn't recognize, which instantly sent her heart racing. The twenty-something baby-faced young man did not look dangerous, but as with mock apple pie, looks could be deceiving. Young men were recruited as street-level soldiers in both clans, and this fresh-faced stranger could be there looking for trouble. Plenty of people knew Willie's girlfriend worked at the bakery.

Erin forced a smile to her lips and inquired pleasantly. "Welcome to Auntie Clem's Bakery. How can I help you?"

The man pulled something out of his pocket, and for an instant, the sun's reflection off a metallic surface convinced her it was a gun. But before she could react, the young man held a phone out in front of him, and the shutter-click whir told Erin that he had snapped a picture of her. She kept her smile steady.

The customer stepped up to the display case and scanned the rows. The camera tipped Erin off as to what he was looking for.

"Morning sunshine muffins?" she guessed.

His face lit up. "Yes, how did you know?"

The late Gerald Montgomery's social media followers were still making pilgrimages to Bald Eagle Falls to eat the last thing he had sampled before his death.

It still bothered Erin that the strawberry compote surprise at the center of the morning sunshine muffins had given Montgomery an anaphylactic reaction that had killed him within minutes. But she wasn't about to stop making them as a result. Not when people traveled across the country and around the world just for the chance to eat one of the muffins.

She took a muffin from the display case and placed it on one of the garish gold paper plates they now stocked for just such an occasion. If people were going to make the purchase of a morning sunshine muffin a social media event, Erin was going to get as much mileage as she could from it. She inserted a toothpick mounted with the words *Auntie Clem's Bakery* into the top of the muffin. She set it in the best position for the Instagrammer to take pictures from the most advantageous angles.

He snapped a few more pictures, but as the young man reached out to take it, Erin removed it from the top of the display case and put it on the counter beside the till. "Payment before tasting," she informed him, and rang it up. He paid with a twenty-dollar bill and a smile, telling her to keep the change. Erin put the change into the tip jar to be divided among the employees.

He recorded himself taking a big bite of the infamous muffin, pausing a dramatic moment to see if it would kill him, then declaring how delicious it was and giving a thumbs-up and a challenge to his followers to make the trip to Bald Eagle Falls in Tennessee to taste it for themselves.

Erin smiled and nodded and saw the customer out the door. As much as she disliked the morbidness of people's fascination with the "murder muffins," she couldn't deny that she made a very good profit on them—this latest customer was not the first to give her twenty dollars, or even more, for a single muffin—and the muffins attracted a lot of customers to Auntie Clem's that would not otherwise have even been in the vicinity. They often stayed at the bed and breakfast and came back again to sample her other wares.

"Erin, have you heard anything from Charley?"

Erin turned to look at Vic, who was standing in the doorway of the kitchen, frowning.

"Uh, no, I haven't heard anything." Erin looked at the clock on the wall. Charley was on the afternoon shift and should have been there twenty minutes ago. "She must have slept in. Can you give her a call?"

"I already have. There's no answer."

"Oh, good grief," Erin snapped. She wasn't irritated at Vic, but at Charley. Her half-sister had been a much more reliable employee than Erin had expected her to be, but occasionally she still flaked out and didn't show up on time for her shifts. They only scheduled her for the afternoon shift so she could sleep until noon and still get there in time. If they were really stuck for help with the early morning time slot, Charley would arrive at the end of her day, after partying or whatever else she did past midnight, and would put in a few hours before going home and going to bed.

Erin wanted to gripe about this not being a good day for Charley not to show up for work, but in truth, it wasn't any worse than any other day; she was just tense and wound up.

That was just Charley. She would end up calling them at three o'clock, embarrassed that she had slept in and asking whether they needed her to help with the last few hours.

Erin relieved her stress by swearing quietly under her breath, and she addressed Vic in a calm, cool voice. "Would you see whether Bella is free? I think she only has morning classes on Wednesday."

"Sure," Vic agreed. "No problem."

She returned to the kitchen. The bells tinkled and Erin turned her attention back to her new customer. Mary Lou usually came either first thing in the morning when the bakery opened or at the end, just before Erin locked the doors; it was unusual for her to be there in the early afternoon. Mary Lou worked down the street at the General Store, so she usually worked the rest of the day and didn't come to the bakery on her break, if she took one.

"Hi, Mary Lou," Erin greeted her warmly. "It's nice to see you."

"Good afternoon," Mary Lou returned. She smoothed her

unwrinkled pantsuit over her hips and perused the display case. "I only have a minute, but I just found out that Cam will be coming for supper and wanted to make sure I had something nice for dessert. I think maybe... a variety of cookies?" she suggested, with slight frown lines between her eyes. "Yes... a selection of twelve cookies. Then everyone can be sure to have one of their favorites."

"Sure," Erin agreed. She got out a box and selected several different kinds of cookies for the Cox men. Mary Lou's husband, Roger, and sons Joshua and Campbell, would enjoy the sweets. However, as this order was over and above Mary Lou's usual carefully-budgeted order, she worried it would strain the family's meager finances. "Can I unload some day-old goods on you?" she asked. "My freezer is full to bursting, and I'm going to have to start throwing stuff in the garbage. Maybe... some rolls for dinner tonight, bagels for breakfast? I know you always plan your menu beforehand, but if you could see your way to taking some off my hands, that would be helpful. Maybe Cam will stay over for breakfast?"

Mary Lou glanced over her shoulder to verify that she was the only customer in the store and none of her friends would hear about her accepting charity. Then she gave a quick nod. "Rolls and bagels would be lovely," she agreed.

"And maybe a couple of pizza shells?" Erin suggested, "Just in case Cam is looking for a midnight snack?"

"Okay," Mary Lou agreed. "Thank you, Erin."

"I'll just be a minute," Erin promised, and hurried into the kitchen to grab what she had promised from the day-old freezer. She wanted to make sure she handed it to Mary Lou and gave her a chance to get out of the store before anyone else arrived. Returning to the front, she bagged everything and rang up the cookie order at the till.

"You know you can always pop in the back door if you know of anyone who needs help," Erin reminded Mary Lou tactfully. "We always have day-old available, no questions asked."

"Of course," Mary Lou agreed with a nod. "You are very generous for caring for the community as you do."

She counted out change to pay her bill to the penny, and then was gone, headed back to the General Store.

Bella came in the front door just as Mary Lou left, turning her head to look at Mary Lou's retreating figure. She knew Mary Lou's schedule as well as Erin and was obviously surprised to see her.

"I thought I saw Campbell earlier," she said to Erin. "I guess that *was* him, and Mary Lou needed a little something extra for supper tonight."

"You guess correctly," Erin confirmed. "Thank you for coming in. I don't know what happened to Charley."

"Sure, no problem. Luckily, I was in town already, so getting here didn't take long."

Bella and her mother lived on a farm outside Bald Eagle Falls, and it would have taken her at least another half hour to get in if she'd not already been there.

"I appreciate you being able to drop everything to help us." Erin sighed. She moved back to give Bella room to pass her so she could wash up and get her apron on. Erin poked her head into the kitchen to talk to Vic. "Did Harold get on his way already?"

Vic nodded. She looked at her watch. "He should have made it back to school in time."

Both Harold and Bella were still in school, and worked around their class schedules. Harold had relief time for work experience some mornings, and Bella had organized her class schedule to give herself afternoons off a couple of times a week. Both were able to put some time in after school dismissed or on weekends. Erin enjoyed the younger employees' energy and interest level. Bella was a business student and hoped to run her own business after college. Not a bakery, but she hadn't yet decided what kind of a business it would be.

"Great. We're good for this afternoon, then."

CHAPTER 3

Charley did not call in when she woke up in the afternoon as Erin had been expecting. Vic tried to reach her a couple of times as the afternoon wore on, and Erin even called her once or twice. But all they got was crickets. No answer, no apology.

At first, Erin was irritated. Then angry. But by the time they closed the doors at Auntie Clem's, her irritation had turned into worry. It was not unheard of for Charley to get her schedule mixed up or to sleep in, but to go all afternoon without answering her phone *was* unusual. They went through their closing checklists as quickly as possible, and then Erin and Vic got in the yellow VW bug to drive to Charley's house and make sure she was okay.

"You don't think there is anything wrong, do you?" Erin asked anxiously as she drove toward Charley's house.

"Well, you know Charley," Vic said with a laugh. "She's probably just fine. Had a bad night for one reason or another. Partying too hard."

"Yeah," Erin agreed. That was what she wanted to think. She certainly didn't want to believe anything had happened to her half-sister. "That's probably all it is."

Vic shifted in her seat and readjusted her clothing. "About being prepared for what is coming…"

Erin glanced over at her in confusion, then remembered the beginning of their discussion at Auntie Clem's. "Oh. With the clans?"

Vic nodded. "With the clans. And any other possible problems. I know what you've said before about carrying a gun…"

"I'm *not* going to carry a gun," Erin insisted. They'd had enough discussions about it in the past. Vic knew very well that Erin didn't want anything to do with guns.

If Erin carried a gun, then she would have to be willing to use it, and she didn't know how she could ever shoot at a person, dangerous or not. If she accepted the need to do so, then she would have to train and practice shooting, because just pulling the trigger without knowing what she was doing was not a good idea and would likely get someone she knew hurt, if not get herself killed. She knew that women could carry guns just as well as men and be as good as or better than their male counterparts in accuracy. Still, she just couldn't get over her discomfort around guns.

Most of the time, she could forget that Vic carried a gun, since it was out of sight in a concealed holster. And, of course, Terry carried one as a law enforcement officer. Both of them had protected Erin on more than one occasion. But there were some times when guns were just not the solution or would even escalate the trouble.

Erin rubbed her forehead, shaking her head. "I'm not going to carry a gun," she repeated.

"Even knowing that anyone could walk into Auntie Clem's and pull one?" Vic challenged.

"That hasn't changed. Of course, I know that."

"And you don't think it is more likely to happen now that… now with this clan stuff?"

"I know… but someone coming into the bakery? Why would they?"

Erin tried to push out of her mind how she had reacted when the young Instagrammer had shown up unexpectedly and pulled out his phone, scaring Erin when she thought for a split-second that it was a weapon. Obviously, she knew in the back of her mind that it was a possibility. And she knew that Vic was a potential target for someone who thought that a Dyson and a Jackson should not have anything to do with each other.

"You never know who might show up," Vic answered, "If they wanted to target... one of us, and didn't want to catch us at home where there might be other guns around, then the next most likely place to confront us would be at the bakery. Especially early in the morning when it is still dark and no one else is around. Or coming to the back door for day-old bread..."

Considering some of their other experiences at the bakery, Erin couldn't deny the possibility.

"I just... don't think I could do it." She glanced aside at Vic. "Can you really picture me carrying a gun? And pulling it out and using it on someone?" Erin shook her head at the thought of it.

Vic giggled. "No. I mean, I can picture it, but it's so ridiculous, it makes me laugh."

Erin nodded. "Exactly. Like giving a toddler a pen and expecting them to write a book."

Vic snickered at that. Erin reached Charley's house and pulled over to the curb. They both looked at the house, trying to assess whether Charley was home and what she was doing. Erin didn't see any lights or movement inside.

"You don't suppose she took a vacation without telling us, do you?" Erin asked.

Vic shrugged. "She could. And with the clans being so volatile right now, it would be a good time to be somewhere else."

Erin nodded. She wondered briefly if Vic had thought about being somewhere else, but didn't ask. She probably didn't want to know the answer to that question. Of course Vic had considered her options and what she might have to defend herself against. Of course, she had considered whether she should just disappear until everything blew over. But how could she leave Willie behind to face it all on his own? Even if Vic disapproved of what he had done and his renewed involvement with the Dyson clan, could she really leave him alone?

"Well, let's see if she's here," Erin said, straightening her shoulders. She opened her door and stepped out. She walked determinedly up the sidewalk and pressed the bell firmly. She heard Vic trailing her. While they stood on the front steps, they both looked around, for anyone on the street who might be watching them, any movement inside the house or other sign that Charley was home.

After a minute, Erin knocked sharply on the door and called out to her. "Charley? Are you home? Wake up. It's Erin. Come to the door."

They waited again. There was no sound at all from the house. Erin knocked once more.

"I don't think she's home," Vic said with a shrug.

"Maybe. Or maybe something happened to her. What if she is sick or overdosed or something? I can't just leave without being sure."

"Do you have a key?" Vic tilted her head slightly, looking at the doorknob and lock on the door. Erin had already assessed it herself to evaluate how difficult it would have been for someone from one of the clans to break in without actually breaking the door or doorframe. A spring lock on the handle. A basic, single-action deadbolt that needed only a pick, tension wrench, and a little patience to tease open. Charley didn't have a burglar alarm, unless she had acquired one recently.

"Key," she said, holding up her keychain with Charley's house key selected. In case she needed to feed Iggy, the chameleon. Though she hated anything creepy-crawly and the fact that the chameleon could roll his eyes in different directions independently freaked her out.

She inserted the key in the lock and turned it. The bolt was not engaged. She inserted the key into the handle lock and unlocked it. She opened the door quietly, listening closely for anything indicating the house was occupied, either by Charley or someone with nefarious plans.

There was no sound. If it had been a mystery movie on TV instead of real life, there might have been a teakettle whistling, water running, or loud music playing to ramp up tension and inform the viewer that the sleuths were about to find something shocking and distressing. Maybe the silence was good. No dead body to find.

Erin took a steadying breath and stepped into the house. Vic followed close behind. Erin looked around the living room, but there was no body. Nothing seemed out of place. Of course, Charley was messy, so someone who didn't know her might think the room had been tossed, but Erin knew the difference.

Dirty glasses, dishes, and cutlery around the room were not evidence that Charley had entertained several people, but just several days' worth of meals eaten in front of the TV. DVD cases and storage cubes scattered around on the floor were not evidence that someone had been going through her possessions looking for something; it was just that Charley had not put things away after using them. Even the one seat cushion removed from the couch and lying on the floor did not mean that someone had been searching the couch for something that had been hidden, just that Charley had been searching for the keys or phone she had dropped while sitting on the couch and hadn't bothered to put it back in place.

It was messy, but not the disaster area it had been in the early days after Charley's boyfriend had been killed and she had been trying to reopen the Bake Shoppe. Erin and Terry had found Charley there in a terrible mess. Emotional as well as physical. But this time, there was no sign that Charley had been drinking excessively. Just that she didn't concern herself with keeping her Bald Eagle Falls home tidy as she had her Moose River apartment. Erin had been startled at the difference between the two. But maybe in Moose River, she had kept it clean so her boyfriend could be comfortable seeing her there, or maybe her adoptive mom had been by every so often to tidy things up. Or maybe she'd had a cleaning lady.

Erin forced herself to go on. They couldn't tell anything from the living room. Charley might be passed out in the bedroom. Or she might be out. There was no way to know without a thorough look around.

Charley's bed was unmade, but there was no telling how long it had been that way and if Charley normally made it every day. There was no sign of her in the bedroom, bathroom, or kitchen. Looking into Iggy's enclosure and trying not to see anything crawly, Erin observed that enough crickets were jumping around to keep him happy for a few days.

Erin breathed a sigh of relief when they had checked each room. Despite the fact that there was no kettle whistling, she had still been worried that they might find out that Charley had been attacked or had taken her own life, too upset to face the impending clan war when she had family and friends on both sides.

"Well, what do you think?" Vic asked, looking around. "I don't see a note or anything that indicates where she has gone or how long she plans to be."

"Would you leave a note behind to tell everyone where you had gone? If you were running away from something?"

"Nope," Vic agreed.

They looked deeper. There was food in the fridge, including milk that had passed its best-before date. There was no sign of Charley's phone or purse, but also no obvious indications that she had packed a suitcase. Erin figured that if Charley had been packing, there would have been a lot more outfits discarded on the floor and bed. There was a toothbrush, toothpaste, and makeup in the bathroom, but no telling whether those were the only ones she had or whether she kept a separate travel case already stocked with those items.

"What do you think?" Erin asked Vic.

Vic grimaced and shook her head. "I don't know. It doesn't feel like she's been gone for a long time. She might have just made a trip into the city. Maybe for the day, or maybe for a few days. I don't see a calendar where she writes down her shifts, so they must be on her phone, and she might have forgotten to write down today's shift or accidentally put it on the wrong day."

"Yeah."

"There's no sign that anything happened to her," Vic tried to reassure Erin.

There was no blood, no sign of a struggle except Charley's

constant battle with entropy. Nothing that Erin could point to as a sign that Charley had been attacked, threatened, or stalked. Erin blew out her breath.

"I guess… maybe she's just gone to the city or something. There's no sign of her car."

"So we just wait?" Vic suggested. "See if she shows up for her next shift?"

"We can't really report her as missing. There's no evidence that she is."

"Not yet," Vic agreed.

"So I guess… Yeah. We just lock it back up and hope she shows up. She probably will. She just missed one shift. It isn't the end of the world."

Erin knew it sounded like she was trying to convince herself.

Because she was.

A tight ball of anxiety in her stomach told her that something was wrong, but she couldn't tie it to a single piece of evidence.

She pulled out her phone and tried again to call Charley. Somewhere in the back of her mind she expected to hear the phone ring inside Charley's house and to find it discarded in the couch or under the bed. But there was no sound. Wherever Charley was, she must have her phone with her. When she reached voicemail, she left a rambling message asking Charley to call her back.

She slid her phone back away and shrugged. "I guess that's it."

Vic nodded. They walked back out of the house, and Erin locked it, being sure to lock the deadbolt as well this time. She wished as she left that there was a burglar alarm. She always felt better leaving her own house when she had armed the burglar alarm and knew no one could get inside without either having the unlock code or setting off the alarm so that everyone in the neighborhood knew there was a problem and the police were alerted a few blocks away.

"I'm sure she's fine," Vic assured Erin. "I'm sure everything is just fine. You know Charley. She just messed up her schedule or stayed out too late drinking with friends last night."

"Yeah," Erin agreed, though she wasn't convinced it was true.

CHAPTER 4

*I*t was getting late, and it was time to get home and make something for dinner. After a little bit of quiet time, unwinding from the day, it would be time for bed. She had to be in bed pretty early to get up in time for the early shift at Auntie Clem's. Baker's hours started very early in the day. They needed to get the first loaves of bread in the oven and muffins baked for the before-work crowd.

Erin pulled the bug into the garage behind Clementine's house. She didn't have to drop Vic off somewhere else; she lived in the loft apartment over Erin's garage. Erin loved having her best friend so close. They were always doing things together in the kitchen at home as well as at Auntie Clem's. Other people might have thought it too stifling to always be together. They might have thought that it would be hard to work and live so close, but it felt good to Erin. She enjoyed the close companionship.

"You got any dinner plans?" Vic inquired.

"Nothing special. There's some cooked rice and some salad in the fridge. Maybe a can of soup with the rice and a salad on the side." She shrugged. She wasn't sure whether Terry would be home for supper, so she was only cooking for herself, and she kept it pretty simple. No point in putting a ton of energy into cooking after a full day of baking.

"Some bread or rolls and cookies in the freezer," Vic added.

"Well… yes," Erin agreed. They always had lots of baking on hand. Not all of the day-old baking ended up in the freezer at the bakery. "You want to stay for supper?" Erin offered, "Assuming Willie will not be around?"

Vic sighed. "I wish I knew when he would be around. It's been so crazy lately. I think part of it is that he doesn't want to be predictable and doesn't want people to know where he will be. It's 'cloak and dagger' all the time now. Secret assignations might be fun to begin with, but they get old *fast*. I just want what we had before—a predictable life: home together during the week and some adventuring on the weekends. But… I guess that is off the table."

"Until Willie gets things sorted out," Erin suggested hopefully.

Vic opened her door and climbed out of the car. "I really hope so. I miss the old Willie. I miss seeing him most nights. He's always had his own life, too, and that was fine when he was just doing his own thing, running his businesses. I knew he was happy and that he'd be back when he was finished running into the city or checking on a mine or whatever he was doing. Now…" She shook her head and didn't finish the sentence.

Erin got out of the car and followed Vic out of the garage. Vic hesitated for an instant at the bottom of the stairs that led up to her loft apartment.

"Come into the house," Erin told her immediately. "I need someone to keep me company."

Vic gave her a grateful smile and followed across the yard to Erin's back door. Erin unlocked it, punched her code into the burglar alarm, and stepped into the kitchen.

They were met with the thrum of soft paws across the floor and Orange Blossom's raucous meows. To listen to him, one would think he had not been fed for days. Of course, he'd had plenty of food during the day. There was dry kibble in his bowl that he could have eaten. But this state of affairs was apparently intolerable, and the fact that Erin was ten minutes late getting home because they had popped over to Charley's apartment had been noticed. A cat could have *starved* to death during that time.

Erin laughed and petted him and scratched Blossom's ears. "Oh, I don't think it's as bad as all that," she soothed him.

Despite his obvious enjoyment of her attention, Orange Blossom continued to demand food. Before long, Erin headed to the pantry to get it out. Marshmallow, the brown and white rabbit, came lolloping into the kitchen, quiet and serene, to await his meal as well.

Erin got out Blossom's treats and skimmed a few of them across the floor for him to watch him chase them and burn off some energy. When she had first taken him in, he had been a tiny, scrawny kitten, but those days were long behind them. He was now a very large cat, bordering on being overweight, if she was to listen to Doc Edmunds's warnings. She needed to play with him more often and feed him less.

Tell that to Blossom. He would keep the whole block awake if she didn't satisfy his demands.

After a bit more teasing and chasing after treats, Erin got out the canned food and dished up a small amount for the cat. Blossom made loud noises as he snarfed it down, clearly *starving*. Erin got a carrot out of the fridge for Marshmallow to supplement his diet of green pellets and hay, and he ate it delicately, his eyes rolling over to Orange Blossom occasionally to watch him eat.

"You don't know what he is doing?" Erin asked. "Willie, I mean? I thought he said that he would unwind things, get himself removed again as the leader of the Dysons."

"It's not as easy as all that," Vic said. "He can't just step down."

"No, I know. But he sounded pretty confident. I thought he would be able to smooth things over pretty quickly."

"I thought he'd sort it out right quick... But he can't change the fact that he acknowledged himself as the direct descendant of Hannah Dyson and the heir to the throne, so to speak. He can't change who he is or deny the people who have been waiting for him to take over leadership of the clan since he was born."

Erin sighed.

"If there is a way to do it, he'll find it," Vic affirmed.

"He'll find what?"

CHAPTER 5

*T*he male voice startled both of them. They spun around, turning away from the animals to see Willie standing at the threshold of the back door, which Erin had left open.

He was similar to Vic in height, but broad across the chest and shoulders. The dark stain of his skin from his mining and processing work was starting to fade as he used safer practices, having recently undergone chelation therapy to treat heavy metal poisoning. Erin was used to seeing him in casual work clothes, looking a little ragged and unkempt, but now he was clean and tidy in a suit jacket. He moved to the side slightly to let Nilla, Vic's small white dog, run into the kitchen.

"Willie!" Vic hurried over to give him a welcoming hug and kiss. "I didn't know if I would see you tonight!"

He nodded and didn't comment on whether he would stay the night or was only there for a quick word. He held her to him for a moment, kissed her gently one more time and then released her. Nilla chased Orange Blossom and Marshmallow out of the room, wanting to play.

"How are you?" Erin asked Willie. "Is everything... going okay?"

"It is what it is," Willie said, his dark eyes darting around the room. He checked the yard and shut the door. The burglar alarm beeped its acknowledgment that the door was closed, and thirty seconds later, the bolt automatically slid into place.

Erin heard Nilla's sharp bark followed by Orange Blossom growling. But she wasn't particularly worried about either of them. They would sort it out.

"We were just wondering… whether you were going to be able to do like you said," Erin said awkwardly, "and get back out of the clan."

Willie's lips pressed together. He shook his head in irritation, obviously not planning to tell Erin anything about what was happening in the clan.

"It's not that simple," he said, echoing Vic's words without knowing it. "I am… exploring my options. Seeing what I can do."

"Vic said you can't just step down."

"No. There are those in the clan who would like to see it happen, but others would take a very dim view of such a betrayal. After previously separating myself from them and denying that I was the heir, they finally have me in place. And… getting out of that will not be easy."

"I'm so sorry," Erin apologized. "I know it is my fault that you are in this position. You told me to stay out of it and stop asking questions about Hannah and Otis and your relationship with them. And I tried to stay out of it, but…"

"It's not your fault. A series of events was triggered that you would not have been able to stop… you were not the one who stole the recipe book. And I knew I was a descendant of the two of them, whether I wanted to be acknowledged or not. Mona has been determined for some time to force me to take my place."

"Was she the one who stole the recipe book?" Erin thought about the figure on the scooter that had knocked her off her feet, and then of the older woman holding her gun pointed steadily at Erin and Terry, and shook her head. "No, it couldn't have been her…"

"Mona had a whole army at her disposal," Willie said with a

shrug. "I don't know who it was she recruited to steal it. That doesn't really matter. It was her doing, no matter who she sent."

"And she did it just to prevent anyone from finding out that Hannah Dyson and Eleanor Jackson were once friends? That their children falling in love started the whole feud?"

Willie's face flushed. "After all of the trouble this has caused, you still want to discuss it openly? It is none of your business, Erin. This is my history, not yours."

Erin nodded meekly. "I'm sorry, it's just hard for me to fathom how something so small could spark so much trouble across generations. It's... mind-boggling."

"Wars have been started over love affairs throughout time. What is more likely to get people fired up?"

"Did you... want to stay for supper?" Erin offered, dropping the subject.

Willie looked at Vic for her opinion. At that moment, there was the sound of a key in the front door and the beep of the burglar alarm as Terry punched his passcode in to prevent the alarm from going off. Nilla barked excitedly.

Erin heard Terry's "There you go, boy" to K9, releasing him from duty, and the dog ran across the house to reach the kitchen first, Nilla hot on his heels.

"Hello, boy!" Erin greeted, scratching the German shepherd's ears. "How's K9? Did you have a good day today? Did you bite all the bad guys?"

Terry followed his dog into the kitchen at a relaxed pace, then saw Vic and Willie in the kitchen with Erin.

"Miss Victoria," he greeted in a low, controlled voice. He looked at Willie and didn't say anything at first, studying his upgraded look. Then politeness won out, and he acknowledged, "Willie."

Willie nodded back. "Officer Piper."

They stood there staring at each other for a moment, the tension between them clear. Willie shifted.

"Thank you for the invitation, Erin. But I think Vic and I will eat on our own tonight."

Vic nodded. "We don't get the chance as often now, so we'd like some private time."

"Sure, of course," Erin agreed. "Have a good evening. I'm glad... everything is good," she said lamely. Of course, everything wasn't good, so it just made her sound stupid. But she didn't want to jinx anything by saying "safe" or commenting about clan politics in front of Terry.

Willie just nodded. He put his arm around Vic and turned her toward the door.

"See you in the morning," Vic offered. She called Nilla to her and picked him up, ignoring his protests.

"See you," Erin agreed, "have a good night."

Vic punched her burglar alarm code to allow her to exit, and the door locked again behind them.

Terry sat down at the table. "Did you know he was coming?"

Erin shook her head. "I don't have any idea where he will be when. Even Vic doesn't know. He just shows up when he does. She said he doesn't want to be predictable, doesn't want people to know where he is."

"I don't blame him. He's got a pretty big target painted on his back."

"You don't think... anything will happen, do you?"

Terry watched the couple make their way up the stairs to the loft apartment through the kitchen window, then sighed and sat down.

"I reckon a lot will happen. I just don't know what. But when the leadership of an organized crime cartel changes, things are never quiet for long. There will be plenty of people inside the organization who don't believe that Willie is who he says he is, or that he should inherit the leadership of the clan. People who think they could do a better job want him out permanently."

Erin puttered around the kitchen, looking through the leftovers and the cupboards to decide what to pull together for their supper.

"And that's just the internal politics." Terry went on. "To say nothing of what the Jacksons are planning to disrupt the Dysons and try to take them while they are off-balance. You haven't noticed how everyone in town has been lately?"

Erin shook her head. "Everything has been quiet. No one has said or done anything."

"Exactly. Everyone is being extra careful not to say anything in public. Not to align themselves with either clan. Not to speculate on what the clans are going to do now that Willie is at the head of the Dysons. People that the police keep an eye on have been lying low. Avoiding being seen in public. Willie hasn't been around town like he usually is, doing odd jobs."

Erin nodded. "Yeah. You're right. I keep thinking that it is too quiet. I don't want terrible things to happen, but the silence is wearing me down. I want... everything to be okay. Normal, not quiet."

"I suspect it will be a while before we see anything like normal in Bald Eagle Falls again."

Erin stopped for a moment, resting her hand on Terry's shoulder. He was solid and strong and safe. She didn't like to think that Bald Eagle Falls was not a safe place. Terry and the other members of the small police department were on the alert. They knew what was going on and would do their best to keep Erin and the other residents of the town safe from the gang unrest.

If Erin was to be honest with herself, Bald Eagle Falls had never been a particularly safe place since she had returned. And apparently not before she had gone on that last car trip with her mother, either. People had been killed. People really did do terrible things to each other, and in the small-town community, people were far more aware of what was going on with their friends and neighbors than in the city. Although some of the secrets that Erin had discovered had been well buried for many years.

"Bald Eagle Falls has probably never been the sleepy little town that it pretends to be," Terry said, echoing Erin's sentiments. "Just being aware of the secret tunnels that once ran between some of the buildings on Main Street, it becomes clear that there is more going on under the surface than you could ever know. People have been hiding behind masks for generations here."

"It really is a nice town… I love it. But it's true. It really isn't the sleepy little town people pretend it is."

Erin knew more about some of her neighbors and the families whose histories intertwined than she would have liked to. She had been caught up by too many of those secrets, both old and new.

She put a pot on the stove to warm up some soup and put the dish of rice in the microwave.

"We went over to Charley's house after closing." Erin unnecessarily readjusted the temperature dial for the stove element, turning it an eighth of an inch. "She didn't show up for her shift or answer her phone."

Terry stretched his legs under the table, pointing and flexing his toes. He had probably been on his feet for most of the day. K9 was snuffling around under the edge of the cupboards, looking for anything interesting. Erin took one of the gluten-free dog biscuits from the cookie jar and offered it to him. He took it politely from her fingers with his lips and lay down beside Terry to nibble the cookie while Erin moved around the kitchen making the dinner.

Orange Blossom, who considered K9 his sworn enemy at any time other than when he had food, returned to the kitchen and followed him around, sniffing the floor to check for any crumbs the dog might have dropped, and then crouched, staring at him, while he ate the cookie. K9 gave no indication that he was interested in sharing the treat. Still, Erin knew that if he were distracted for an instant or left any crumbs on the floor or on his face, Blossom would be on them in an instant. The only time he ever appeared to be affectionate with K9 was when he had food crumbs on his face.

CHAPTER 6

"*W*as she okay?" Terry asked.

Erin looked at him and remembered her previous comment. Charley. Was Charley okay.

"Well… everything looked okay at her house. There was no blood or… more disorder than usual. But she wasn't there. No note to say where she had gone, no call or text or voicemail from her. She's just gone."

Terry considered this, nodding slowly. "Well… Charley definitely needs to be careful of the clans. She probably decided that things are too hot in Bald Eagle Falls and decided to go for a trip."

"Without telling anyone?"

"If someone came and asked you where she had gone, what would you say?"

"That I don't know, I guess. She left without telling anyone."

"So even if someone was to press you, threaten you, or even fool you, going about it circumspectly, you wouldn't tell them where Charley has gone."

"Well, no."

He shrugged. "If you don't know, you can't tell anyone. Even by accident. Even by talking in your sleep."

"The only person who would know if I said something about it in my sleep is you," Erin pointed out teasingly. "And *you* wouldn't tell anyone."

"Maybe she doesn't want the police to know, either. She doesn't exactly… have a great relationship with Bald Eagle's finest."

As a former member of the Dyson clan, Charley didn't want anything to do with the police. She was now an independent, law-abiding business owner, but she still didn't like to have anything to do with the authorities. Even when Erin needed to renew her business license, Charley—her half-partner in the bakery—would not go to the town hall to do it.

"No, I guess not. But I wish she'd at least told me that she was leaving town. She wouldn't have to say where she was going. Just say she wanted to get out for a while because it was too hot."

"And you wouldn't have tried to dissuade her?"

"No." Erin would not want Charley to stay where it was dangerous for her. Though she really didn't know why anyone would be concerned about going after Charley when the leadership of the clan had changed. She had been booted out of the clan when her biological parentage had been revealed. Why would anyone care about her? "But I don't know that she was in any danger. I mean—"

"But you wouldn't have tried to talk her out of it."

Erin huffed and shook her head and gave her attention to the meal rather than to Officer Piper, who didn't have to be such a know-it-all about Charley and the clans in the area.

"I don't see why anyone would care about the fact that Charley was in the clan a couple of years ago when it was discovered that her father was Adam Plaint. It wasn't like she knew anything important about the clan."

"She was spending time with Bobby Dyson. Bobby Dyson might not have been big-time, but Dwight, his father, is. That means Charley knows something about the bigger players in the clan."

"Knew. Two years ago. How is that a danger to anybody today?"

"We don't know," Terry said slowly. "Unless she talks to someone."

Erin struggled to wrap her mind around the fact that Charley could hold such dangerous information. She was Erin's younger sister. She was flaky, immature, and a party girl, different from Erin in almost every way imaginable. Erin had trouble seeing Charley as she once had, as a tough gang chick who had been dating the heir to the throne. Or at least, Erin thought that Bobby would have been the heir to the throne since his older brother Nelson had very different ideas about running the clan from his father's.

She hadn't known then that Dwight had only been a figurehead and that the Dyson clan was really run by a matriarch. A woman named Mona, who Erin knew little else about. And the matriarchs were only ruling until Hannah's heir stepped up to the plate.

"You really think that Charley knows something about the Dysons that could be dangerous for them?" she asked skeptically.

"Whether she does or not, and whether I think she does or not, isn't the point. It is whether anyone in the organization thinks she does."

"Huh." Erin stirred her pot, the fragrant steam filling the room. "I guess that makes sense. You think she did the right thing by disappearing?"

"I have no idea. I can only guess. She's the best judge of that. You know Charley. She may come across as a flake sometimes, but then you find out that it was a front, that she was drinking with someone just to get information out of them, or that she's there when you really need her." Terry met her eyes.

Charley had rescued Erin when the first Auntie Clem's Bakery had burned down, and she didn't have any way to get it rebuilt. She had been there for Erin when she had been concussed and unable to run the bakery for several weeks. She was the baby sister Erin had longed for as a girl and never had.

"You're right. Charley is not as silly as she puts on," she admitted. "So if she decided she needed to get out of Dodge until this blows over, and not tell me so that I don't have anything to tell anyone else… then okay. I guess it was probably the right choice."

"You're not going to report her missing?"

Erin hesitated, then shook her head. On one hand, it made sense to report Charley missing, because that would be the normal thing for a sister to do. People would be less suspicious. But she didn't want to end up causing more problems for Charley, who would not want to deal with the police.

"No, I guess not. Although… if she is gone for too long, or I see or hear something that worries me… I still might. I don't want to be oblivious if something happened to her and she *didn't* leave of her own choice."

"But you didn't see anything at her house that would make you think that?"

"No. There wasn't any sign of violence or that someone had been through her house. Everything seemed pretty normal."

"For Charley."

Erin smiled. "If you came home and *this* house looked like hers did… you'd better make a report. But for Charley… it was tidier than some other times I've seen it."

She put some rolls from the freezer in the microwave to thaw and started to set the table. "Sorry, it's nothing fancy today, but…"

"When was the last time we had something fancy? Maybe Easter? We can do fancy for the big occasions, when everyone can help out. When it is just you and me, I'm a meat and potatoes guy. I'm happy with whatever you put in front of me."

Terry suddenly grimaced.

"I should not just be sitting here while you do all the work. You started earlier than I did and have been on your feet all day." He stood up belatedly, since there was nothing left to do but put the food on the table. "It isn't because I think cooking is women's work."

He helped bring everything to the table, his face a little flushed. "I got too used to you cooking when it was just your house. When I moved in… I should have started doing more."

The transition had been so gradual Erin had hardly realized, until Terry sat her down one day to discuss whether it was necessary for them to continue to keep up two houses when he was spending all of his time there. That had been months ago, and they had never really discussed a realignment of their roles. Erin kept cooking and baking, and Terry maintained things like the burglar alarm and outside lights, and other chores and roles had gradually been worked out between them.

Sometimes, Erin asked Terry to put a dish in the oven for her if he was home in the afternoon, and he had cooked for her while she had been sick, on the days she had been able to keep food down. But they did not divide the chores evenly.

They finished setting the plates and food on the table and sat down together.

"You work hard," Erin said with a shrug, "I'm used to getting supper ready when I get home from the bakery and I really don't mind."

"That's not very fair to you, though."

"Neither is expecting you to do it when you have night shift."

"If I'm working the night shift, I have time before you get home to make something. And then we can eat together instead of in two separate shifts."

Erin had to admit that they could do a better job of coordinating their schedules when she and Terry were working wildly varying shifts. It seemed like they just passed each other in the hallway instead of finding time to talk together or share a meal.

"Well, maybe," she agreed. "We can talk about it."

She knew Terry *could* make dinner; he just didn't do it very often. He didn't complain if she asked him to take care of meal preparations. She just felt like it was easier to do it herself than to arrange for Terry to do it. But maybe they could get around that if they planned it ahead of time, like she had done when she'd been working on Melissa's wedding.

CHAPTER 7

They started to dish up. Erin caught Terry looking out the kitchen window toward the loft again. She glanced over her shoulder quickly, wondering if Willie was leaving already or if he and Vic were going out together for dinner. But Erin supposed they wouldn't go out for dinner, not if Willie wanted to keep a low profile. She didn't see anything.

"What's up?" she asked, her stomach clenching. Had Terry seen a shadow flit past the window that she had missed because she had looked too late? Were Willie and Vic in danger?

"Nothing," Terry assured. If he had seen something worrisome, he would have reacted to it. He would be walking to the back door and maybe calling the police dispatcher for backup, not dishing up his meal.

"Nothing?" Erin pressed.

"No."

"What were you looking at?"

"I didn't mean to worry you. I was just… looking at the apartment. Nothing is wrong. No movement. Just…" Terry sighed and shook his head, looking irritated. "Having him out there… knowing that he is the boss of the Dyson clan now and being unable to do anything about it…"

"You can't arrest him if you don't have evidence of him committing a crime."

"Yes. That's what I'm saying."

"But if he hasn't done anything, that's good. You don't want to arrest him for nothing!"

"If I could arrest people based on what I knew about them, about their positions or professions and what that involved... then I would. That would be much better than having to wait until I can catch someone red-handed or until they have hurt someone before I can do anything about it."

Erin shook her head and gave a little laugh. "You don't really mean that, though. You're the *law-and-order* guy."

"That doesn't prevent me from wishing that I could put someone dangerous behind bars before catching them red-handed or being able to prove they had done something. Wanting something and being determined to follow the law are not mutually exclusive."

"Willie isn't dangerous," Erin said flatly.

Terry raised an eyebrow and stared at her. "He isn't dangerous? Are you really going to tell me that? The leader of a notorious crime family? Of course he is dangerous. Not just because he carries a gun and is capable of physical violence. And has a temper."

"He wouldn't do anything to hurt anyone."

"The side of Willie that *you* see is very limited. I agree that he wouldn't hurt you. And I don't think he would hurt Vic, except in a knock-down, blow-out lover's quarrel." He put up a finger to stop Erin from protesting the impossibility of Willie hurting Vic. "And I know you have been concerned about some of their fights, so don't try telling me that the possibility has never occurred to you."

Erin almost said, "They're just two passionate people," echoing Vic's explanation for their arguments. But she didn't like it when Vic used that excuse, so she wasn't going to parrot it. The problem was, Terry was right. She just didn't want to admit it.

"Okay. I've worried about it. But I don't think Willie would actually do anything to hurt her. And Vic is pretty good at defending herself."

"I'd rather see her kill Willie in self-defense than for him to kill her in anger. But the fact is, he is much more experienced, twice her weight, and a trained Dyson soldier. Her chances of besting him in a fight are… slim."

"I still say Willie isn't dangerous. His temper has been a lot better since he went through chelation and got all of those heavy metals out of his system. He and Vic have been getting along pretty well. No loud arguments or slammed doors."

Or not as many, anyway.

"You're ignoring the fact that Willie is the head of the Dyson clan. And the fact that Vic is a Jackson, his sworn enemy."

"It hasn't bothered him before, why would it now?"

Terry looked at Erin, a frown line creasing his forehead. "Because he wasn't the leader of the clan before."

"That won't change his feelings for her."

"He'll be under all kinds of pressure to get rid of her. And I don't mean sending her home to her family farm or off to the Bahamas for a vacation."

"He's not going to do anything to hurt her."

"You don't know what pressure he is under or what kinds of threats he faces. He might think it is more merciful to find a way to take her out kindly than to let one of the other members of the clan get his hands on her."

Erin caught her breath and stared at Terry in horror. "He wouldn't!"

"You don't know him. He isn't the big, kindhearted hick you think he is."

"I don't think that. I know Willie is a real person and that he has a history. But…" she shook her head, "he would never do anything to intentionally hurt Vic."

Terry tore a piece from his roll. "Agree to disagree."

Erin wasn't sure how to respond to that. She knew they had very different perspectives. But she knew she was right. Willie would not do anything to hurt Vic. No matter what sort of political problems and terrible people he was dealing with in the clan. It was Terry's job to be suspicious, and his job put him in contact with people on the worst days of their lives—people who did terrible things to each other.

"Willie is in this position because he wouldn't let you and me be harmed by someone in the clan. And he'll find a way out of it. Without hurting Vic."

"I wish I could believe that. But a single person cannot change the clan and the only way for him to get out of his position is to die. It's an inherited position, and he can't just quit now that he's accepted it."

"Willie will find a way. There's a loophole somewhere. Willie will find it. He'll find a way to make it work. Or he'll find a way to steer the clan in another direction. Maybe he'll legitimize them. Get them into something legal. He and Nelson have already been working on... whatever they're working on. Computers or security or something. If he gets them into something lucrative but legal, who would argue with it? If they can get what they want without the danger of getting caught and going to prison, they'll jump at the chance, won't they?"

Terry eyed Erin while he sipped a few spoonfuls of soup. "I think you're speaking from personal experience," he said slowly. "When you were struggling, you didn't want to be in anything illegal. You wanted a way to earn a living legitimately and not have to worry about getting caught and sent to prison. So you think everyone else feels the same way."

Erin caught herself nodding along to his words and tried to stop. She didn't want him to be able to see that clearly into her soul. She wanted there to be more... mystery between them. A safe distance.

"But not everyone sees life that way," Terry went on. "You only wanted to make enough to survive on. These guys aren't looking for a few honest dollars. They want to make six or seven figures personally. With as little effort as possible. And that means drug trafficking, human trafficking, contract killing, grand larceny, stuff like that."

He took a few swallows of his beer and wiped his mouth.

"A little guy can get started with burglary, if he's got some good targets with nice jewels or other valuables to start with. But sooner or later, he ends up face-to-face with the owner or another household or staff member, and there's only one way to get out without getting caught. Or he can get a start cooking meth. These are not nice guys, Erin. You saw Bo Biggles. You ended up face-to-face with Crazy Theresa. These are not the type of people who are *happy* to legitimize."

"He'll find a way," Erin maintained. "Willie decided long ago that he did not want to be a part of the clan. He's fought against being a part of it. He'll find a way out."

Terry looked at the apartment over the garage.

"I'm not so sure of that. And I don't like having him right there. I think we should make it clear to Vic that we don't want him here. He still has a place of his own. If they want to get together, they can meet there. I don't want him drawing members of either clan into the neighborhood."

Erin's jaw dropped. "I'm not telling Vic that Willie can't come over here."

"You want a gang war taking place in your backyard?"

"That's not going to happen."

"If the leader of the Dyson clan and his Jackson soldier-turned-girlfriend rendezvous here, what makes you think it won't?"

CHAPTER 8

*A*fter the serious discussions of the day, Erin found it hard to settle for the night. She couldn't stop thinking about Charley's disappearance and whether she was doing the right thing by assuming Charley had disappeared on purpose and she should not report the disappearance. What if Charley was actually in trouble and in need of rescue?

Terry's comments about Vic and Willie were even more disturbing. She didn't believe that Willie would do anything to hurt Vic and wanted to believe that no one in either of the clans would come after Vic and Willie while they were together in Vic's apartment. But what better place to take Willie unaware and kill or harm Vic in front of him?

She'd seen too many thrillers on TV. That wasn't going to happen in real life. That was just overblown Hollywood stuff.

But still, she couldn't put it out of her mind. She tossed and turned and occasionally cuddled with Terry for a few minutes, trying to make herself go to sleep. Still, when her alarm sounded in the morning, she felt like she had only had a few minutes' worth of sleep, and those few minutes had been riddled with nightmares and anxiety.

Despite her sleepless night, it was a relief to get up in the morning to prepare for the morning baking at Auntie Clem's. It was pleasant, routine work that Erin enjoyed and would help her to stay calm. It was a relief to escape the tossing and turning and the nightmarish feelings.

She put on a pot of coffee and looked over at the loft to see whether Vic's light was on yet. Vic was a late riser compared to Erin, often only rolling out of bed minutes before they needed to head to the bakery. Despite the quickness of her preparations, she still always looked better than Erin did. Her sleek blond hair seemed to always knot up effortlessly into a bun, whereas Erin's shorter hair was always poking out from under her cap and getting in the way despite numerous bobby pins to hold it in place.

Vic's light was already on. Willie had probably gotten up early to tend to his business and Vic had been unable to get back to sleep after his departure.

Which meant that she probably wouldn't be in the best mood.

Before the coffee was finished perking, Vic's door opened and Erin watched her descend the steps with Nilla. Erin called for K9 and let him out into the yard as well. The two dogs enjoyed playing with each other. Their antics would wear Nilla out so that he would behave himself while Vic was working, and she wouldn't come home to a disaster area when she popped back at lunch to take him outside.

Vic let herself in through the back door a minute later, standing on the threshold and looking back for a moment to smile at the dogs greeting each other and starting to race around.

"Mornin', sunshine! Can you imagine having so much energy at this hour?" she drawled.

"Morning," Erin greeted. She shook her head. "I'm no good till I've had my coffee."

"Amen."

Erin handed Vic a mug, and the two of them nursed their drinks for a few minutes as they waited for the scalding coffee to cool enough to have a few sips.

"You don't look like you slept a wink," Vic observed. "Do you want me to cover the morning shift and you get a few more hours of sleep?"

"No, I'll be fine. Do I really look that bad?"

"I just know you," Vic assured her. "That look you get when you've had a rough night. You look fresh as a daisy, but I know you were fightin' to get to sleep all night long."

Erin inclined her head in agreement. She hoped the part about looking fresh was true and her customers wouldn't notice her fatigue. She would be better after a cup of coffee anyway. Everything would be just fine once she got into the regular routine at Auntie Clem's.

"How did last night go?" she asked Vic, changing the subject.

"Last night?" Vic gave Erin a long blink and lowered lashes. "Well, Willie and I had a very nice time together, thank you. And you and Officer Handsome?"

Erin looked away from Vic, laughing. "Well, I didn't mean to ask anything... personal," she said uncomfortably. "I just meant how did you enjoy each other's company?"

"So did I," Vic said, deliberately increasing the innuendo in her tone. "And you and Terry...?"

Erin waved the inquiry away, her cheeks getting hot. "We just talked," she insisted. "There's plenty going on, and... I was worried about Charley and everything."

"It's no wonder you had trouble sleeping. You should try alternate ways to work your anxiety out. A little... physical activity would be good for you."

Erin loved it when Vic teased her, even if it did embarrass her.

"I know, I know. We shouldn't talk about worries before bed, or I just get all wound up. We should just do relaxing things before bed. But it's the only time I have to discuss things with him face to face and find out what is going on in Bald Eagle Falls."

"So that you have something good to worry about all night."

Erin shrugged and shook her head. "I just want to sort things out..."

"But everything isn't sorted out, is it? You need to put all of that aside before you go to bed. Just *enjoy yourself with Officer Piper* and worry about it during the day."

Erin sighed and nodded. It was true that worrying things over in discussion with Terry before bed was not a very functional behavior. But she didn't know how to just put it aside and focus on intimacy.

She looked at the clock on the wall. "We'd better get going."

They took care of the dogs and were out to the car and to the bakery in a few minutes. One of the benefits of living in a small town was how close everything was. The bakery was within easy walking distance from the house, so buzzing over there in the car was very quick. Before opening the bakery, Erin had anticipated being able to walk to and from Auntie Clem's and get her exercise that way. But it was still dark out when she got to the bakery in the morning. And she often had things to bring home after work, which required the car. She couldn't very well take the car in only one direction.

"Ahh." She breathed in the warm, clean air of the bakery after letting them in through the back door. She could smell the yeasty batters that had been soaking overnight. "This is what it's all about!"

Vic smiled, and they got to work pulling out the prepared batters and pouring them into loaf pans and muffin tins. Before long, the air was redolent with the smell of baking bread, sweet cinnamon, and the other spices in the muffins. Vic started cracking eggs for the mini breakfast quiches.

By opening time, Erin was in her groove, happy and relaxed despite the difficult night and everything she had been worried about. Baking was her happy place; she looked forward to opening the doors and inviting the morning customers in to make their selections.

The rest of the world could do whatever they were going to do. Erin would bake and feed the town good, wholesome, safe foods.

She flipped the door sign from Closed to Open, turned the bolt, and opened the door for her first few customers. She was surprised to see Campbell Cox as part of the morning crowd. He was not a morning person and did not live in Bald Eagle Falls. She couldn't remember ever seeing him there in the morning before, especially not first thing.

"Good morning," she greeted everyone as a group. "How is everything today?"

Most of them smiled and greeted her; a few murmured something about the evening before or what they were looking forward to today. Erin noticed that Cam hung toward the back of the group and didn't have anything to say. She supposed he was picking up something for Mary Lou while she opened up the General Store. Maybe they planned to have muffins together before Cam returned to the city.

"How could anybody be cheerful this morning?" Lottie Sturm challenged, looking straight at Erin. Her grumpy head shake made her too-juvenile blond pigtails flap, contrasting with her worn and creased face. "How can you be so happy with all the clan activity and the coming storm?"

Erin pressed her lips together. It wouldn't do to engage Lottie in the town politics or the trouble with the clan. She would just make everyone else miserable. Lottie had no idea that Erin had just spent the night worrying over everything and that talking about it more would make her feel even worse.

"Even in times of trouble, you can count your blessings," she pointed out to Lottie. "Isn't that what your religion tells you?"

As Erin was an atheist, she rarely brought up religion with anyone, and when the subject was brought up, she usually went out of her way to avoid it and to change the topic if someone else brought it up. But Lottie was one of the church ladies who often brought up religion and God's commandments around Vic and Erin, hoping, Erin supposed, to turn them from their sinful ways and convert them to the truth. Vic was Christian, but due to being trans, was not accepted by the Bald Eagle Falls church ladies and usually went into the city for Sunday services at a church that welcomed the LGBT community.

Lottie glared at Erin as if she were the devil quoting scriptures, and scowled.

"I count my blessings every day," she told Erin. "But in times of trouble like this, it is impossible to escape the evil that pervades our society, even here in Bald Eagle Falls. It drags me down," she announced soulfully, "It makes me so sorrowful."

Erin didn't know what to say after that. She glanced at Vic, who was communicating with her glance that Erin had done the wrong thing by mentioning religion.

Erin looked around for a solution and was inspired. "You know what's good for that?" she asked. "Chocolate. Double fudge brownies. And if you're feeling really sad, you go to the grocery store and pick yourself up some whipped cream, chocolate sauce, and cherries to top them with."

Vic started grinning, and despite Lottie's dramatically upset expression, Erin saw the corners of her mouth twitching as well, her eyes wide and bright with the thought of the delicious dessert.

"Dang, girl," Vic said admiringly, "I think you've hit on the solution. We'll have to bake a couple more trays once word of this cure gets out!"

From the looks being exchanged among the customers waiting for service, Vic was right. It might even be a good idea to run to the grocery store to pick up whipped cream, chocolate sauce, and cherries to sell at a slight markup to save people having to go to the grocery store to enhance their double fudge brownie experience.

Lottie didn't have anything else to say about Erin looking too happy considering what was happening in Bald Eagle Falls. Erin could see her eyeing Vic, trying to decide whether she dared say anything to her. She had, in the past, been thrown out on her ear without any purchases for making comments about Vic's gender or her having an intimate relationship with a man she was not married to.

But the brownies had apparently worked their magic, and Lottie kept her mouth shut so that she could purchase her baking —including the brownies. She looked sideways at Erin and apparently decided she'd better not push her luck today. She kept her lips primly pressed together.

There were a couple more orders for brownies before the group of early customers dispersed. They definitely needed to put another batch in the oven.

CHAPTER 9

*C*am had hung back until the others had made their purchases, and stepped forward now, a little hesitant. Erin suspected he was concerned that she had a poor opinion of him since he had been arrested for drug trafficking. But Erin had gone to the city to find the people Cam associated with and prove he had been framed. She knew the truth. She gave him a warm, reassuring smile.

"Hi, Cam. What can I get you today?"

Cam looked around. He didn't look into the display case to make his selections, but maybe he had just memorized what Mary Lou told him to purchase.

"Look, Miss Erin... have you seen my mom?"

Erin drew in a breath, shocked. She blinked at Cam. It was too early for Mary Lou to have gone anywhere but the General Store or the bakery.

"No, usually she is here when I open. Grabs a quick muffin and then goes to the General Store to get ready to open."

"That's why I came over here... I thought if Mom was anywhere, she would be here. Or the General Store."

"Didn't she tell you where she was going this morning?" Erin looked at the clock, "It couldn't have been that long ago."

"No. When I got up this morning, she wasn't there."

"She wasn't there?" Vic frowned at Campbell. "I know she must get up early, but... you couldn't have missed her between the house and the bakery, could you?"

"I was watching for her. Didn't see her."

"Well..." Erin tried to think of an explanation that made sense. "Maybe she had to go into the city for a doctor's appointment or something like that."

"She would have told me."

"Maybe she didn't think to, because you aren't usually there. Or it was private and she doesn't want people to know about it. Sometimes women—people—are very private about their medical information, even with their family."

"We talked last night. She could have told me then that she wouldn't be around. That she had to go into the city or somewhere here in town. She didn't say anything. I told her I would probably get a pretty early start, and she said I could come here with her, and we would have a quick bite together before I left."

That *was* odd. Erin shook her head slowly. "Something must have happened... was Joshua home? Is everything okay with your dad? Maybe she had to take Roger in unexpectedly."

"Mom would have told me. Why wouldn't she have woken me up to let me know what was going on? Dad was still there this morning. Joshua was... taking care of things. Helping Dad get ready for the day before the care worker gets there. He was worried. He didn't know where Mom was either." Cam shook his head. "Nothing like this has ever happened before. She's never just disappeared... been gone when we woke in the morning." He swallowed hard. "It's like... when Joshua disappeared. Mom just got up in the morning and he wasn't there. You don't think..."

Erin rubbed her forehead, which was starting to pulse with pain. She thought of Charley's disappearance. Of Willie not being there at predictable intervals. That was all explainable. But Mary Lou disappearing without a word to her family, when she had one son visiting from out of town and a disabled husband who relied heavily on her, that made no sense.

"No… I can't think of anywhere else Mary Lou would have gone, but that doesn't mean that something happened to her. But maybe we should talk to Officer Piper. Have him look into it."

Cam's jaw clenched. "I don't want to pull the cops into it."

"If something has happened to her, you don't want to delay. You need to get the police on to it as soon as possible. So they can start investigating before the trail grows cold."

"You *do* think something happened to her."

"I don't know. I can't think of why else she would just disappear. But maybe there is a logical explanation. Terry can help. You know he won't make trouble for you. He's not going to accuse you of something."

"No, that would never happen," Cam said sarcastically.

"Campbell," Erin said firmly. He was very young, and though he had been living on his own for a year, that didn't mean he knew how the world worked. "Listen to me. You need to step up. You can't afford to be the resentful kid in this case. You can't let your feelings toward the police and what happened to you keep you from doing what you have to do."

He swallowed again and bit his lip, considering her words. "Reckon I ain't got much choice, do I?" he asked eventually.

"No. Do you want me to call Officer Piper here? Or do you want to go there to make the report?"

"I don't really want to go there. To the police station where they held me."

"Okay. Sit down over there," she directed him to one of the cafe chairs at the front of the bakery. "I'll get him to come over so the two of you can talk. Can I get you a coffee and a muffin while you wait?"

He nodded, but she didn't think he was really thinking about his answer. It was just an automatic reaction. But a nice hot coffee and sweet muffin were probably just what he needed.

"Good. Go have a seat. He'll be here in a few minutes."

Erin headed for the kitchen. She didn't want to make the call from the public section of the bakery. Someone might come in and overhear the call. Word would spread quickly enough about

Mary Lou's disappearance; Erin didn't want to contribute to the gossip.

CHAPTER 10

"Mary Lou Cox is missing?" Terry demanded. "What makes you think that?"

"Campbell is here. He has been visiting since yesterday. But when he got up this morning, Mary Lou was gone. They were going to come to Auntie Clem's together this morning, so this was the first place he thought to come when he couldn't find her. But we haven't seen any sign of her."

"Where would Mary Lou go?"

"I don't know. If we had any ideas, we would look there. But he checked the General Store, and he checked here and kept an eye out for her on the way. Where else would she be?"

"She could have gone anywhere. You can't assume she is missing just because she didn't go to the bakery first thing. Something else could have come up. She could have had to go to the grocery store or a supplier to pick something up."

"You need to come to talk to Cam," Erin said firmly. "You can discuss all of that stuff with him. But he was up early this morning, and she wasn't there. No note. Joshua and Roger didn't know where she was. She left without taking care of Roger."

"Okay," Terry conceded. "I'll be there in a few minutes. There are a couple of other fires to be put out, but I'll be there as soon as I can."

Erin couldn't fathom anything more important than finding out what happened to Mary Lou, but she didn't argue. Terry was the only one who could make that judgment. She would have to trust what he'd decided.

"Okay, but don't be long. If something happened to Mary Lou..."

"I'll be there as soon as I can, Erin."

Erin said goodbye to him and returned to the front of the store to update Campbell. She took coffee and muffins to him and sat in the chair across from him. Cam was looking out the window at the street. Erin turned to look out at Main Street. It was quiet, just as it had been the day before. She remembered thinking it was too quiet. She hadn't wanted to jinx it.

Now look at where they were.

Erin put her hand over Cam's. "Officer Piper says he'll be here as soon as possible. He had a couple of other calls to clear first, but I'm sure it won't be very long."

"Sound like he's putting a real high priority on it," Cam said bitterly.

"We know Mary Lou. I'm sure he *is* putting a high priority on it. You just have to remember that this is a small town, and its police force is very small."

"I've lived here all my life. I know all about the limitations of the police department."

Erin nodded. "I'm sorry. Here." She slid a mug of coffee and a small basket of assorted muffins to him. "You probably haven't had anything this morning."

"No." He rubbed his eyes, looking fatigued. "I know I should force myself, but..."

He picked up the cup of coffee and sipped it, but didn't touch the muffins.

"You can go back to your work. You don't need to babysit me."

"I can keep you company..." Erin offered.

"No. I'll just wait for Officer Piper to show up. I don't want to attract any more attention than necessary."

Erin nodded and stood up. "Okay, I understand. Just flag one of us down if you need anything."

It was only a couple of minutes later that the bells at the door rang loudly, and Erin looked up to see Melissa Lee had burst through the door. Her curly hair was wild, falling around her head in dark ringlets she had to push back out of the way. She looked around the bakery and saw Cam sitting at the table. But she spoke to Erin.

"Mary Lou too?" she demanded. "What is going on here?"

"Mary Lou too?" Erin repeated.

Cam stood up from the table. "What? What do you mean 'Mary Lou too'?"

Melissa shook her head, her brows up and eyes open wide. "What is going on with people going missing? It's like half the town done disappeared."

Vic came around the counter to join the conversation. There were no other customers to panic.

"Half the town?" Vic asked.

"No, not half the town," Melissa admitted. "That's an exaggeration. I just... I just don't understand what is going on."

"Who else? Charley and Mary Lou, and who else?"

"Charley?" Melissa asked.

"She didn't show up for her shift yesterday, but there isn't anything about it that looks suspicious... but she isn't at her house and she hadn't been to work."

"A few men or women who are..." Melissa hesitated, choosing her words carefully, "associated with one of the clans. But the sheriff doesn't think they are missing, just that they... decided not to be here."

They all looked at each other.

"Men from the clans that have disappeared. You mean they are gathering with the clans or hiding from them?" Erin asked.

"Well, how am I supposed to know that?" Melissa asked in exasperation. "You think they told me that? I'm just a part-time admin assistant over at the police station. I'm not an investigator. How am I supposed to know the difference?"

Cam's jaw clenched. "My mom doesn't have anything to do with any of the clans. We have stayed far away from any clan stuff."

"Are you related to either of them?" Melissa asked breathlessly, pushing another lock of hair back down behind her ear.

Erin remembered Mary Lou's declaration, "If you're kin to Clementine, you're kin to half the mountain."

"Everyone is related to one of the clans. Or to both of them, Mary Lou said so."

Melissa looked aghast. "Not both of them."

"If you really know your family history. The feud hasn't been going on for that long, compared with how long ago people started settling the mountain. It was only a few generations back that the Dysons and Jacksons stopped intermarrying. And even then... there have probably been a number of secret relationships. Or people who weren't close enough to realize what blood they carried."

Melissa was shaking her head, disbelieving.

"None of that has anything to do with what happened to my mom," Cam reminded them. "She wasn't involved with either of the clans. Or related to any of them. Not closely enough for anyone to know it, anyway. And this morning, she's just *gone*. So, what does that have to do with anyone else? We need to find her! Something has happened to her."

"We're going to find out," Erin soothed. "Officer Piper will be here soon."

She couldn't promise that Terry would be able to find Mary Lou immediately, but it seemed so bizarre to her that Mary Lou would just disappear. There had to be some kind of explanation. Mary Lou wasn't the type who would just take off like that. Not like Charley.

Cam ran his fingers through his hair, making it stand on end. He curled his fingers and pulled his hair. "Where is Officer Piper, then? Don't tell me the cop disappeared too." He gave a sharp laugh that was more of a sob.

"No, I talked to him on the phone. He'll be here soon."

"He should have been here by now. Nothing else should take precedence over this."

Melissa shook her head at this. "Why is your mom more important than the others who have disappeared? There are other things to be concerned about right now with all of the clan activity."

Erin looked at Melissa, her stomach tightening. Terry had not told her about any clan activity to be concerned about. He had said that people were lying low and waiting for things to happen. But Melissa made it sound like there had already been clan violence.

"What else has happened?"

Melissa pressed her lips together, maybe realizing she had said too much. Not that it ever seemed to stop her. She usually continued until Terry or someone else stopped her, telling her she had said too much.

CHAPTER 11

*I*t was then that the door jangled all their nerves. Erin was relieved to see Terry in uniform with K9 alert at his side. Terry looked them over, and his eyes stopped on Melissa. "Miss Lee. Or rather, Missus Davis. Did you have something you needed to pass on to me?"

"Uh…" Melissa shook her head. "No, I was just making sure that everything was okay until you got here. I knew you couldn't get here right away…"

But given how quickly Terry had shown up, he must have dealt with his other calls pretty quickly, putting them on hold until later.

"Well, I'm here, and I'm sure Cam would prefer to discuss this privately, so…"

"I'll get back to the office," Melissa agreed, reddening. "I just stepped out for a short break."

The police department was within walking distance, like most of Bald Eagle Falls. Far enough that Melissa was sweating from hurrying over on a warm day. What Erin would have called a blazing hot day before moving back to Tennessee.

Flushed, Melissa saw herself to the door and headed back to the station.

Terry turned back to the rest of them.

"I'm needed in the kitchen," Vic said, raising her hands in defense and heading toward the back without being told. Terry looked at Erin.

"Maybe we could talk at the police department offices," Terry suggested to Cam. "It's just down the road and would be more private. We're likely to be interrupted here."

Cam shook his head. "I know exactly where the police offices are, in case you forgot. And I don't have any desire to go back there."

"This isn't the best place to have a private conversation."

Terry didn't say that the bakery was where everyone gathered to hear the latest gossip, but Erin knew he was thinking about it. He had understated the case; it was pretty much the worst place to be trying to hold a private conversation.

"This is where we are going to talk," Cam told him flatly. "To start with, anyway. I want to hear what you have to say about this. My mom was supposed to be coming here this morning before opening the General Store. But she never got here. And never got to the General Store."

"What time did she leave the house?" Terry asked, sitting across from Cam in the chair Erin had vacated. She worked at the counter, readjusting items in the display case, wiping down the counter, and doing various other unnecessary jobs so she could listen in on the discussion as much as possible.

Cam hadn't left or asked her to go, so that meant he wanted her to hear his story, didn't it?

"Dunno. We were going to come over here together. I got up early, but she was already gone. Don't know what happened to her. She never leaves that early. She has to... you know, help Dad to get ready for the day before she goes to work. And make sure that everything is okay with Joshua and that he's going to school. She doesn't get up and leave before everyone else."

"But today, for one reason or another, she did."

Cam nodded. He was trying to look strong and unemotional about it, but he was struggling. He was barely out of his teens and had been living with friends or on the streets for a year. He had broken away and struck out on his own rather than try to live up to everyone's expectations any longer. He associated with people Mary Lou would not have liked or approved of. But rather than looking tough, Cam looked vulnerable and afraid, at a loss for what to do.

"It's just not like Mom. She looks after everyone. She has rules… a routine… I've tried calling her, but she's not answering her phone."

"Give me her number to see where it was last used and if it is still on. Does she share her location with you or anyone else through an app?"

Cam shook his head slowly. "No, I don't think so. Not with me. I don't think that is something she would know very much about doing."

"Does she have an app to find her phone if she can't find it?"

"She never loses her phone. She always has it with her or knows where it is."

"So you don't think she has a 'find my phone' feature?" Terry persisted.

"No. Don't think so."

"Tell me what happened last night."

"What do you mean?"

"When you got up this morning, she was already gone, so you can't help us much with that. But what happened last night that you can tell me about? What did you do? What did you talk with her about? You said that you talked about what you would do this morning. What else?"

"Oh… okay." Cam took a drink of his coffee. He looked at the muffins, but didn't pick one out. He was probably way too anxious to force himself to eat anything.

K9 made grumbling noises as he settled down beside Terry and looked up at him to see if he was eating anything. But Terry hadn't helped himself to the muffins either. He took out a notepad and pen.

"Yeah… I got into town yesterday afternoon, and Mom was home for supper. We all ate together. Everything was pretty normal… as far as spending time together, I mean. We talked a bit about... well, the clan stuff. But Mom didn't want to talk much about it. It was always sort of a forbidden topic in our family. Like we might attract trouble just by talking about it."

Erin had noticed a lot of people who avoided it and pretended that there wasn't anything going on. Avoidance seemed to be a very common way to deal with anything to do with the clans.

"But you *did* talk about it?" Terry pressed.

"Well, a little bit. I had heard through the grapevine about what had happened... Willie taking over leadership of the Dysons, I mean." Cam looked around, checking the bakery's interior and outside on Main Street as if Mary Lou would pop up to tell him that he shouldn't be talking about it. But she didn't appear out of nowhere to stop him.

Terry nodded. "Did she say what she thought about it?"

"No. I said that I couldn't believe Willie could do that, or would be able to stay in power. She just looked at me and said I knew nothing about it. And I guess I don't. I knew he was a Dyson soldier, but that he'd broken ranks with them years ago. I don't know how he got back in, or how he replaced Dwight in some kind of coup. I didn't think he wanted anything to do with the clans. Whenever I saw or talked to him—I didn't much, because Mom didn't think we should have anything to do with him—he always said it wasn't something he wanted to get into, and that we should stay clear of the clans."

Willie had always told Erin that he had nothing to do with the Dysons anymore, even though she knew he still had some contact with Nelson about computer systems. People like Terry and Mary Lou had not believed that he'd made the clean break he said he had. They insisted that he was still involved with them. *Once in the clan, always in the clan.*

"Did she say whether she had discussed it with anyone else?" Terry asked.

Cam shook his head. "No. And she wouldn't. I know my mom. It wasn't just us she wouldn't talk about Willie or the clans with. She wouldn't discuss it with anyone. And we were supposed to stay away from Willie and anyone who might be involved with either of the clans. She didn't want us to have anything to do with them." Cam scowled, his brows drawn down. "Do you think this has something to do with the clans? That doesn't make any sense."

"What do *you* think happened? Where do you think she is?"

"I don't know. I just keep thinking about Joshua when he disappeared like that. Mom got up in the morning and he was gone, taken right out of his room. That's what it was like for us. We got up this morning, expecting everything to be normal, but she wasn't there. She wasn't anywhere."

"So you think she was kidnapped."

"That's the only thing that makes sense."

"Kidnapped by whom?"

"I don't know. Isn't that for the police to figure out? You must know who around Bald Eagle Falls would be likely to do something like that. We can't have too many kidnappers around here."

"No, it isn't something you see very much of. And usually... it is children or teens. Not grown adults. And it is even more rare for someone to come right into the house, right into the person's bedroom to kidnap them. What happened to Joshua is very rare."

"But look at it. What else do you think happened?"

"I'd like to come to your house to look around. See if I can find evidence of what might have happened."

Cam nodded. "Yeah, I guess."

"Can you tell me whether her bed was slept in? Was it made this morning? Did you see her go to bed last night? And what about her car?"

"Her bed was made," Cam said slowly, his eyes far away, reviewing what he had seen that morning. "So... she wasn't taken from her bed. A kidnapper wouldn't have bothered to make the bed while snatching her. Then it was either... before she went to sleep last night, or after she got up this morning."

"What time did she say she was going to bed and when does she usually get up?"

"It was... maybe ten when she was going to bed. She had to be up early to get Dad ready for the day and get to work. I don't know what time her alarm was set for. She was usually up and around at six if I was ever up that early… or late."

"And what about her car?"

"It was in the garage. I thought… she must have gone to the General Store for something. I couldn't figure out why she would leave so early without seeing to Dad, but that was the only thing I could think of."

He wiped his face with both hands, rubbing the heels of his hands into his eyes and then blinking as if he were just waking up.

"What happened to her?" He looked at his watch. "I have to call Joshua and update him…. but what do I say?"

CHAPTER 12

"Tell him the police are on it," Terry said calmly. "We'll sort it out. I will make some inquiries to see if anyone saw her along her usual route this morning. She made the bed before she left, so it is most likely sometime this morning. You were still up when she went to bed last night? So you would have heard if there was someone else in the house. Especially if there was a struggle."

Cam's face cleared, the stress lines softening slightly. "Yeah. We were both up for a while after she got ready for bed. Joshua and me. Dad was already in bed."

Terry's pen paused in his note taking. "They don't sleep together? No, not if Mary Lou's bed was made, but Joshua was the one to get Roger up."

Cam shrugged. "No. Not since..." He shifted awkwardly and looked away from Terry. Erin put extra energy into polishing the glass on the inside of the display case, pretending that she couldn't hear their discussion. As if the display case were a cone of silence. "Not since *before*," Cam finished.

There could be a lot of *befores*. Before Roger had returned home? Before he had been at the institution? Before he had been brain-damaged in his suicide attempt? The Cox family had been through such a long list of tragedies; it was amazing that the boys were doing as well as they were. Or that Mary Lou hadn't run away from home several years before.

"When Mom found out he'd lost all of their money," Cam clarified.

Before the suicide attempt, when Roger had invested everything with a friend. Instead of the returns they had been promised, it had all disappeared. Erin could see how that would have caused a rift between the couple. But Mary Lou had still been there for him throughout everything that had happened after that. Erin admired her immensely. Erin would have run away after all that Mary Lou had been through. She would have run away at the first sign of problems.

"They have different schedules," Cam went on. "Mom doesn't sleep a lot. She always has things to do. Dad sleeps longer. Goes to bed early in the evening and doesn't get up until just before the care worker is due."

"Did your dad see or hear anything? How close are their bedrooms together?"

"I don't think he heard anything. You can ask if you are going to the house to look around. He might be able to answer you. Sometimes, he is really good, and it is almost like nothing ever happened. But usually, he's on the other end... easily confused, difficulty speaking. He's taken his morning meds by now, and it might be harder. Better at suppertime before he takes his night meds."

Terry nodded. "Okay. I might try a couple of times then, see if I can catch him at a good time. Of course, I might not need to. We might have found her by then."

Cam sighed. His face remained a mask, though his fingers clutched the edge of the table, his knuckles turning white. "Do you think so?"

"Most adults who are reported missing show up within twenty-four to forty-eight hours. Usually within a few miles of home. And usually, it is voluntary."

"Mom wouldn't just walk out on us. Not for anything."

Terry didn't argue. He wrote down a few more notes. "I will follow up on all of this," he promised. "Please don't worry if I am not talking to the people you expect on the timeline you expect. A lot goes on behind the scenes that you don't see or hear about. And I won't be the only one working on the case. Some of the inquiries will be made by other law enforcement officers."

"Okay." Cam nodded stiffly. "As long as you promise me you'll do everything you can to find her. And that nothing else will take priority."

"Priorities are fluid. If the bank was held up or there was a shooting, you wouldn't expect me to ignore it. I promise we will not ignore the case or put it on hold because she hasn't been gone for forty-eight hours. We will be doing everything we can to find her."

"Yeah."

"I'll follow up with Joshua later. But I want to make some other inquiries first. Did he go to school?"

"Yeah. I told him Mom would expect him to, and Dad told him he needed to go." He snorted. "Kind of hypocritical for me to tell him he has to go to school, but it was what he needed to hear. It wouldn't have done him any good to stay home all day waiting for her."

"No. So tell him we are on it, and I will catch up with him later today. Roger is at home with this worker?"

"Yeah. While Josh is at school."

"Can you leave word with them to let me in to take a look around?"

"I'll be back there. I will let you in."

"It isn't going to drive *you* stir crazy to sit around all day waiting for her to come back?"

"Someone has to do it. I know I don't live there, so I can't say I'm the man of the house since Dad can't take care of things. But... I wouldn't put it all on Josh. I'll do whatever I can to lighten his load." He swallowed, staring off into space. "I didn't really do much for him when Dad... did what he did. I threw myself into sports at school and didn't want to be home. So he went through a lot of that alone, when I should have been there for him."

"The past is the past. You were a teenager. You couldn't be expected to be an adult."

"No?" Cam smiled wryly. "Mom expected me to be. She expected both of us to just… go on with our lives. Step up and do whatever needed to be done." He drank the remainder of his coffee. "I couldn't hack it. I had to get out of there."

And he had. Eventually, he had dropped out of school and run away to the city, where he had pursued a life without any expectations. Where he didn't have to play football or basketball, look after his brother, work a part-time job, and do whatever household tasks Mary Lou had expected of him. Instead, he could crash on a friend's couch, eat whatever was in the fridge, drink whatever he and his friends could get together, and do other things Erin probably didn't want to know about.

But she knew what it was like to be on the street at a tender age, expected to support herself as soon as she had aged out of foster care. She knew that it may have sounded like an easy, responsibility-free life, but it was not. And from what she could gather from references Mary Lou made and the fact that Cam came home now and then for dinner, a weekend, or the holidays, he was holding his own. He had a car or access to one. He didn't look like he was sleeping rough. She hadn't ever heard of his stealing from Mary Lou or asking her for money.

"I'm going to get started on making some inquiries," Terry said briskly. "Give me your cell number so I can catch up with you if I need to."

Cam gave it to him and Terry wrote it in his notepad, then put it away. "I'll let you get back home. Keep an eye on Roger; I know he can get agitated when things do not go how he expects them to."

Cam nodded somberly. He shook hands with Terry and nodded to Erin before leaving the bakery. Terry approached the counter, and Erin dug a gluten-free dog biscuit from the cookie jar for K9.

"Mary Lou's usual schedule," Terry said, "she would be here when you opened?"

"Yes. Not every day; she couldn't afford to get that much baking. But once or twice a week to pick up a few supplies. Always first thing in the morning, waiting outside the door when I opened. It was rare for her to stop by later in the day like she did yesterday when she found out that Cam would be home."

"So this wasn't a planned visit?"

"Uh... no. If it was, she would have picked up what she needed earlier in the week, when she made her usual bakery run. Coming by for a breakfast muffin was not part of her usual routine."

"Did she say why Cam was coming into town?"

"No. I don't know why he was coming back... just to visit, I thought. But... it's not the weekend or a holiday. I'm not sure why he would come back now."

"But Mary Lou wasn't upset about it."

"No, no. She was happy about it."

Terry nodded. "Okay. Thanks. I will start making inquiries, put out the word that she is missing, and see if I can find out why she would leave like that without telling her family. You're not aware of her ever doing anything like this before?"

"Mary Lou? No! She's always been the most level-headed, reliable person... focused on her family. Even after everything Roger has put her through, she is still devoted to him. She knows that he can't take care of the family. None of them could take over in her absence. Even though Joshua is older now and making strides toward independence... she still tries to shelter him. Keep him away from any bad influences and make sure he keeps going to school. I think maybe she knew she had put too much pressure on them after Roger's suicide attempt and was trying to ease some of the pressure on Josh."

"And leaving him in the lurch to look after Roger's needs would not qualify as sheltering him and letting him be a teenager."

"No."

Terry nodded, leaned over the counter to give Erin a quick kiss, then left. She watched him turn down Main Street to begin his investigation.

CHAPTER 13

As soon as Terry was out of the bakery, Vic came through the kitchen door eagerly to get the scoop. Erin related as much as she could to Vic without breaking confidences. Cam had chosen to stay at the bakery rather than go somewhere more private. He had spoken with Erin standing right there, so he couldn't be too concerned about any details Erin had overheard getting out.

Vic shook her head. "I just can't imagine where Mary Lou would go! She wouldn't just leave without making sure that her husband and son were taken care of!"

"Well, she didn't. Not exactly."

Vic shook her head. "What do you mean?"

"She left when Cam was there to look after things. Both boys are used to helping with Roger, and they have a care worker for him when Joshua is at school. And Cam is an adult, so she hasn't left either of them without an adult to make the decisions."

"You don't think that she left because Cam was there and could take over!"

"I don't think so... but it's interesting timing. If it was something like a kidnapping, then wouldn't they wait until Mary Lou was alone and or away from home? They wouldn't go into the house and take her from there. She walks to work every day. It's not hard for someone to drive up in a van and snatch her."

"I've heard of that happening." Vic frowned. "But sometimes people *are* taken from their homes, with other people in the house."

"Sometimes," Erin agreed. "But the reason they are such a big deal and you hear about them is because it is so rare."

"Okay, yes. But it does happen."

Erin shrugged. "I'm just saying... that you don't usually wait until there are *more* people in the house to kidnap someone."

"Reckon they didn't know that."

"Or it wasn't a kidnapping," Erin agreed.

Vic was opening her mouth to say something else when she looked suddenly at the door, an instant before the bells jingled and a new customer arrived.

Only it wasn't a new customer. Erin turned to see who had arrived, and saw Terry and K9. She looked immediately over to the table they had been sitting at to see if Terry had left his phone or something else at the table and was returning to collect it.

Terry's mouth was a grim line. "Erin... do you know who is supposed to be opening the Book Nook today?" He tilted his head slightly in the direction of the bookstore.

"Well... it should be Naomi, unless she had an appointment somewhere this morning. And then she would have gotten a staff member to open it up. Mr. Foster has been helping out over there for a while."

Terry nodded and pulled out his phone. Erin and Vic exchanged glances.

"There isn't anyone there?" Erin asked with concern.

"No. The closed sign is still up. There isn't any sign saying they would be closed today."

"Naomi didn't say anything to me about not being there today. I was over yesterday to pick up the trays from the book club meeting. She didn't say anything."

"I'll see if I can find anything out," Terry said, and walked back out of the bakery with his phone to his ear.

"Naomi?" Erin asked, looking at Vic. "What is going on here?

Where is everyone going? Charley, I could understand, but Mary Lou and Naomi? And Melissa said other people were missing; Mary Lou wasn't the first."

"They couldn't all have been kidnapped," Vic pointed out. "Charley probably just left on her own. I don't know who else is missing, but some are probably just... out of town. Avoiding any clan unrest. Either because they are associated with one of them or they don't want to get caught in the middle of anything."

"Yes, but this is... it's crazy. Where would Naomi go?"

"I don't really know very much about her. Do you know if she is closely related to either of the clans?"

"I have no idea. She's never said anything. And she isn't the *type*, if you know what I mean. I don't think she would have anything to do with them."

"What type?" Vic asked. "Would you have thought that Mona was the acting head of the Dysons? Would you have pictured Crazy Theresa as a Jackson soldier? There *are* women in the clans. Some of them very prominent."

"Well, yeah... I guess," Erin admitted. She was still having trouble wrapping her mind around the fact that the Dysons had been led by women for generations. That the whole feud had been started by a woman. She would have thought that women were just caught up in the middle of it, like Vic's mother, surrounded by boys who thought membership in the clan was the best thing since sliced bread.

But Naomi? She couldn't have anything to do with the clans. Erin was sure of that. She was always busy. There was so much for a small business owner to do. Naomi was every bit as busy with the demands of the bookstore as Erin was with the bakery.

"Is Terry still there?" Erin asked, trying to crane her neck to an angle where she could see Terry out the front window without abandoning her workstation and admitting that she was snooping.

If people were disappearing from Bald Eagle Falls, that impacted everyone. That *made* it everyone's business.

Didn't it?

Vic walked to the end of the counter, then through the hinged portion so she could walk to the front of the store and see where Terry was.

"He's still there, in front of the Book Nook."

"This is just too bizarre."

A couple of older women came up to the door and entered, setting the bells jingling. Erin forced herself to focus on the women and find out what they needed.

After they were dealt with, Vic again walked to the front of the bakery and looked out.

"Mr. Foster is coming," she reported. "He'll have keys and unlock the doors to make sure Naomi isn't there… if she had a heart attack or something."

Naomi was older than Erin, but she didn't think she was old enough to suffer a heart attack or stroke.

Erin had taken care of elderly people in the past, before she had come to Bald Eagle Falls. She knew how devastating something like that could be.

"Even young people can have heart problems," Vic murmured, apparently thinking along the same lines as Erin. "Even athletes. You've seen pro athletes go down on the field."

"Don't tell me that," Erin begged. "Now you've got me worried. Naomi never said that she had any heart problems."

"She wouldn't necessarily know."

"I don't think she's missed a day of work since I opened Auntie Clem's. She's healthy and takes care of herself."

Vic just nodded. "They're going in," she reported.

Erin held her breath. She probably shouldn't. Who knew how long it would take before Terry or Mr. Foster returned and reported what they had found out. She should keep herself busy and try to take her mind off it.

She and Vic went back to work and tried to stay focused on their baking and customers until Mr. Foster himself came into Auntie Clem's.

He gave Vic a disapproving look before focusing on Erin. "Miss Erin. I guess you heard…" he nodded toward the Book Nook. "Naomi didn't show up to open today."

"Do you know what happened to her? Is she okay?"

"We still don't know. The police were going to send someone to her house for a welfare check. See if she's there and if she is okay."

"Was everything okay over there?" Erin motioned toward the bookstore. It was hard to get the image of a death at the shop out of her mind. As soon as she had started to worry about Naomi, her mind had been filled with images of the man she had previously found dead there. A man she had once known, in her past life.

"It was fine," Mr. Foster assured her. "Everything was just as it was when we closed up last night. It hadn't been broken into. Nothing has been touched."

CHAPTER 14

*A*t the end of the day, they were no closer to finding out what had happened to Naomi or Mary Lou. Maybe that was because Erin was not a police detective, and Terry was unwilling to part with any information on the investigation and whether he felt they were any closer to finding either of the missing women.

Erin sat on the couch with Orange Blossom in her lap, purring away as she stroked him and scratched his ears. The last time she had talked to Terry he had been on his way to the Cox home to talk to the boys again. Erin was afraid that meant he was no further along than he had been when he had started that morning.

Blossom's ears twitched and he looked toward the front of the house. Erin focused on the figure that crossed from the side yard to the front. She tensed. She was not used to visitors who came around the house from the backyard. She didn't like people lurking around the yard. She grasped her phone, ready to hit Terry's number if there were any danger.

There was a quick knock at the door. No doorbell to begin with. Someone who did not want to startle her.

Erin had to stand up to answer the door, upsetting Orange Blossom from his comfortable spot. He protested, yowling at her in irritation. Erin ignored the complaint and went to the door to peer out the wide-angle peephole to see who it was. She should get a doorbell camera for a better view of who it was, and a recording in case they ever needed evidence for a court case.

But in this case, she was not worried about vandalism, porch theft, or violence. She opened the door to a lanky, shaggy-haired young man with hair the same color as Vic's.

"Jeremy! Hey, how are you? I didn't know that you were coming by."

"Well, I didn't either, to tell the truth. I was just around back looking for my sister."

The last Erin had seen Vic, she had been headed to the loft apartment. She'd said she was tired and ready to crash for the night. A lump rose in Erin's throat, making it hard for her to swallow.

"Isn't she there?"

Jeremy shook his head. "Door's locked. I knocked, but there was no answer. Reckon she an' Willie might be out somewhere."

"I haven't seen him tonight. He was by yesterday and hasn't been here very often lately, so I didn't figure he'd be back that quick. Are you sure…?"

"Sure that Vic wasn't there? Well, I'm sure no one answered the door. Maybe she doesn't want any visitors tonight."

Erin frowned. "She's always happy to see you. And if Willie isn't there, you aren't interrupting anything. Unless he sneaked in while I was out here, and I didn't hear anything. I usually hear his truck, but Orange Blossom was purring," she stooped to pick him up and held him up to her face. "You know how loud he is; he might have drowned out a jet plane landing in the backyard."

Jeremy shook his head. "Willie's truck ain't back there. Nothin' parked behind the house. Unless he parked a few blocks away and walked in, and I don't see why he would do that unless—"

"He is being kind of… covert lately. Trying to avoid trouble with the clans. So it's possible. If they were busy, Vic might not have answered the door."

"If they're busy, I don't want to interrupt them," Jeremy said, his cheeks getting pink. "We'll just let them have their romantic interlude."

"I don't think he is there, though," Erin said. "And with so many people disappearing lately, I don't want to assume…"

She sat back down with Orange Blossom in her lap, but he wanted to show her his displeasure at being dumped off, so he jumped down and stalked away. Erin shrugged and looked down at the phone she was still holding in her hand. She tapped Vic's number and the speaker button, and waited, holding her breath, heart already pounding hard.

What if Vic didn't answer?

What if Vic's apartment was empty, just like the Book Nook and Mary Lou's bedroom? What if she had disappeared just as easily, right under Erin's own nose?

"Erin?" Vic's voice clicked in. "What's up?"

"Oh, thank goodness. I was afraid that you had disappeared."

"I'm still here," Vic said, sounding just slightly irritated at Erin's concern. "What's up?"

"Are you in your apartment? Sorry to interrupt, Jeremy is looking for you."

"Oh. I'll give him a call."

"You're on speaker."

"Well, thanks for telling me, girl," Vic drawled, "Good thing I didn't say anything inappropriate in front of my baby brother."

"I'm your big brother," Jeremy corrected. "And I've heard you say plenty of inappropriate things in the past."

"You're my youngest brother. So you're my baby brother."

Jeremy shot Erin an exasperated look, rolling his eyes. "So, where are you? If you're busy, I'll head home. I just dropped in to say hi."

"I'm home. I'll just get dressed and pop over. Give me five."

"Are you in bed?" Jeremy looked at the clock on the wall, then pulled his phone out, foiled by the analog dial. "It's still early, but I know you gotta be up before dawn for this slave driver," Jeremy teased Erin.

Erin's phone gave a short beep, indicating that the call had ended. She looked down at the screen and decided not to call back. The call hadn't been dropped; Vic had ended it. She would explain when she arrived. Prolonging the call would keep her from being able to get ready and over there to discuss it in person.

"I guess she's okay," Erin told Jeremy with relief.

He gave her an odd look, cocking his head slightly. "Why wouldn't she be?"

CHAPTER 15

*E*rin sighed. She glanced at the clock. Vic had told her five minutes. So there was enough time to give Jeremy a brief rundown of the disappearances.

He sat down at the other end of the couch while she explained about the missing people she was aware of. And there were undoubtedly more, or Melissa would not have said what she had. Jeremy's eyes grew wider as she ran through each of the names. Then his brows drew down.

"What is the thread that connects them all?" he asked. "There must be something that is the same between all of them, right?"

"I don't know. Terry said people are either running to the clans or away from them. Some people find safety on one side, and some on the other."

"But someone like Mary Lou… it doesn't sound like she ran away. Cam thinks she was kidnapped? That someone came into the house and took her?"

Erin nodded. Jeremy considered this thoughtfully. He shook his head. "I didn't live in Bald Eagle Falls when he was around, so I don't know Cam that well, but I was aware of him, and I know other people who knew him or mentioned him. And… he never struck me as the kind to let his imagination get away from him."

"No, he's pretty down-to-earth. Both of those boys are. They had to grow up pretty quickly, with everything that happened to the family."

"And his dad... I mean, he had a brain injury, right? It wasn't something genetic that... made him the way he is?" Jeremy tried to address the question sensitively.

"Right...?" Erin wasn't sure why Jeremy brought that into it.

"So Cam hasn't turned into some kind of conspiracy theorist, right? He's... grounded."

"Oh." Erin nodded. "Yeah, it's not some wild flight of fancy. The police department is investigating. And honestly, I can't think of any reason Mary Lou would have to just abandon her family like that. I mean, logically, she could have, but why would she? Why, after everything she has done until now?"

"You never know what's going on in other people's heads," Jeremy pointed out. "Maybe it was just too much. She knows it will never be over. Roger isn't going to suddenly recover. He's going to need to be cared for the rest of his life."

It was a bleak outlook.

"But nothing has changed," Erin insisted. "Why would she suddenly decide that?"

"Because people get burned out. They put up with conditions for years, and then it is... just too much. Like it was for Cam."

"Hmm."

The back door opened, and Vic joined them. She had a house-coat on over her frilly nightgown, and her hair hung in wet rat tails around her shoulders.

She didn't need to explain where she had been when Jeremy had knocked on her door. Soaking in the tub at the back of the apart-ment, with the door closed, exhaust fan on, and music playing. It was lucky she'd had her phone close enough to hear when Erin had called her. Otherwise, Erin might have let herself into the apart-ment to make sure Vic was okay and found herself in an awkward situation when she found Vic in the bathtub in her altogether.

Erin's cheeks flared with heat. She looked away, not wanting to draw attention to how red her face had turned. She made noises to call Marshmallow to her, since Orange Blossom had spurned her.

"Come on, Marshmallow. Come get some ear scratches."

The rabbit hopped over and accepted the affection, closing his eyes in bliss.

"Hey, sorry to interrupt your bath," Jeremy apologized. "Like I said, I just stopped by to say hi. You could have just told me to go home."

"I was nearly done anyway. It's fine. You got me out before I fell asleep and woke up in cold water, so you did me a favor."

"If you're that tired, I won't stay long."

Vic shrugged and sat down in her favorite chair. "So, how's my baby brother? Glad to see you haven't disappeared anywhere."

"Erin was just filling me in on everyone who has disappeared." Jeremy grimaced. "That's... weird."

"For most of them... it's *not* that weird. But Mary Lou and Naomi? I can't think of any reason either of them would want to disappear. If they had said they wanted to get away from any clan violence that might come out of Willie becoming the leader of the Dysons, I'd get it. But just to disappear without saying anything... I can't make heads or tails of it."

"You think Cam is lying?" Jeremy asked.

"I don't know Cam well enough. Maybe he's lying. Maybe Mary Lou didn't tell him for a reason. Or maybe it was a kidnapping, like Cam thinks. But why would anyone want to take Mary Lou? It isn't like she's a high-value target. Or like she knows anything about Willie or the Dysons that someone would want to keep from getting out. It don't make a lick of sense."

"You don't *know* what she knows," Jeremy disagreed.

"Even if she knows something, Mary Lou isn't the kind of person to blab. If she was going to spread around stories about Willie or the clans, don't you think she would have already? I just can't see a more unlikely person to kidnap."

"Naomi?" Erin suggested.

Vic looked at her, lips pursed, then nodded. "Or Naomi," she admitted. "You think someone took both of them? What's your theory?"

"I don't have one yet," Erin admitted. "I keep going around and around in circles, saying she wouldn't have done something like that and then wondering if she did. Thinking it couldn't possibly have been a kidnapping and then deciding that's the only thing that makes any sense."

Vic nodded with wry amusement. She took a deep breath and let it out. She turned her focus to Jeremy. "What does Beaver think?"

"Ro?" Jeremy asked, using his own nickname for Rohilda Beaven, federal agent. "What makes you think that she has any opinion on it?"

"Well, Cam is *her* informant, isn't he? She's his handler? So she must have some opinion when it comes to the disappearance of his mother."

"Well, maybe she does, but I have no idea what it is. I haven't seen her for a while. Certainly not since Mary Lou's disappearance."

Beaver and Jeremy were romantically involved, so Erin was surprised he hadn't seen her recently. Unless she had dumped him.

"You haven't seen her for a while?" Vic fastened on to this comment, sounding protective of her "baby brother." "Why not? Where is she?"

"I don't know. She doesn't usually tell me what she's working on. It's classified. Sometimes, she'll tell me a few stories, but nothing that would identify anyone or tell me where she was working or on what kind of files. You know as much as I do about her working with Cam."

"She *is* still working with him, right?" Vic drilled.

"As far as I know. But I don't talk to him, and like I said, she doesn't tell me a thing about him."

Erin pondered the possibilities. Maybe Beaver was already working on files related to the clans. Sooner or later, there would be a federal case against them, if there wasn't one already. Probably several of them. Organized crime cartels racked up charges for trafficking drugs, guns, and humans. They evaded taxes. They contracted murders and committed all other sorts of crimes.

There had to be a lot of things that the feds were interested in. A lot of things that Beaver might be looking into, knowing the disruption that was going on in the Dyson clan right now. There were bound to be people who objected to Willie being appointed the clan's leader. A lot of people in the Dyson clan considered him a traitor and wouldn't have anything to do with him, and now they had to report to him or be subject to him. Beaver would dig into those cracks in the organization to see where she could get a foothold and start prying them apart...

"I'll be sure to ask Ro what she's up to and whether she knows who kidnapped Cam's mother the next time I see her," Jeremy said dryly.

Vic snickered. "Are you saying she wouldn't help you out with that?"

"Maybe she would talk to Terry, though," Erin suggested thoughtfully. "I wonder if he's already talked to her to see if she knows anything."

Beaver had been involved in a number of cases since she had first shown up in town during an attempt by the Jacksons to take over a Dyson drug way station. She seemed to be able to insinuate herself into any case that interested her, and to show up as a player in all kinds of cases. Erin still wasn't even sure which agency she worked for.

"I wouldn't know," Jeremy said, putting his hands up. "Seeing as I haven't seen her."

"Is she in town?" Vic asked.

He looked like he was about to repeat the same gesture and answer, and Vic made a disgusted noise and waved his response away.

"Well... I'm worn slap out," Vic excused herself. "So unless you have news of anyone else who has disappeared, I'm going to dry my hair and go to bed."

Jeremy stretched. "Then I guess it is back to my lonely little hovel I go. Nice talking to you ladies. Glad you're both okay."

Vic stood up, but stopped, twirling one lock of hair around her finger and looking at her brother with a question in her eyes.

Jeremy raised his brows.

"You haven't heard anything from Pa, have you?" Vic asked. "I mean… everything is okay with him and Ma, and they aren't trying to get you involved with the clan again, right?"

Jeremy nodded slowly. "It's been pretty quiet. They're okay, as far as I know. And… I'm not getting involved in any clan stuff."

"With Daniel and Joseph in prison, he's not trying to recruit you… to take their place? To be *his* heir if something happens to him?"

"I'm not getting involved in anything with the clan," Jeremy said firmly.

"And he's not trying to get you to?"

Jeremy just looked at Vic and didn't answer, which was an answer in itself.

CHAPTER 16

*I*t was another restless night. Erin was relieved when Terry finally got home after a long day of investigation into Mary Lou's disappearance and whatever other complications there were to the case. Erin couldn't imagine trying to solve a growing number of disappearances from the small town. It felt like living in a sci-fi movie where people were being kidnapped by aliens.

She would have to watch out for the pod people. If people who had disappeared suddenly started coming back and were behaving suspiciously...

She got more sleep than she had the previous night due solely to her level of exhaustion, her body taking over from her anxious brain and dragging her into the depths of sleep until her alarm went off in the morning. Terry shook her awake and asked whether she needed someone else to take her morning shift for her because she was too tired or sick.

"You could still be suffering concussion symptoms," he reminded her. "We were told that they could last for months, and that you might need more sleep while your brain finishes healing."

"I'm fine," Erin snapped. "I'm up."

She didn't like his jumping to the conclusion that something was wrong with her when she had just not awakened to the opening notes of her morning alarm.

But when she looked at her phone after leaving the bedroom, she realized that she had not just slept through the first few notes of her alarm. It had actually been sounding for ten minutes before Terry had woken her up.

Grumpy, she put her phone on the bathroom counter while she had a quick wake-up shower and got dressed for the day. Her hair would not behave and go in the direction it was supposed to, increasing her irritation. She knocked her phone off the counter when she slammed her brush down in her frustration. When she picked it up, she saw that there was a crack across the corner of the screen.

"That better not be a sign of what today is going to be like," she muttered aloud. "Maybe I *should* just go back to bed."

But there was no way she would sleep now anyway. She was awake, and she was angry. Her heart rate spiked, and she wished that she could go for a run to burn off the adrenaline. If she had been a runner. And if she'd actually had the time to go for a run.

She just felt like she needed to do something. It felt like everything was falling to pieces, and she didn't like the out-of-control feeling.

When she got to the kitchen, she found Vic there, the coffee perking, and toast in the toaster.

"What's all this?" she asked grumpily, rubbing her eyes.

Vic laughed. "Mornin', sunshine. I just woke up with all this nervous energy this morning. So I figured I'd put it to use."

Erin wondered whether Terry had texted Vic and asked her to help get Erin on track for the day.

She didn't like to be *handled*.

"I don't know if I can eat anything," she grumbled. "But the coffee is welcome."

Vic seemed unperturbed by her mood. "Your caffeine should be ready in a minute." Vic stifled a yawn. "I'm not worth a hill of beans without the stuff some mornings. You didn't sleep well?"

"I did... better than the night before. But I feel like..." Erin rubbed her head and tried to find the words to express it. "I feel like I was down a well... with some big guy sitting on my head. I slept, but it felt more like it was a sickness than actual rest."

Vic opened her mouth to make an observation.

"And it isn't my concussion," Erin told her. "I am over all of the concussion symptoms. This is something totally different."

"Okay," Vic didn't try to talk Erin out of it and tell her that it was just a new manifestation of the concussion, which had already kept Erin away from the bakery for way too long. "What do you think it is, then? Worried about... everything that is happening?"

Erin nodded. "Probably," she agreed. "It seems like everything that I've gotten used to in Bald Eagle Falls is changing. I don't like people disappearing. I could always depend on Mary Lou and her routines. And with our partnership with the Book Nook for the book club, I thought we had a relationship with Naomi. I can't imagine her leaving without saying something to us."

"Well, apparently, she didn't even say anything to Mr. Foster, her employee, so you shouldn't feel bad. I don't think that... *all* of them just disappeared voluntarily without telling anyone." Vic shook her head and put her hand over her stomach. "I'm worried sick, if you want to know the truth."

Erin was sorry for assuming that Vic's chipper attitude meant the unrest in Bald Eagle Falls hadn't affected her. They were both feeling the same thing.

"Well, let's do something about it," she said briskly.

Vic raised her brows. "Exactly how are we going to do anything about it?" she inquired. "Do you have a time machine? A solution to Willie's little problem of now being the head of an organization he didn't want anything to do with and all of the people who would rather kill him than have to obey him?"

"No," Erin admitted. "I thought we would take a care package to the Coxes and see how they're doing. Maybe ask a few questions to see if... the police have missed anything."

Vic took the coffee pot from under the spout and filled two travel mugs. She leaned back against the counter, holding one of the mugs under her nose and inhaling the steam.

"Did Terry tell you anything about their investigation? Do they have any idea what happened to Mary Lou?"

Erin rolled her eyes. "He won't tell me anything. I don't know if they've found any clues or picked up any chatter." She caught herself clenching her teeth and tried to relax her jaw and the rest of her tense muscles. "Maybe that's what's got me so frustrated. I need to hear something. I need to know that they're making progress and that Mary Lou will be back, and she'll be okay."

Vic nodded. She sipped her coffee. "I can't help thinking... she would never leave voluntarily. She would fight to get back to her family, and how would a kidnapper respond to that?" She sighed. "I'm probably catastrophizing. I can't help thinking of the worst possible outcomes." She indicated the coffee with her eyes. "And I'm sure this will improve my mood, right?"

Erin chuckled and took a large swallow of her own piping hot coffee. It brought tears to her eyes.

"Roger likes the chocolate muffins with the cherry jam inside. Let's make some of those. And we'll take them over this afternoon, along with some pizza pretzels and... what's something Mary Lou really likes? She liked those onion rolls. They weren't very popular, so I haven't made them since. I'll make some of those too. For when she comes back."

Vic swallowed hard and nodded. "Yeah, that sounds good."

"We'll get the afternoon and close covered, and pop over to the Coxes to give them their treats and see how everything is going. Maybe there will be some good news by then. If not, we can see if they need anything. Help with Roger so they can take a break, running errands, whatever."

CHAPTER 17

$\mathcal{H}$aving a purpose for the day really helped, even knowing that it wouldn't actually change the situation with Willie and the clans. It didn't make Bald Eagle Falls safer or bring back anyone who was missing. But doing something, anything, gave Erin a sense of purpose and the illusion that she might uncover what had happened to Mary Lou.

Cam answered the door, looking a little haggard. Erin hoped they hadn't woken him from a nap. He was probably getting less sleep than Erin, worrying about what had happened to his mother.

He looked at them and his eyes went to the box in Erin's hands.

"Come on in."

They entered the house and Erin carried the box of fresh baking over to the dining room table, where a number of other offerings were arranged. Apparently they were not the first to try to offer comfort by the way of food.

"There are some of those muffins that your dad likes," Erin offered, putting them down.

"Thanks. He's down for a nap right now. He was pretty agitated last night, with Mom not being here."

"Poor guy," Erin sympathized. She and Vic sat down with Cam

in the living room. Erin wrapped her arms around herself, feeling chilled even though it was a warm day. "I feel so bad for all of you. I wish there was something more we could do. We're yours for the afternoon, if you want us to run any errands for you, or to keep an eye on things here while you take a break. What would help the most?"

"That's great, but I don't think there's anything right now. We're just… waiting for the police to find something." Cam shook his head. "I got no use for cops."

Erin knew it wasn't anything personal against Terry, but she still felt a stab of anger and defensiveness at his vitriol against the Bald Eagle Falls police department. But she remembered being in the house after Cam's arrest for a crime he hadn't committed. How unfair it was and how bereft everyone in the house had felt. And it was difficult to think about Mary Lou's absence without remembering Joshua's kidnapping. She remembered Mary Lou taking her up to Joshua's room as they both looked for anything that might be a clue to where he was or what had happened to him.

The family had been through so many tragedies. Mary Lou should be there. Let something happen to another family for once.

She knew it wouldn't help anything if bad things happened to another member of the community. Melissa had already said that there were others. The Coxes were not alone in their confusion and anxiety over what had happened to Mary Lou. There were others.

She felt a twinge of guilt over not being more worried about Charley. She *was* worried about Charley. But in all likelihood, Charley was just fine. She was just being Charley. She was looking after herself, making sure the clans could not reach her.

It was different with Mary Lou. It was out of character and she had people at home who needed her.

"They haven't been able to find anything…?"

Cam shook his head. "Not that they've told me about. Of course… why would they? They say they'll keep us updated on what they know, but you know it isn't going to happen. They'll keep us in the dark with platitudes until…" He choked off the sentence and shook his head, eyes glistening.

"She's going to be okay," Vic comforted. "They'll find something."

Cam's eyes shot daggers. Vic looked away, her cheeks turning pink.

"You can't know that," Cam told her.

Vic bit her lip. "I just think... I guess I hope and pray that it will all turn out. We want to help in any way we can. I'm sorry for sounding like I'm just placating you or promising something I can't control."

Cam nodded. "I've had enough of the old ladies around telling me everything is going to be fine; I don't need to hear it from you, too. You can believe whatever makes you happy," he waved the idea of religion away, "but God isn't the one who is going to bring Mom home. If the police can't find her... then that's it. I don't know what happened, but if she could come back here on her own, she would."

Erin and Vic nodded sympathetically.

"Did she keep a journal?" Erin asked, "Or a planning calendar? She always seemed very organized, so I assume she has a system in place."

"She had journals and a planner," Cam said. "You can look at the planner if you want, but not her journals. I'm not reading those until... I know for sure. I don't want to invade her privacy. Mom has always been very sensitive about that." He stood and went up the stairs to Mary Lou's bedroom. Erin wanted to follow him and have a look around Mary Lou's room, but he hadn't invited her along, so she didn't dare. He had just finished saying how protective Mary Lou was of her privacy. She would not want Erin snooping around in her room.

In a couple of minutes, Cam came back with a binder. It was larger than Erin's, full letter size rather than the executive size book she carted around with her in her large shoulder bag. Unlike Erin's, there were no stickies or odd-sized pages sticking out of it. Everything looked neat and clean, as if Mary Lou always knew exactly what she was doing and didn't have to rewrite anything or make an addition, flag a reference, or leave anything incomplete.

Cam handed it to Erin, and she opened it carefully, respectful, mindful that even this was an invasion of Mary Lou's privacy that she would probably not be happy about when she returned.

CHAPTER 18

*E*rin opened the daily pages to the page Mary Lou had left the plastic "today" bookmark in. Two days before. Wednesday. Erin skimmed over the calendar and the reminders and tasks that Mary Lou had left for herself. Everything was written in precise, even printing. She saw ACB marked in the afternoon to remind Mary Lou to hop over to Auntie Clem's Bakery to pick up the things she wanted for the dinner with Cam, which was also neatly lettered in the 6:30 time slot.

There wasn't anything else written in the evening. Erin turned the page and looked at Thursday's plan. Mary Lou had her shift at the General Store written in. Above it, she had written "Cam?" with a question mark. What was her question? Whether he would be there in the morning, or already gone back to the city? Whether they would grab a muffin together at the bakery as they had planned? There had obviously been some question in Mary Lou's mind as to whether they would follow through.

Erin frowned, thinking about it. She skimmed over the rest of the day and the tasks and reminders she had made for the day. Nothing about any unusual appointments or plans. It looked as if she had planned to breakfast with Cam and then to open at the General Store, work her shift, and go home. Just like any other day.

There were notations for when Joshua would be at school and when the care worker would be at the house. Making sure that someone was always there to keep an eye on Roger to make sure he had the support he needed and couldn't go wandering without supervision.

Erin reviewed Mary Lou's plans for the weekend and into the following week. Everything seemed perfectly normal, the schedule Erin had been familiar with. No doctor appointments. No mysterious meetings with a Mr. X. Nothing about the clans, warning about what they might be doing.

Cam was watching Erin closely to see if she had found anything enlightening. Erin shook her head regretfully. She looked through the rest of the planner. The week view. The monthly calendar. A year-at-a-glance with holidays marked off.

In the reference section, she found a detailed list of Roger's medications, daily schedule, and upcoming doctor's appointments. She knew that if she looked back at the day planner views, she would see each doctor's appointments carefully slotted into place so they wouldn't miss anything.

"Everything looks perfectly normal," she admitted with a shrug of her shoulders. She coughed and cleared her throat several times. "Uh, do you think I could get a glass of water?" she asked, shifting to stand up.

"I can get you one," Cam offered, his hospitality training kicking in. "Sorry. I should have offered both of you beverages. Miss Victoria, can I get you anything?"

"No, I'm okay," Vic told him.

While Cam's back was to them, Erin turned on her phone video and recorded Roger's information and a quick page flip of a few days of Mary Lou's schedule. She didn't have more than a few seconds because she didn't want Cam to turn around and catch her at it.

Cam returned with a glass of water and Erin sipped it. "Ah, that's better. I just had a bit of a tickle, you know?" She cleared her throat experimentally. "Yeah, that's much better. Do you want me to put this back for you?" She stood up, holding on to it, aiming to get to the stairs before Cam thought to stop her.

Cam's hand closed over the book and he pulled it from her grasp. "I'll take care of it. Thanks."

So much for Erin's chance to get a look at Mary Lou's bedroom. She had to take Cam's word that nothing had been out of place. And the police department's investigation, of course. They would have found anything that seemed out of place.

"Did Mary Lou know ahead of time that you were coming?" Erin asked. "I guess not, because she came to the bakery Wednesday to pick up some things for dinner."

Cam shrugged. "Yeah, it was kind of spur of the moment. I just called her Tuesday night to let her know that I was going to be around, if she didn't mind having company for supper." He blinked and thought about that. "I'm company now," he said with realization. "I don't live here."

Mary Lou still kept a room for him and probably invited him home frequently, so it still felt like the home he had left, but he hadn't lived there for more than a year.

Erin nodded. "I'm sure she would have loved for you to move back any time you wanted to."

"I know. And I left on my own; it wasn't like I was kicked out or anything. I just couldn't deal with living up to everyone's expectations. It was so... stifling. I felt like I couldn't breathe."

Erin nodded. She had lived in many different places in her lifetime, and Vic had run away from home, so they both understood something about the life that Campbell was leading and his reasons for doing it.

"Sometimes... no matter how you want something to work out, it just doesn't," Erin acknowledged. "I know this was your real family since birth, but for me... going from one family to another... I wanted some of them to work out so bad. I could see myself living there, could see the kind of life I would have if I just fit in. For a long time, I thought it was my fault. If I was better at following the rules and acting like a normal person, it would all work out, and I could stay with them forever."

Cam looked at her, waiting for her to finish.

Erin shrugged helplessly. She looked at Vic. "Sometimes, no

matter how hard you try to fit a certain mold, you just can't." She looked back at Cam. "All those expectations... they are just too much, and you can't keep it up anymore."

Vic and Cam both nodded at this.

"So..." Cam rubbed his hands together briskly. "So I left, and I just came home occasionally for visits. And Mom was good about not begging me to stay all the time. She just accepted that I would be here for a meal or two, and then go back to the city."

"And you told her you would be returning yesterday morning," Erin recalled.

"Yeah. She said we could have a muffin or something from Auntie Clem's, and then I was going to head out and she was going in to work."

Erin frowned and turned to look out toward the street. "What are you driving?"

"Uh, nothing right now. Someone dropped me off. And I was going to... I had a ride arranged to get back to the city. But, of course, that didn't work out. I had to stay here. I couldn't just leave Josh to take care of everything."

"Are the two of you managing okay? You don't need any help?"

"I've had lots of offers from the church ladies. We're okay for now, but not indefinitely. Mom has power of attorney for Dad and all that, we don't. We can't make decisions on his medical care or anything. The bills are all on autopay, I think, but if Mom isn't working, putting money into those accounts... I don't think there are more than a couple of weeks in the checking account. And savings... is pretty sparse."

"Does she have life insurance?" the words were out of Erin's mouth before she realized it. She clapped a hand over her mouth, choking. Vic's eyes were wide in horror.

Cam gave a bark of laughter. "Well, you're direct, aren't you? The police didn't ask it quite like that."

"No, no, I didn't mean to say anything. I'm sorry. I didn't even mean to ask. You certainly shouldn't answer."

He chuckled. "I looked through her files to see what she has, but I don't understand all the terms. And they don't cover missing persons. She would have to actually be… dead. With proof and a medical examiner's report. And no suicide. I guess after Dad's attempt, no one would cover suicide for him or the rest of the family."

"No," Erin said faintly. "Oh, I'm sorry, Cam. That's probably up there with the rudest thing I've ever said."

He patted her arm. "I'd rather you said something like that than just sat around thinking it," he assured her. "I'm sure half the ladies who have come to visit and offer their condolences have probably been thinking the same thing. Putting on their long faces and sympathy and wondering whether I did something to her or whether she… did that."

"I'm sure not. They have a lot more faith than me."

"Just because someone says they have faith, that doesn't mean they do. Or that it is anything more than something they just keep in their back pocket for appropriate occasions. There aren't a lot of people who actually… live it." He glanced over at Vic. "At least when Miss Victoria says she's hoping and praying, I believe it. That she actually does it and thinks it will make a difference."

Vic nodded, looking away uncomfortably.

"So…" Erin tried to change the subject. "Did Beaver drive you to Bald Eagle Falls, or was she the one who was supposed to take you back to the city?"

Cam's eyes widened. He considered the question before answering.

"She dropped me off. How did you know that?"

"Was it her idea to come here? Or had you made plans that you needed to be here for something?"

Erin already knew that it wasn't Cam's own plan. He would have known further ahead of time. Not just announcing to Mary Lou that he would be there for supper.

"Beaver said she was driving from the city to Bald Eagle Falls and would be happy to drop me off to see Mom. I figured… why not? I didn't have anything else planned."

"Beaver wanted you to come to Bald Eagle Falls?"

"No, I wouldn't say that. Just told me that she was making the trip if I wanted a ride one way. I figured I could hitch a ride back with someone or grab a bus. It's not convenient, but it works."

"Was she going to stay in town for long? Did she say why she was coming here?"

"I don't know. It wasn't really anything to do with me. I know better than to ask her anything. She'd just tell me that I was the one who was supposed to be giving her information, not the other way around."

There had long been rumors around that Beaver was using Cam as a confidential informant. Erin supposed that confirmed the rumor was true.

"That sounds like Beaver," Vic acknowledged, grinning.

It was always fun to speculate about Beaver. Each time Erin had something to do with her, she learned something new about the complicated woman. At first glance, she seemed like an unsophisticated, ordinary woman. She wasn't particularly beautiful, with a too-large nose and jaw. Her blond hair was usually gathered into a plain ponytail, sometimes threaded through the back of her baseball cap. She wore a bulky coat that hid her well-developed muscles from view. She was stocked with numerous weapons and tools that she might find herself in need of. She was constantly chewing a big wad of gum.

She seemed to enjoy her job and had told them that when she wasn't working, she moonlighted as a treasure hunter and had been to several other continents to look for particular treasures. Somehow, Erin didn't imagine that kind of work was much more relaxing than her job as a federal agent. Erin often wondered how Beaver dug up the information she did. She had to have a very large and involved group of informants like Cam. More than once, she had shown up at the opportune time to help get Erin out of hot water.

"Is she here to look into the clans?" Erin persisted, suspecting that Cam probably knew more than he let on. "Into what's going on behind the scenes with Willie's new... um... position?"

Cam scratched the back of his neck. He had a five o'clock shadow and was looking a little rough. He had probably not slept in the past forty-eight hours, and during that time, had been called on to entertain the various ladies who came over to offer their sympathies and casseroles. Not to mention the police interviews, helping take care of his father and brother, and the anxiety and grief he felt over Mary Lou's disappearance.

"What would I know about Willie and his kind?" Cam asked. "I live in the city. The clans don't have much pull there. They're mostly rural. In the city, they have to compete with all the other organized—and disorganized—crime factions."

"That doesn't answer the question," Erin said, amused by his attempt to deflect her question. "Was that why Beaver was in town?"

"How would I know? I have my own problems."

"You didn't talk on the way here?"

"Listened to the satellite radio. She's got a really nice one. I didn't ask her what she was up to. That would have been… a dangerous question to ask. Beaver doesn't like people who are too curious about her activities."

Erin sighed, figuring she wasn't likely to get any more help from Cam as to what Beaver was involved in.

"How did you know Beaver was in town?" Vic asked.

Erin shrugged and shook her head. "Beaver seems to always be where things are happening. And things have certainly been happening here. And Cam had to get to Bald Eagle Falls somehow."

"But Jeremy said he hadn't heard from her lately."

"That was the other thing," Erin agreed. "I figured he was covering for her."

"Does Jeremy have a tell?" Vic demanded, sitting up and staring at Erin. "You figured out how to tell when he's telling a lie?"

"My lips are sealed," Erin told her, miming zipping her lips shut. "I wouldn't want to cause trouble between siblings."

"You know. You have to tell me," Vic insisted. "The next time I play poker with him…"

"Nope." Erin grinned. "I'm not telling."

CHAPTER 19

Cam looked amused by the teasing between Erin and Vic. Erin knew they were being silly and juvenile, but it seemed like it helped Cam more than sympathy and long faces.

"You want a drink?" he asked, leaning forward in his seat. "I could really use a drink, and I've been waiting all day."

"On, no, I don't think so," Erin protested. "We should probably be on our way."

"Joshua will be home soon," Vic said, looking at her watch. "We probably shouldn't be drinking."

"That's exactly why I'm going to. When Joshua gets home, I'm off the clock. He can take over with Dad for the evening."

"He'll need help, won't he? It isn't really fair to saddle him with it as soon as he gets home from school. He'll be tired and have homework to do."

"And Dad is sleeping. He'll probably sleep most of the evening. I can still help, but I don't need anyone saying that I was endangering him because I was under the influence when I was supposed to be in charge of him."

Erin and Vic glanced at each other, looking for something else to say. But who were they to say that he couldn't have a relaxing drink at the end of a taxing day? He deserved it, after everything he had gone through.

"Nothing for me," Erin said, "but you go ahead."

"When Joshua gets home," Vic added.

Campbell scowled at this reminder that he wasn't quite off the clock yet. He pulled out his phone and tapped out a message, which he then sent out. He leaned back on the couch. "He can't get here too soon."

Erin couldn't help feeling a little twinge of worry. What if something had happened to Josh? What if he was the next missing person?

She pushed the thought out of her mind the best she could.

"What do *you* think of Willie being the new leader of the Dyson clan?" she asked Cam.

"I think it's ridiculous." Cam shook his head, his messy hair getting even untidier. "Ain't no way Willie can lead that clan. And he never wanted anything to do with the clans. Isn't that right? Isn't that what he always told us?"

"That's what he told me," Erin agreed. Willie had always been adamant that he wouldn't have anything to do with the clans. Though he *had* somehow kept his finger in business with Nelson Dyson. From what he had said, it was something that Nelson had wanted to keep separate from the organization, which was supposedly being led by his father, Dwight. A legitimate business, like Erin had suggested to Terry.

"Mom never wanted us to have anything to do with Willie," Cam said. "Told us he was stupid and lazy and wouldn't work for a living. That he was a member of the Dyson clan and always would be, even if he said he wasn't. We weren't even supposed to talk to him. But I did now and then. I mean... you end up standing behind someone in the grocery store, and they say hello; what are you supposed to do?"

"Be friendly," Erin agreed. "I'm sure your mom taught you to do that too."

Cam nodded. "But as far as him leading the clan? There's no way." He looked at Vic and blushed slightly. "No offense, but he'll find a way out of it, or he'll be killed, or someone will find a way to squeeze him out or make *him* disappear. It won't last."

Vic turned very white. Erin put her hand on hers comfortingly. She was really putting her foot in her mouth tonight. She tried to make Cam more comfortable but ended up steering the conversation toward something that hurt her best friend.

There was a noise at the door, and Erin turned to see Joshua coming in. He looked tired and worn. He and Cam were very similar in appearance, both with dark, wavy hair, but Josh didn't have the same hardness in his features that Cam did. He was still trying to do what was right, to live his life the way his mother wanted him to. Cam had thrown off the shackles, but that had made Joshua the sole focus of Mary Lou's efforts, determined to turn out the most mature, responsible son possible. He would be better than his father and better than Cam. A son who would follow her instructions and not be taken in by the wild crowd Cam had decided to ally himself with.

"Oh, hi, Miss Erin, Miss Victoria," Joshua greeted politely. He put his book bag on the floor and dragged himself over to them to shake their hands. "Thanks for coming over. It's nice to know people are so concerned about Mom. Cam said they have been coming all day."

"Well, we'll head out soon. I don't want to wear you both out," Erin told him apologetically. "We brought you some baking. And we wanted to see if there is anything else you need."

His hands were damp with sweat, and he smelled like he had been working out, though he was just in a regular t-shirt, and Erin didn't think he was on any of the school teams. He wasn't a sports star like Cam had been.

"That's very nice of you," Joshua said, clasping Erin's hand for an extra moment. He let it go and shook Vic's, though he barely touched her before withdrawing. Erin knew that Mary Lou did not want Joshua to have anything to do with Vic. She hadn't wanted Erin putting ideas into his head, either, but Joshua had a mind of his own. Mary Lou had given up on being able to control all of the information that flowed to the teenager.

He was determined to be an investigative reporter, and he was very good at it. Erin had no doubt that if he kept working at it, he would one day have the career he hoped for. He'd already had several pieces in the Bald Eagle Falls weekly newspaper. Not just letters to the editor or fluff pieces, but real stories, carefully investigated and written up. Front page headlines.

"Where's Dad?" Josh asked Cam, his mouth tightening.

"Having a nap. He didn't sleep much last night, so he'll probably sleep most of the evening."

"If he sleeps the whole time, he'll be up all night again."

"Then give him something to make him sleep," Cam said irritably. "I know he's got sleeping pills."

"I'm going to go check on him," Josh said, and climbed the stairs to his father's bedroom.

He wasn't gone for long. He nodded his confirmation that Roger was still quiet. He sat down next to Cam, sighing.

"What a day." He rubbed the bridge of his nose. "I don't know why I even went to school today."

"Because it's easier to do something than to sit around here all day doing nothing," Cam told him.

"School is just sitting around while the teachers drone on. It isn't exactly doing something. And every chance people got, every break between classes, or if I tried to sneak off to the restroom… everyone asked questions or told me what they thought about Mom being missing. It was just… exhausting."

CHAPTER 20

*C*am got up and went to the fridge, where he pulled out a bottle of beer. "No one else wants one?" he asked.

Erin was sure Mary Lou didn't keep the fridge stocked with beer. She was unlikely to indulge herself or to want alcohol around her teenage son—or her husband, who was on several potent psychoactive medications. Erin looked at Vic, who shook her head.

"No, we're all okay," Erin said, speaking up for Joshua as well, though she didn't look at him to see whether he agreed. "I've got my water. Anyone else want some water?"

Vic and Josh did not speak up. Josh cast a glance toward the fridge but did not say anything.

"I'm off duty," Cam told Joshua, pointing the beer bottle at him. "I'll help out if you need anything, but *you* are in charge of listening for Dad and making sure he doesn't wander off."

Roger had a tracking anklet now, so they would be alerted if he left the house. It would be quicker to find him, but technology sometimes failed, and they didn't want him to get out of the house and be on his own for any length of time.

Josh nodded and held his palms over his eyes for a moment. "Yeah," he agreed with a groan. "No problem."

"If you're exhausted and want to take a nap, we could stay around and help out for a couple of hours," Erin offered.

"Nah, it's okay."

Erin weighed whether it was time for them to say goodbye and take their leave. Cam seemed to have decided he'd had enough talking and just wanted to relax. Josh was tired from school. They both had to deal with a lot of questions, not only from the police but also from well-meaning friends and community members. All of that interaction, as well as their own grief and anxiety, must have wiped both boys out.

Joshua uncovered his eyes, rubbed his forehead for a moment, then focused on Vic.

"So, how is Willie?" he asked conversationally. "It must be weird for him, all of this attention, and everyone expecting him to lead the Dyson clan now."

Vic grimaced. "He's fine. Yeah, it's a lot of stress, and he's trying to figure out how to manage everything. But I shouldn't be talking about it. Anything that's said between him and me is private. Like going to court," she explained, "you don't have to testify about pillow talk. That's protected speech."

"I think that's only if you're married," Erin pointed out. "And you and Willie aren't, unless you snuck off and tied the knot while I wasn't looking."

Of course, they could have. They often went into the city on the weekend and Erin didn't know anything about what went on there, unless Vic chose to tell her about it.

Vic's cheeks reddened. "No, we're not married! But why should it matter? What's the difference between whether you're married or living together?"

"I don't know." Erin waved her hands in protest. "I don't know anything about it. But I think you have to be married."

"Huh." Vic shook her head. "But that doesn't mean I have to tell anyone else about it. Especially not a reporter."

It was Joshua's turn to blush and pretend that he had only been asking out of curiosity and concern for Willie's well-being, not because he was hoping to write a story about the current clan unrest, Willie's ascension, and how it was affecting everyone involved as well as Bald Eagle Falls as a whole.

"I was just... wondering. You know, Willie was always good to us, even though Mom said he was no good and we shouldn't have anything to do with him. He never acted resentful about it or anything. Maybe he didn't know that we weren't supposed to talk to him or that *people* said he was no-good and lazy, but he is always friendly with us, treats us like we're adults." Joshua stretched, scratched his head, and leaned back, closing his eyes. "In a small town like this, where everyone remembers when you were born or toddling around in diapers, they still see you as a kid even when you're grown. But Willie always treated us like we were grown up enough to understand stuff."

Vic's expression softened as he spoke, and she nodded her agreement. "He's like that with everyone. Treats them like they're real people instead of... by stereotypes and prejudices."

It hadn't been easy for Willie to find out that the girl he was attracted to was trans, but he had seemed more concerned about how much younger Vic was than he was than about the gender complications. And that was before he'd known that Vic was lying about her age and was still a minor.

"I know he probably doesn't talk to you about the clan stuff," Josh said to Vic, "especially since you are—or used to be—part of the Jackson family. But has he said anything to you about... an underground cartel?"

Everyone froze. Erin could have heard a pin drop. They all looked at Joshua, eyes wide and faces pale.

"What?" Cam demanded.

Josh stared into space, either not realizing how he'd shocked everyone or hoping that if he just kept cool they would not make a big deal about it. "Just something that I heard," he said. "I don't know if it's true or not. That kind of thing is pretty hard to investigate."

"I would think so!" Erin agreed, her voice more explosive than she had intended. Josh raised an eyebrow at her.

"*Who* told you about this underground cartel?" Cam demanded.

"I'm not revealing my sources."

"Come on, li'l brother, don't try that reporter stuff with me. Where did you hear this? Who is talking about an underground cartel?"

Josh folded his arms across his chest and looked smug.

Erin heard a noise upstairs. Everyone's eyes went to the top of the stairs, and in a moment, Roger came out of his bedroom and down the stairs. He looked over the people gathered in his living room and smiled uncertainly.

"Havin' a party?" he asked. He made his way down the stairs more slowly than Erin would have expected, but she knew that the medications he was on slowed him down and had some side effects. When she had first met him, he had been quick on his feet and his speech had come more easily, though he had been easily confused or upset.

"You have a good nap, Dad?" Josh asked. He didn't get up to give him a hug or redirect him; he just watched him as he made his way down the stairs and then into the dining area, where he looked down at the various food offerings.

"Feeling better," Roger confirmed, rubbing his head. His eyes went over the table, and he eventually reached for the box of goodies from the bakery. He opened the box and brightened at the sight of the chocolate muffins. He turned toward Erin after taking one of them out. "Filling?" he asked.

"Cherry filling," Erin confirmed.

He grinned and picked up a dessert plate to catch his crumbs.

"Cherry's good," he told her through the first big bite of chocolate muffin.

"I knew you like those."

He looked back at the spread, a slight frown line between his eyes. "Someone die?"

Cam made a choked sound and took another quick swallow of his beer.

"Nobody died," Joshua told him. "It's just to help us out while Mom's away."

Roger considered this for a while as he worked his way through the muffin. "Where's Mary Lou?"

"She's just taking care of some things," Josh said in a calm, even voice. He didn't look at Cam, but Erin felt this was the approach they had worked out between them to keep Roger from being upset by Mary Lou's disappearance. He could get angry, confused, and violent despite the drugs he was on. It was best to keep him calm.

Roger nodded. He looked over the other food that had been left out and collected some on a dinner plate. The muffin had quickly disappeared, Erin noted with pleasure. Dessert out of the way, Roger helped himself to one of the pizza pretzels and some salads and finger foods others had brought to the family.

Roger joined them and sat down next to Josh.

"Help yourself," he said to Vic and Erin, motioning to the table.

"Oh, yeah," Joshua agreed. "There's more than we can eat. Please help yourselves. You might as well avoid having to cook and do dishes tonight."

"Maybe in a few minutes," Erin allowed. She wasn't hungry yet, but before long, her body would decide it was suppertime. In the meantime, she wanted to learn more about the bombshell Joshua had dropped.

"So, what is this about an underground cartel?" she asked him.

Everyone glanced covertly in Roger's direction to see if he would pick up on this conversation or be upset by it. He ate without any indication he was listening to the conversation.

"I don't know much yet," Josh told her. "Obviously, it isn't public knowledge at this point."

"Being *underground*," Vic contributed dryly.

Josh nodded his agreement. "Because of all of the unrest, with Willie doing his thing and the disruption between the two you-know-whats, there may be another player positioning itself to get in on the business."

"Where did they come from? Who is it?" Cam demanded. "Is that why—" he cut himself off.

"Why Beaver is here?" Erin suggested. "There must be something going on that caught her interest. Or the interest of her agency."

"It isn't enough that everything is already getting close to exploding between the two... organizations?" Cam protested, even though he was the one who had started to make the suggestion in the first place.

"I guess," Erin said. "But it would make more sense that she would come if there was something unusual going on. Any normal activity would already be covered by their usual staff, right?"

"Willie becoming the... head of the organization isn't unusual enough?"

Erin shrugged. Cam seemed awfully concerned with Beaver's activity and what was going on with the clans despite his previous assertion that he didn't know why she had decided to come to Bald Eagle Falls or what she was doing there.

"I don't know a lot," Josh said. "I'm going to try to find out more. But there aren't a lot of sources who will know anything about what is happening who will actually talk to me."

"You be careful," Erin warned. Mary Lou would not be happy to hear that he was investigating something so potentially dangerous. "If you start asking questions about a third *organization* trying to push its way into the business here, someone might get... upset."

"I know. I am being careful," Josh dismissed her concern. "I'm not going to just charge into the middle of things like an idiot. I know what I'm doing."

What a teenager perceived as being dangerous and what an experienced adult perceived as dangerous could be very different. While Joshua was a skilled investigative reporter, he wasn't always as careful as he should be. That would come with maturity and experience. Hopefully.

"Really," she emphasized. "I don't think this is something that you should be getting into. It could be really dangerous. Things are really explosive right now."

"I know," he agreed bullishly, sticking to his guns. "And I told you I'll be careful. I'm not a little kid."

"I know that. I just... you know what Mary Lou would tell you. She's not here, so I'm just telling you... listen to what she would tell you."

"Listen to your mother," Roger echoed.

Erin looked at him, wondering how much of what they had said he had followed. Or was he just echoing what Erin had said?

Roger picked up on more than they knew. He had previously told them about Joshua carrying a gun for protection, something that no one else had been aware of. Josh hadn't thought that Roger would tell anyone else what he had seen, but when they had needed to know, he had done his best to communicate it, despite his challenges.

"I will, Dad," Josh answered in a slightly lower, more compliant tone.

Roger nodded. "Be safe," he said, and patted Josh on the shoulder. "Safe, safe."

CHAPTER 21

"I feel so bad for those boys," Vic said as Erin pulled the car into the garage. "I can't imagine what it must be like for them to deal with Mary Lou missing right now. After all they've had to go through, they shouldn't have to deal with this too."

Erin swallowed. "What would be worse is if they lose her permanently." Her chest felt paralyzed as she considered this. She could hardly draw breath, and her heart physically ached for them. She had grown up without a mother, but that was different from the two of them growing up so close to Mary Lou and then losing her. Especially with the care of their father to consider. Would Joshua have to give up his career dreams to look after him? Would Cam decide to step up and leave his wild life behind? She didn't see a lot of indications that he would be willing to deal with a disabled father long-term.

"Don't even say that," Vic whispered. "They are not going to lose her. The police will find her. They will bring her home."

Erin swallowed and nodded, hoping it was true.

They closed the car doors and silently stepped out from the stifling hot garage into the cooler air outside. The sun was setting, the heat of the day dissipating.

A figure loomed up in front of them and at first, Erin thought it was Willie, standing there in the dark waiting for Vic to get home. But it was not Willie, and the knit balaclava over the man's face was obviously not a fashion statement or to protect him from cold weather.

Vic gasped, and her hand snaked under her shirt to grab her gun from its concealed holster. The man struck out, shoving her back into the wall of the garage and pressing his gun to her chest until she withdrew her hand and held both hands at shoulder level to assure him that they were both empty and she wasn't a threat to him.

"Okay, okay," she protested. "What is this? A mugging?"

"The girlfriend and the baker," the man snarled in a guttural voice. "Always sticking your noses where they aren't wanted. Don't you know when to quit?"

"We haven't done anything," Erin said. Her throat constricted with fear. She could barely get the words out. "We just got back from visiting a friend."

The gun pointed at her now, and the food she had eaten at the Coxes' threatened to come back up.

"They've just suffered a family tragedy," she explained, as if she needed to. The gunman probably knew more about what was going on than Erin and Vic did. "We were there to take them some baking and offer our sympathy and support."

"And to ask questions," the gunman snarled. "You can never mind your own business. Stick with the bakery and your cookies."

"Okay," Vic agreed. "We get it. We'll mind our own business. We'll stay out of it."

The gun turned back to her and again pressed against her chest, even though Vic's hands were still held up and empty.

"We'll stay out of it," Erin echoed.

Where was Terry? Where was Willie? Where was the increased police presence that the police department had promised, knowing Vic might be in danger when people heard about Willie's new position? Neither clan liked the fact that the leader of the Dyson clan was intimate with a woman from the Jackson family, even if she had been disavowed.

The intruder looked from one to the other, the eyes visible through the mask dark and hard. Erin felt like she was smothering just looking at the balaclava. He must have been cooking, sweat soaking into the material.

He pointed the gun at each of them. "You just stick to your work and stay out of clan business," he warned one last time.

They both nodded and agreed. He withdrew the gun and slid it into an underarm holster. He turned his back on them and walked away. Erin felt rather than saw Vic grab for her gun in its holster. She reached out a hand to stop her.

"No, Vic, you'll get us killed!"

Vic pulled away from her, but the split-second that Erin had stopped her for was enough that Vic was no longer sure of her shot, and she let the gun go, leaving it in its holster. She scowled at Erin.

"I had the shot."

"In the back? How are you going to explain that to the police?"

Vic considered this for a moment. "I wasn't planning on telling the police."

"So, what, you and me would get rid of the body? Load him into the bug and dump him somewhere? Dig a shallow grave out in the woods and hope nobody finds him?"

"I wasn't thinking about all of that." Vic gazed at the place where the man had disappeared into the woods. "It grates on me to let him just walk away. I don't do kindly with people threatening me with a gun!"

"I can't say I do either," Erin admitted shakily. But she didn't feel like going after the guy with a gun. She wanted to call Terry and cower under the blankets on her bed with her eyes tightly shut, trying to wipe the images from her mind.

Vic grasped Erin's arm. "Let's get you into the house."

Erin didn't protest. She let Vic escort her to the back door and input her passcode to let them into the house.

Of course they didn't get far before Orange Blossom was underfoot meowing that Erin hadn't been home to feed him when she was supposed to.

"Git out," Vic said irritably, pushing Orange Blossom away with her foot. "Quit complaining for once and let Erin sit down."

The pressure on Erin's arm was directing her to the living room, where she could sit down on the couch, but she didn't know if she could make it that far. She wobbled toward the kitchen table and Vic ensured she landed in one of the chairs.

"There, you just set a spell and get your legs back under you," she told Erin, moving immediately toward the teakettle.

"I should call Terry," Erin murmured. But her phone seemed far out of reach. She couldn't impress upon her brain the need to reach out to pull out her phone. She felt like she was separated from her body, watching herself. She was a little disgusted with herself for being so weak, collapsing in the chair and slumping there like a jellyfish.

"Don't worry about it," Vic told her. "We'll call him in a minute. Whether it is now or in five minutes don't make no difference now."

Erin watched Vic prepare a cup of tea and stirred in extra sugar. She knew this was supposed to help her recover faster from the shock of the confrontation, but she didn't think it would make any difference to how shaky and overwhelmed she felt.

"Drink it," Vic told her firmly.

Erin nodded and sat with it in her hand, waiting for her strength to return to the point where she could raise it to her mouth without shaking so badly that she spilled it. The hot tea warmed the mug and felt good in her hand.

Vic pulled out her own phone. Erin knew she was calling Terry and wished they could skip this part and the drama that would follow. Her bed was calling her. She would rather skip over all of the drama and just bury herself in layers of blankets until she was warm and cozy and safe and could just sleep.

Vic spoke into the phone. "Terry, we had an intruder," she told him baldly. "You need to get home." She paused to allow Terry time to react to this announcement. "She's okay. Everyone is fine. But

Erin needs you. And if there's any chance the police could catch up to this guy... I don't think you can do anything, but you can try."

She again waited for a moment, then gave a description of the gunman and the direction he had gone so Terry could start the others conducting a search.

"We'll be here," she said unnecessarily, and ended the call.

CHAPTER 22

*E*rin took a sip of the oversweet tea. It flowed down to her stomach and spread out to her limbs in a warm rush. She closed her eyes and took another drink.

"He'll be here in a minute," Vic advised.

"Can you feed the animals?"

"Sure."

Vic went to the pantry to get Orange Blossom's food out and apologized to him for being so stern when she had spoken to him earlier. "Sometimes you just have to wait," she explained. "Sometimes Momma needs something before you."

She got some vegetables from the fridge for Marshmallow, who waited patiently as usual. Then Terry was at the front door, letting himself in and hurrying to Erin to brush her cheek with a kiss and ask if she was okay.

"I'm fine," Erin said, "just fine. Nothing happened. Everyone is fine."

"What happened?" Terry asked Vic. "An intruder in the house?" He looked around for any sign of trouble.

"Not inside," Vic said. "Out in the yard beside the garage. We got in from work and he was waiting there for us."

"He had a gun?" Terry already knew this from Vic's description of the man, warning him that he had a concealed weapon.

Vic nodded. "Yeah. Handgun in an underarm holster. Sig Sauer."

"Did he threaten you?"

Erin nodded, not wanting to be excluded from the conversation. She was not just a bystander or a child to be coddled. She had been there, and she had eyes, too. He would need both of their statements. "He had his gun on Vic before she could pull hers from the holster. He pointed it at both of us, but mostly at Vic."

"What did he say? Did you recognize him?"

Erin shook her head. "I don't know who it was. I was trying to recognize him... his body or voice, but I don't think it was anyone I have ever met."

"What can you add to Vic's description? Or do you disagree with anything?"

Erin thought Vic had done a good job giving a general description of the intruder, including his height and weight and what he had been wearing. The whole time he had been threatening them, she had been looking for something identifiable.

"Uh... white guy. Light-colored eyes. It was too dark to see them very well, but they weren't brown. Lighter. Probably blue. Maybe green. His hands..." Erin closed her eyes. The images kept intruding on her thoughts; she might as well let them come now and try to use them. She pictured the man's hand holding the gun. She could see little but the gun when he had been threatening them, but the image was still there in her mind. "The hair on his knuckles was dark. Not blond or red. Brown or black. I think he had a tattoo, but I couldn't see it very well because he was wearing a windbreaker. It was here," Erin touched the inside of her wrist. "I could just see the edge of it under his jacket."

"What could you see of the color and shape?"

"Uh, hard to say. I think red or orange, but the light wasn't good. It was round. Or that edge of it was rounded."

Terry nodded encouragingly. "Anything else?"

"One of his nails was blackened, down at the base. Like he'd shut it in a door or hit it with a hammer." Erin had done both things on previous occasions and knew how painful they were, and knew how the blood under the nail turned black and stayed there for ages until the nail grew out.

"Which finger?"

"Uh... index finger on his gun hand. His right hand."

"Was his finger through the trigger guard?"

Erin nodded. She searched the image for anything else that might help to identify the man, or at least to confirm his identity if they found him on a nearby street during the search. She didn't want him slipping through their fingers because she hadn't been able to give a good enough description.

She opened her eyes. "That's all I can think of."

"That's very good, Erin. For the two of you to be able to give such a good description of a man wearing a balaclava is... it's extraordinary. Nice job." He looked at Vic. "Can you tell me any more details about the gun?"

Vic obliged, giving him several technical specifications that went over Erin's head. About all she would have been able to tell Terry was that it was a silver handgun.

Terry's radio had been squawking as they talked, but he had turned down the volume so it was barely audible. There was a knock on the front door, and Terry answered it, checking through the peephole before opening the door to Sheriff Wilmot.

"Sheriff," he greeted.

"How are the ladies?"

Terry nodded. "They're doing pretty well, considering. How is the search going?"

"We've got a perimeter and everyone is out looking for him."

Considering how few officers were actually on the Bald Eagle Falls police force, and that two of them were now inside Erin's house, Erin didn't see how they could have established any effective perimeter or conducted a proper search. A couple of cops searching the surrounding streets would be pretty easy to avoid. And the intruder had left through Erin's woods. There was no way for them to search the woods, especially at night.

Wilmot could likely see the doubt in her eyes.

"We have volunteers helping surveil the perimeter," he said. "And I have the staties coming in to help beat the bushes. A couple have already arrived. I know it isn't much, but we're doing our best with limited numbers."

"How about Beaver? Is she helping?"

"Haven't been in contact with Miss Beaven, sorry. I don't know where she is right now. She's not often in town."

"She is. She brought Cam on Wednesday."

"She might not still be here today. I'll leave it to the dispatcher to reach out to whatever agencies she thinks will be able to help." He looked her over. "You're still a mite pale."

Which probably meant she was as white as a ghost. Erin took another long swallow of the hot tea. The sooner she could get back to normal, the more she would be able to help. If she could remember anything else that might help them.

"Well… thank you. I appreciate you helping."

"Don't count us out yet," he said, interpreting her tone as doubting they would be able to find the man. "You never know. We might be able to catch this lowlife."

Erin shrugged. "Maybe," she agreed. She wasn't counting on it. If she hadn't stopped Vic from plugging the guy in the back, they wouldn't be having this conversation. She gave Vic an apologetic look, which made Vic grin. Terry raised a brow, inquiring what the inside joke was.

Erin shook her head. "Nothing."

Vic chuckled. "She's regretting that she stopped me from shooting him in the back."

"Oh." Terry chuckled at that, too. "Well, you know we can't have you going around shooting private citizens in the back."

"When he threatens my life and is still on my property…"

"He was no longer threatening you if his back was to you. And he was on Erin's property, not yours."

"The law doesn't care who owns it. If my castle is on this property, I have a right to defend it."

"Not when he is walking away."

Vic shrugged. "It's probably a good thing she kept me from going to jail for shooting a guy in the back, but I think I could've gotten off."

"Probably," Terry agreed. "People tend to be very sympathetic toward pretty young ladies. Poor, defenseless things being threatened by a big, strong man."

"That's right," Vic agreed pertly. She took a deep breath and released it in a long, controlled exhale. "I'll admit, my heart is still racing. I was pretty cool while it was happening, but now..." She held her hands out in front of her. They were trembling very slightly. "Just look at that," Vic said in disgust.

The men, looking at her barely shaking fingers, did not share her negative opinion.

"You're still cool as a cucumber," Wilmot told her. "Most people do not stay that calm when threatened at gunpoint."

"Most people didn't have the upbringing I did. My Pa woulda given me an earful for letting the guy get the drop on me. And letting him get away like that... He woulda tanned my hide for being such a coward."

Erin had met Vic's pa, and it was no exaggeration. The man was not the tolerant sort. He had raised his boys, including the former James Jackson, to be tough clan men.

"We're asking folks to check their doorbell cameras and any other surveillance video they might have. See if anyone managed to catch this guy on camera. What about you?" He looked at Terry. "I don't suppose you have a camera out back?"

Terry shook his head. "Certain people would see it as an invasion of their privacy." He looked at Vic. Both she and Willie had objected to any video surveillance of the backyard, despite the breaches they'd had in the past.

Vic shrugged, but didn't say she wished they'd gone ahead with video surveillance of the backyard. She still preferred her privacy over being able to get a picture of the intruder.

"If you had video of him, you still wouldn't have any more to go on than we already gave you. It would see a black figure in the dark wearing a balaclava. How would that help you find him?"

"You never know what it might have shown, since you don't have it. Maybe he came with someone else. Maybe he didn't put the mask on until he saw you guys pull into the garage. If someone dropped him off here, maybe we coulda got their plates."

"Maybe. And maybe all you would have is a black blob in the dark."

CHAPTER 23

*A*fter getting all of the information they could from Vic and Erin, Terry and Sheriff Wilmot got back to work, joining the rest of the law enforcement officers looking for the mysterious intruder. Erin and Vic were both yawning, and Erin knew she had reached the point where her brain and body would not allow her to go on. She had been longing for her bed ever since the man had left and she was finally ready to give in.

"You look as plumb tuckered out as I feel," Vic said. "I know I should be worked up and too wired to do anything for hours, but I'm not. I just feel… shut down. And like I need to shut out the rest of the world."

"Exactly," Erin agreed.

"So… I'd love to stay and keep you company tonight, but…" Vic barely covered another yawn. "I'm not going to be able to."

"Go to bed," Erin told her. "That's what I'm doing."

Vic nodded. "Okay."

Erin watched Vic walk across the backyard and climb the stairs to the loft apartment. Once Erin saw her close the door, she started to prepare for bed herself.

She wanted to just slide into bed without taking care of anything else first, but she needed to do the rest of her wind-down bedtime routine, including saying goodnight to the animals, checking her planner for the next day, brushing her teeth and washing her face, moisturizing, putting on the shorts and t-shirt she wore for pajamas. It took longer than it should have because she was so tired, but she held herself accountable and would not skip any of her responsibilities.

She was checking the burglar alarm and making sure it was properly armed before bed when a shadow crossed the window. Erin jumped, then froze, staring out into the night. She was sure she had seen a person cross in front of the house. She pulled her phone out and prepared to call the police emergency number.

There was a knock on the door.

Erin jumped again. She looked around her for the animals. Marshmallow's toes were just visible behind the couch, where he was sleeping. Orange Blossom yowled behind her. He went up to the door and sniffed along the bottom edge. He looked back at her and yowled again.

The knock was repeated, this time followed up with a voice. "Miss Erin? Are you all right?"

Erin swallowed and stepped up to the door to look through the peephole.

She blew out her breath and unlocked the door. She punched her passcode into the burglar alarm and opened it.

"Officer Stayner."

He nodded and touched the edge of his cap in acknowledgment. "Sorry, Miss Erin. Just checking in with you to make sure you are all right."

"Yes. You scared me half to death. I thought he was back again! And this time, I don't have Vic with me. I'm totally unarmed. Other than this furball," Erin indicated Orange Blossom with her toe.

Blossom looked up at Stayner and hissed. Erin laughed. "*Now* he decides to get protective. Officer Stayner is okay, Blossom. He works with Terry. He's one of the good guys."

Stayner looked down at Orange Blossom. "I heard how he's attacked an intruder before. He doesn't look that menacing, but I remember the cat my grandma had when I was little. I wouldn't want to face those claws again!"

Orange Blossom put his ears back, growled low, and hissed again, his fur fluffing up.

"He won't hurt you. Will you, Blossom?" Erin demanded. "You be good now." She addressed Stayner again. "I appreciate you checking in. I'm just about to head to bed. Burglar alarm is set, so everything should be fine. I'm exhausted. I feel like I could sleep for the next three days."

"Okay. I'm going to walk around to the backyard and talk to Miss Victoria, too. As long as everything checks out, you won't hear from me again tonight."

"Okay, thanks. I'll probably see you tomorrow."

He touched his cap again and withdrew.

Erin closed the door and headed to her bedroom.

Erin watched through the window as Stayner crossed to the side of the house to go around to the backyard and check on Vic.

It was nice to know that the police were keeping an eye on things even though the man who had threatened them had gone away. Though it wasn't very likely, he could still come back. If he found he couldn't get out through whatever perimeter the police had established, he might decide to stay there until they had all given up and the hunt was called off. Terry was still working with the rest of the police department to track the man down, and he probably would be until morning.

She considered walking through to the kitchen to observe Stayner as he searched the yard for any intruders and knocked on Vic's door, but she decided she didn't have the energy. She walked to her bedroom and fell into bed. She didn't check her phone alarms or send a good night text to Vic; she just pulled the covers over herself and closed her eyes.

She was vaguely aware of Orange Blossom jumping up onto the bed and snuggling up with her, but beyond that, everything was lost in the void of unconsciousness.

∽

Erin awoke to her alarm in the morning. She was momentarily disconcerted that it was so late, but when she looked at her phone and the schedule, she saw that it was Saturday. The students were off school, which meant that they would take the opening shift. It was a rare day off for both Erin and Vic, which was good, since they could both do with a little extra sleep after the previous evening's drama.

Erin texted Bella's number to ensure everything was okay, that she was on track and not having any issues. Bella responded within a few minutes to say that all was well and that she didn't need Erin to come in.

Erin lay back down, nestling into the warm indentation on her pillow. Terry's arm encircled her. "You going back to sleep?" he questioned.

"Yeah. Maybe."

"Good."

Erin snuggled into him. She didn't remember when he had gotten back home. He might have just barely gotten into bed as her alarm went off. At any rate, she had not gotten in any cuddle time the night before, and enjoyed it now, knowing that she didn't have to get up for work.

But she was used to getting up early, and her brain wouldn't settle back down to let her go to sleep even though she had the opportunity. She squirmed around for a while, but didn't want to keep Terry awake with her restlessness, so eventually, she slipped out of bed to let him sleep while she had a long shower.

When she put the coffee on in the kitchen, she looked over at the loft to see whether Vic was awake, but the apartment was still dark. Vic was much better at sleeping late when she had the chance than Erin. She would probably sleep until mid-morning.

CHAPTER 24

*E*ventually, Terry was up. Erin looked for any sign of life at Vic's, but if she was up, it wasn't obvious. The sun was up, so she could no longer judge by Vic's lights.

"Well, how do you want to spend your day?" Terry asked with a yawn, scratching his chest. He sat down at the table, still sleepy-eyed, dressed in a worn gray t-shirt and cargo pants. Five o'clock shadow softened his jaw, and Erin thought he looked adorable.

"I have a list," Erin admitted, looking around for her planner. She knew she had updated it before going to bed. "I have a few errands I wanted to run. They can wait until this afternoon. What do you want for breakfast?"

There was always a variety of baked goods in the freezer to warm up for breakfast. Terry considered. "Saturday morning. It seems like a waffle kind of day. And then I need to check to see what happened in the games last night. Watch the highlights. I didn't get the chance for anything last night."

"No." Erin bent down to brush his cheek with a kiss. "Instead, you had to rescue me. I guess you guys didn't manage to find and arrest my intruder."

He shook his head. "Unfortunately not. We'll go through the

descriptions of some of the clan members we know are more active right now. See if anyone matches the description you and Vic gave."

That didn't sound too promising. Not when they couldn't even look at mugshots to confirm what he looked like. With all of the technology and databases that were available, a balaclava was still a pretty good way to avoid being identified.

"Well, I appreciate everything that you did," Erin said with a sigh. "You did everything you could." She popped a couple of frozen waffles into the toaster, placing a muffin in the microwave for herself. It was later than she usually had breakfast and she was starving.

Terry nodded. "I wish we had found him. We'll do a bit of follow-up today, see if we can find any footprints or other signs, now that it's light out. You never know, he might have dropped something or given us some way to identify him or at least to narrow it down."

Erin nodded as she bussed the butter, maple syrup, and a couple of jars of jam to the table.

"You never know," she agreed unenthusiastically.

Terry opened his mouth to add something else, but Erin was distracted by the vibration of her phone. She pulled it out of her pocket and looked at the screen. It was Willie. Erin glanced out the window toward the loft apartment and answered it.

"Hello?"

"Erin, do you know where Vic is? She was supposed to meet me this morning."

"She's probably still asleep. Last night was kind of... exhausting. And we didn't have to get up for Auntie Clem's this morning, so she probably turned off her alarms."

There was a pause before Willie answered. "What happened last night?"

"Oh... I thought you had heard." Erin looked at Terry but didn't want him to know she was talking to Willie. He was not happy about her having anything to do with him. Even though they were friends, Terry thought Erin should cut off contact with him now that he was back with the clan. Which might be a good idea, except that he was still associating with Vic, and Erin couldn't very well avoid having anything to do with her best friend's partner.

"Just a sec," she murmured, leaving the kitchen. "I'll be right back," she told Terry. "Make sure your waffles don't burn."

Erin went into her bedroom and shut the door so she could talk more freely.

"Last night when Vic and I got home, there was a… someone waiting for us here. He told us to mind our own business." She shrugged and tried to think of what else to say. It wasn't the first time someone had told one of them to back off. All they had been doing was visiting a friend. A friend whose mother had disappeared mysteriously. "He, uh… well, he threatened us, and then he left. We called Terry, but the police couldn't find him."

"I heard something was going on last night," Willie said. "But I couldn't get a reliable account of what."

"Yeah. Well, that was it, I guess. They brought in extra people to form a perimeter and keep an eye out, and the state police helped with the search… but they weren't able to find him. They're going to look around again now that it's light out."

"These threats… what exactly was threatened?"

Erin cleared her throat. "He had a gun. Held it on both of us. But mostly on Vic, because she went for hers."

Willie swore under his breath. "And you don't know who it was? Which clan he was with? Who sent him?"

"No. He didn't exactly say.."

"No, of course not. What did he look like?"

"He had a balaclava on. We couldn't see his face." Erin did not offer Willie the rest of the details they had given to the police.

"Does Terry know who it was? Have any suspicions?"

"I don't think so. Not that he would tell me."

"What exactly did this good-for-nothing say to you?"

"To stop asking questions… stay out of clan business. All we had done was to go visit Campbell Cox."

"In the city?"

"No. He's home. At Mary Lou's."

"I didn't know you were friends with Cam."

135

"Well, no, not really. He's closer to Vic's age. But he's helping Josh with Roger. We just wanted to offer our support..."

"I'm missing something here, Erin. What's going on with the Coxes?"

Erin rubbed her forehead. She had assumed that Willie would be up on everything that was going on in Bald Eagle Falls.

"Vic didn't tell you?"

"We haven't talked for a few days. We were supposed to get together today. If she hadn't slept in."

"Oh... well... Mary Lou is missing."

Willie drew in a sharp breath. "What do you mean, she's missing?"

Erin cleared her throat. "When Cam and Josh got up on Thursday, she wasn't there. Her bed was made, and she wasn't there. She hadn't gotten Roger up. She and Cam were supposed to come to the bakery for a breakfast muffin, so Cam came to Auntie Clem's looking for her. But she never came to the bakery or opened the General Store. No one has seen her."

Willie swore under his breath. "I hadn't heard. There's... a lot going on right now."

"I know. What about Charley? Did you hear that she is gone? And Naomi, at the bookstore? Melissa said there are a lot of people missing right now. I don't know who else."

"What does Terry think happened to Mary Lou?"

"You would have to ask him. I don't think he's turned up anything. Not that he's told me. The police just keep saying that it is voluntary. There's no sign of foul play, everyone is just missing voluntarily."

"Everyone?" Willie repeated. Erin didn't answer right away; she knew it was not actually a question. "Maybe some of them are voluntary. People who are gathering to the clans or going underground to keep from getting pulled into something. But Mary Lou." She could hear him breathe out in a long, controlled exhale. "That concerns me."

"A lot of this concerns me!" Erin told him, sounding a little angrier than she intended to. "But no one else seems to be taking it seriously."

"Does 'no one' mean Office Piper?"

"Not just him. I don't understand how no one can be concerned with the number of people who have disappeared. I mean... it's like some magic trick gone bad." Erin vaguely remembered her former foster sister Reg Rawlins calling almost a year ago and talking about people disappearing in her town. Erin had brushed it off as Reg's usual attention-seeking drama. Now, she wished she had been more supportive. "I know I can't take care of everyone, I can't make sure that everyone is okay, but Charley, Mary Lou, Naomi... those are people in my circle and I just... want to know that they are okay. Then some puke comes and waves his gun around and tells me I'm asking too many questions."

Willie chuckled. "Such language, Erin. I can see why you're so frustrated, and I'm sorry. I wish I could give you all the answers you seek. I am aware of some people's movements through clan channels, but most of the people you have mentioned... they are off my radar, and I don't know what's going on with them."

"Is there any truth to the rumor of an underground cartel trying to take advantage of the disruption between the clans and force their way into the market?"

Willie was silent for several long seconds. "Where did you hear that?"

"I can't tell you. Is it true?"

The bedroom door opened, and Terry stood there looking questioningly. He held a plate with Erin's muffin on it as if he had just wanted to bring her breakfast in case she was getting too hungry while talking on the phone. But Erin knew he had only come into the bedroom to find out who she was talking to and what they were discussing.

"Oh, I have to go. We'll talk more later."

"Erin—will you check in on Vicky and make sure everything is okay? Just have her text me."

"Sure," Erin agreed. "No problem."

She pressed the End button to terminate the call and put her phone back in her pocket, smiling at Terry.

"Thanks, that was so sweet. I'll come out and eat with you. Sorry to take so long."

"I didn't mean to interrupt your call…"

"No, it's okay. We were done."

"Was it the bakery?"

Erin shrugged and didn't say anything. She returned to the kitchen and put her muffin on the table. She looked out across the backyard toward Vic's apartment.

"I'm just going to see if Vic wants to join us or for me to thaw something out for her."

Terry sighed and sat down at the table with his waffles. He started to drizzle syrup on them.

Erin slid into some sandals at the back door, and after punching her clearance code on the burglar alarm, opened the door and walked across to the stairs on the outside of the garage.

She climbed the stairs quickly and knocked on the door. She knocked loudly, remembering that Vic hadn't heard Jeremy knocking when she had been in the bathtub. And if she were asleep, it might also be difficult to get her attention.

There was no response. Erin knocked again as loudly as she could. "Vic! Are you awake?"

She hoped that if the knocking did not wake Vic, her voice would.

But there was still no answer. Erin fingered her key ring, worrying about using her landlord key to enter Vic's premises. Vic had not been happy with her for using it once before in an emergency. Not at all happy.

But Vic would want to know that Willie was trying to reach her. She would want to know that she had overslept and Willie was worried about her. Even if she were too tired to go out with him, she would still want to text him to confirm she was okay.

Erin knocked again. She heard the back door of the house open, and Terry stood on the back porch looking up at her.

"If she isn't home, can we just have our breakfast?"

Erin scowled. She dialed Vic's number on the phone and waited for her to answer, but it went directly to voicemail. Out of juice or on Do Not Disturb? Erin pounded on the door again. "Vic!"

Terry walked over to the bottom of the stairs, frowning. "Is something wrong? What's going on?"

"She isn't answering," Erin pointed out. "Willie is worried about her."

"She's not answering Willie?"

"No. She was supposed to meet with him and didn't show up."

"You didn't see her leave this morning? She could have twisted an ankle on the way or something like that…?"

"No. I've been watching for her because I wanted to talk…"

Terry took his time climbing the stairs, thinking about it. He knocked on the door louder than Erin had. "Victoria Webster! Police welfare check! Open up!"

They both stood there. Nilla barked at the noise, but otherwise, there was no stirring of life within. Erin felt a weight growing in her stomach. "No," she whispered. "Not Vicky."

"Do you have your key?" Terry asked.

"Yes." Erin took it out. "I'll go in. If she's just in the bathtub or something…"

"No." Terry shook his head. "This is a welfare check now. I need to go in while you stay out here. I want you safely out of the way."

"There's no one else in there. There isn't any danger."

"Erin, you don't know what kind of things you can walk into in a situation like this. I've seen all kinds of things that I don't want you to be exposed to."

Erin felt even sicker thinking about what some of those things might be. The police were first in line to see a lot of horrible things.

She reluctantly handed the keys to Terry. He selected Vic's apartment key and inserted it into the lock.

CHAPTER 25

erry gave Erin one more stern look to warn her to stay out of the apartment, and she did not follow him in when he opened the door. She kept thinking of all of the horrible things he had seen walking into people's residences. She couldn't believe that anything awful could have happened to Vic. If she had been depressed or sick, she would have told Erin, wouldn't she? Or if she had started seeing someone other than Willie or gotten into something that could lead to trouble? She and Vic talked about everything.

Not everything.

There was still plenty Vic didn't know about Erin's past, and she suspected, a number of things that Vic had held back about hers.

But Vic's troubles were in her past. Her abusive family, the Jackson clan, the dysphoria, anyone in her former life as James Jackson.

That was all behind her.

Wasn't it?

Erin stood there, still as a statue, listening for any hint of what Terry might have discovered. She chewed her lip. It seemed like an eternity had passed before Terry finally returned to the door. He carried Nilla in his arms, the dog struggling to get away. Erin stepped forward to enter the apartment, but he shook his head and motioned her back. He closed the door.

"She's not there. There isn't anyone home."

At first, Erin was relieved. Nothing horrible had happened to Vic.

But Vic's absence opened up a whole host of other questions. Erin had been keeping half an eye on the backyard since she got up and hadn't seen Vic leave. So when had she left? And where had she gone, if she had not rendezvoused with Willie? If Willie didn't know where she was, then where was she?

Terry motioned for her to go down the stairs, and followed her. He released Nilla into the yard once they got to the bottom. The little dog immediately ran to his usual bathroom corner.

"Do you think... Vic went out?" Erin asked.

"I guess she did. She didn't tell you her plans?"

"No. She didn't tell me anything. Willie said she was supposed to meet him."

"You'd better call him back."

Erin hesitated, then nodded. She pulled out her phone and tapped Willie's name to call him again. She put Willie on speakerphone this time.

"Erin?"

"Willie, you're on speaker. With Terry."

"Willie, Vic isn't in her apartment," Terry advised. "Could there have been any confusion about where or when she was supposed to meet you?"

"No." There were a few beats of silence as Willie thought about this further. "I don't see how. We've met up before, and there haven't been any problems. We change the time and place, but... she knew the details."

"Could something have happened to her on the way? I want to follow the path she should have taken."

"Through the woods," Willie told him. "Come out the back by Canyon Park. A couple of blocks to the west, there is a little convenience store. Used to be run by Mr. and Mrs. Mayer. You know it?"

"I know it," Terry agreed. "I'm going to walk the route now. Will you stay there?"

"Yeah."

Terry led the way down the stairs. "Take a minute to get proper shoes on," he told Erin. "You don't want to walk through the woods in those."

Erin wanted to tell him no, that they couldn't stop to do something so unimportant. But he was right. They would save more time by being in proper footwear than by leaving immediately without taking care of their feet.

"What are you going to do with Nilla?"

"I'll leave him in the run to get some fresh air and exercise. One of us will be back here within the hour."

Erin went back into the house to put on socks and walking shoes. Terry retrieved his radio and a couple of other items normally in his duty belt. He didn't stop to get completely geared up, but had enough pockets for the miscellany, and grabbed the concealed carry holster for his gun. He was ready almost as quickly as she was. He called K9 to accompany them.

Terry made several calls on his radio, reporting Vic missing and trying to get a search party started for her and for the suspect from the previous night.

They armed the burglar alarm and headed out, following Willie's directions. Erin had been to Canyon Park before. It wasn't very big, just a small public park with a bench or two and a large sandstone rock with the words *Canyon Park* chiseled into it. And the last time she had been there... she really didn't want to remember the details.

The wood behind the house, once a wild, mysterious place when Erin had first come to Bald Eagle Falls, was much more familiar to her now. She didn't know all of its secrets, but she was familiar with the main pathways, the location of the summer cottage where Adele, her gamekeeper, lived, and some of the other buildings that had aged, and in some cases, collapsed over the decades. There were a couple of fire pits where teenagers had partied before Adele had shooed them on their way.

They both moved quickly, eyes sharp for any sign that Vic had been that way, but not expecting to find her. She was another of the missing. Erin was sure Vic hadn't gotten lost or twisted her ankle on the way to meet Willie.

"Find Vic," Terry told K9.

He wasn't a scent dog, but he was smart, and he knew their names. He led Terry eagerly along the main path. He did not appear to be tracking Vic by scent; Erin didn't see him put his muzzle to the ground or lift his nose up to scent the wind.

Erin heard the cawing of crows and looked toward them. There was a path that branched off toward Adele's house. Probably it was just Skye, Adele's crow, maybe with a few friends. She looked into the trees to see what they were making a fuss about. Was Bernt, the little black cat Adele had nursed back to health, harassing them? Or, more likely, were the birds teasing the cat?

There was something off to the side of the pathway that was attracting the crows' attention. Erin didn't want to be distracted by something unimportant. They needed to find Vic, especially if she was hurt.

But the dark form in the long grasses and weeds next to the pathway...

Erin called Terry back and took the side path.

"Erin, what is it?" Terry sounded irritated as he turned around and followed her.

She didn't answer, because she wasn't sure what she was going to find.

But she approached the dark form and could see before she got there the general shape of a torso, two legs, and two arms. Terry, catching up to her, put his hand on her shoulder to stop her.

"Wait," he instructed, and moved forward, looking at the dark form and shooing the noisy crows away. Erin couldn't tell whether Skye was among them. One crow looked like another to her.

Erin sneaked forward a few shuffling steps to adjust her angle and position for a better view. It was clear that the form on the ground was not Vic. Too big and bulky, not Vic's tall willowy form.

Black shoes. Dark pants. Black windbreaker. He wasn't wearing a balaclava any longer, but she was sure it was the man who had threatened her the night before.

"Stay there," Terry warned, looking up and frowning at her sternly. "Don't get any closer."

"Is it him? Is it the guy who threatened us?"

"I can't tell you that for sure. We are going to have a difficult time identifying him positively, since you never saw his face."

"What about the tattoo? And his gun?"

"I can't touch anything until the tech guys get here to document everything. You know what kind of trouble it will cause if I touch the body and mess up the evidence."

"It's got to be him."

Terry looked at her, his mouth a grim line. "You said that Vic did not get a shot off at him."

"She didn't! I stopped her. She didn't fire her gun."

"We'll need to get a look at it. Compare the ballistics with the bullets that killed this guy."

"We have to find her." Erin looked back at the trail they had been on. "We need to keep going and see if something happened to her."

"I can't leave the body. And you can't go wandering through here alone when there could be an armed suspect hiding anywhere, waiting for the opportunity to get a shot at someone else."

"We have to find her," Erin insisted, her voice cracking.

"We will. But we have to wait for someone else to get here and protect the scene. And we do have someone coming from the opposite direction. Be patient; he'll be here in a few minutes. Everything will be looked after; we just have to be methodical about it. Take it one step at a time."

Erin hated to be told that she had to wait. She was worried about Vic. It seemed impossible that she could have joined the ranks of the missing without a sign of what had happened to her. Where was she?

"Stayner talked to her last night. How could she have gone missing between then and now? It doesn't make any sense."

"Stayner talked to her?"

Erin nodded. "He came around last night as I was getting ready for bed. I thought you had sent him. He checked in with me and then said he would look around the backyard and make sure Vic was good, too."

"I'll follow up with him. See what time it was and what she said. If there was anything that he might have thought strange at the time, but wrote off as not being important enough to worry about. If Vic said anything that seemed off... He should be here any minute. They've got everyone on this. Again." Terry sighed. Despite having slept in, he looked tired. Who knew what time he had gotten to bed.

"I'm sorry," she said. "You guys can't all keep working every shift. If it was anyone else..."

"We have to be concerned about any reports of missing persons or anything that might be related to the clans. But of course, Vic is extra special."

Erin felt a rush of warmth at his declaration and reassured that Terry really did care about Vic. But he threw ice water over her with the conclusion of his statement. "Her life was threatened last night by a man who has now turned up dead, and she is the girl-friend of one of the most powerful cartel bosses in the area."

"You mean she's a suspect? Or a good target?"

"She's both," Terry admitted. "But I was thinking about her being targeted. I'm sure Willie hasn't been happy about her continuing to live in your backyard without any special protection, rather than living with him in a more secure location."

Erin knew they had argued about it. There had been more than one blow-up about Vic insisting on living her own life without any contact with the clans and Willie wanting to protect her.

"Yeah. He wasn't happy," she agreed.

"I figured as much."

Terry must have been home for one or two of those arguments. But thinking about it, maybe not. He had been working so many extra shifts lately that she felt like he was always out. Maybe he had missed most of the domestic drama.

Erin stood there, feeling anxious and useless. She wanted to go on, looking for Vic, but she knew in her gut that walking the route Vic should have taken to meet Willie wouldn't help. Vic hadn't just twisted her ankle and sat down on a log to wait until someone came looking for her. She hadn't gotten lost.

They weren't going to find her out here unless she was lying in the weeds like the gunman from the night before. The police could look for her, but they weren't going to find her.

Something terrible had happened to Vic. Erin knew it.

CHAPTER 26

"You found another one?" Sheriff Wilmot demanded as he reached them.

Erin rolled her eyes toward the body Terry was still standing guard over.

"Well... could we actually attribute this one to Terry? I haven't actually gotten any closer than this. He was the one who... called it in."

"How did you find this body?" Wilmot called out to Terry.

"I was on the main path, and Erin called me back. She had seen something..."

"The birds," Erin said. "The crows were making a big racket, and I wondered what they were making such a fuss over. They're scavengers, you know, they're attracted to whatever is available in their environment..."

"And that was how *you* found the body."

"Well, yes. That was when I saw there was something lying in the grass, and I told Terry, but he was the one who... identified it as a body," Erin lied. Of course she had realized it was a body before Terry had reached it. It wasn't that hard to tell from a distance away. There had been no attempt to hide the body.

"Okay," Wilmot said with a nod, and wrote a few notes in his notepad. "How are you doing? You okay?"

"I'm okay. I'm worried about Vic."

"Yes, I heard the latest report." He shook his head. "I would really like to know what is going on in our town."

"I heard there might be an underground cartel. A third gang trying to squeeze out the other two."

Wilmot's jaw dropped. "Where did you hear that?" He shook his head. "Wish you'd take some good advice and stop putting yourself into this kind of situation."

"I'm not in any kind of situation. Terry and I were walking together through my private property to see if we could find my friend. I didn't arrange any of that. I didn't ask anyone questions."

"You have obviously been talking to someone if you are asking me questions about an underground cartel." Wilmot looked at her for a moment, evaluating her. "These are dangerous people, Erin. This is not harmless gossip. You are talking about hardened criminals with long histories who will not hesitate to take someone out who is in their way."

Erin thought that was a pretty clear answer that there *was* a third gang moving into the territory. It wasn't just the decades-long feud between the Jacksons and Dysons anymore. Another organization was determined to take advantage of the Dysons and the Jacksons being distracted by the changes in the Dyson clan's leadership.

She looked back at Wilmot, biting her lip. "I don't want to get in the way. I really haven't had anything to do with this third cartel. Or with Willie. The only time I've seen him is when he's been visiting Vic. I haven't had anything to do with anyone else in the Dyson clan."

Except that now, something had happened. Despite whatever precautions Willie had taken not to visit her too often or on a regular schedule, someone had taken it on themselves to take Vic away from him. Away from her home and everyone who loved her.

Erin dreaded the news that another body had been discovered in the woods.

How could this be happening?

A man's voice rose over the rustling of the leaves and calling of the birds. "I want to see this guy!"

Erin recognized Willie's voice. She looked up to see him approaching, Stayner trying to hold him back.

"Look, Mr. Andrews—"

"I want to know who he is and what clan he is with. I deserve to know that, at least. How am I supposed to protect myself and my family if I don't know who is being sent and who they are being sent by?"

"It isn't up to you," Stayner argued. "It is up to the police to enforce law and order in Bald Eagle Falls. If it weren't for your actions, this would not have happened—"

"My actions were taken to protect your citizens, including one of your own. That's what put me into this position in the first place! And now it has put someone I love in the crosshairs of some renegade who has taken action without the authorization of his bosses."

"How do you know that?"

"How do you expect me to confirm it without seeing who it is?" Willie demanded in frustration.

"It's going to be public information once he is identified," Erin pointed out to Sheriff Wilmot. "What good does it do you to keep Willie from finding out? Why not let him see while there's still a chance Vic is still alive and he can do something to find her and bring her back safely?"

"We don't work with criminals."

"Law enforcement works with criminals all the time," Erin scoffed. "Don't try telling me that."

Terry glanced over at her, but he didn't say anything to censure her. Wilmot looked at Stayner and Willie, then made a decision. He flicked a hand over to the dead body.

"Let him see. But don't get too close, Mr. Andrews."

Willie pushed by Stayner and walked closer, staying back from where Terry stood guard. He looked down at the man.

"This is the man who threatened you last night?" Willie asked Erin.

"I haven't gotten close enough to confirm it, but he's the same build and dressed the same way."

"You never saw his face?"

"He was masked. But he had a tattoo on his right arm."

Willie looked over at Terry. "Does he have the tattoo?"

The crime techs had not yet arrived, and Terry had said that he couldn't do anything to try to identify the body until then. He looked at Wilmot, who gave a nod. Terry pulled on a glove and tugged the man's right sleeve up half an inch.

He nodded. "A coiled-up rattlesnake. Orange-red. It matches Erin's general description of a rounded, red or orange shape. Not bad, considering the lighting when you saw it," he told her, "and that you were being threatened at gunpoint."

Erin took a deep breath and let it out again, trying to keep the images at bay. She didn't want to think about the threat. She didn't want to think that this man had returned to take Vic and things had gone horribly wrong.

"You can't tell anything about the bullet?"

Terry pressed the jacket down against the body to get a better view of the bullet or the bullet hole.

"Single gunshot. Small caliber. Maybe a .22."

Erin didn't know much about bullets, but she assumed that the small handgun Vic kept concealed in a bra holster was a .22.

"That doesn't really tell us anything," Terry told her. "It's a common caliber. Nice shooting, to drop someone with a single shot in the back." Then he looked at Willie. "So, do you know him?"

CHAPTER 27

*W*illie gave a brief nod. "Jackson clan," he said briefly. "Could have been sent by Vic's pa. Or someone further up the food chain. Eddie Potter."

Sheriff Wilmot wrote the name down. "How do you know him? When was the last time you saw him?"

Willie shook his head. "I have no idea. You just get familiar with these people if you have been around the clans for long. Potters have been on this mountain for generations. I'm sure you probably have a dozen more living here in town."

"Did Eddie Potter live here? In Bald Eagle Falls?"

"I reckon he was closer to Moose River, but don't take that as gospel. People move around, and with the number of people who live on farms and in other rural areas, it's hard to say who lives closer to what towns."

"But for sure, he is a Jackson?"

Willie nodded. He clenched his teeth and said nothing.

"Did you send someone after him when you heard he threatened Vic?" Wilmot asked bluntly.

Willie looked at him. "If I had, why would I tell you?" He shook his head. "I didn't know anything about it until this morning."

And the man must have been killed the previous night. He wouldn't have stayed in the woods all night waiting for Vic or Erin to come back outside. Not with the police search going on. That meant he must have been killed pretty soon after he had threatened them. Maybe he'd had a partner who had taken him out of the equation to prevent him from being caught, questioned, and possibly implicated.

Vic could not have gone out into the woods looking for him. Erin was sure of that. Was it possible that she had called Willie to report the incident and he had been able to get someone into the woods and to find the intruder before he had managed to get out?

Erin didn't see how Willie could have known or done anything unless he had been in the woods already. Had he been there to see Vic? Vic hadn't said she was planning to see Willie that night, but with all that was happening with the clans, she kept her meetings with Willie secret, even from Erin. Could Willie have been there, waiting for Vic to get home, and witnessed everything? It wouldn't be hard, under those circumstances, for him to follow the man and shoot him in the back once they were out of earshot of the house.

Would Willie shoot him in the back? Or would he think that was cowardly and insist on calling out to the man and accusing him face-to-face?

"Why would Vic's pa send someone out to threaten her?" Terry asked, approaching it from the other direction.

"I don't rightly know. Vic was raised inside the clan, but that doesn't mean she knew any clan secrets. What would you tell a kid that would put anyone at risk a few years later?" Willie frowned at Erin. "What did Potter actually say?"

"He just....he said to quit asking questions and mind our own business. But we hadn't been asking any questions about the Jacksons. I can't think of why he would think we had."

"What had you been doing?"

"Talking to Campbell Cox. About Mary Lou."

Willie's scowl deepened. "Mary Lou?"

"You don't know anything about who might have taken Mary Lou?" she asked him.

"I can't say I do. I assume that if it was a Dyson, I would have heard about it."

"Why would a Dyson take Mary Lou? Or a Jackson, for that matter?" Erin shook her head. "If this guy who came and threatened us was a Jackson, then Mary Lou must have been taken by the Jacksons, right? That is why they wanted us to stop asking questions?"

"Makes sense," Willie agreed.

"But why would a Jackson kidnap Mary Lou?" Terry demanded. "She wasn't involved in the clan. She wasn't related to anyone in the clan's leadership, was she? In either clan? She was just an ordinary Bald Eagle Falls citizen who wasn't involved in anything to do with the clans if she could help it."

Willie rolled his eyes and looked at the sky as if trying to predict the weather.

"Am I supposed to know everything that everyone in either clan is thinking? Who knows if Mary Lou had anything to do with anyone in either clan? Maybe she cut someone off in traffic. Maybe someone had a crush on her in high school. Maybe it was something to do with a deal that Roger made and then reneged on. Maybe he borrowed money from the wrong person trying to get them back on their feet, before he attempted suicide. Mary Lou and the boys wouldn't know. Roger might not remember after his brain injury."

"You think Roger borrowed money from the Jacksons?"

Willie held his arms out. "How do I know? He wouldn't have told me. They wouldn't have told me. There are plenty of bad deals going on with both clans all the time. They don't necessarily reach the ears of those who are in charge. And there would be no reason for me to know about it years ago."

Erin shook her head. None of it made any sense. But she had a different priority. It didn't really matter who had killed Eddie Potter. She wouldn't mourn him. And while she cared about Mary Lou and what had happened to her, finding out who had killed Potter wouldn't necessarily get them any closer to finding out what had happened to Mary Lou or Vic.

"If the Jackson clan threatened us, then did they come back and take Vicky?" she suggested. "Or did Potter get ambushed by a Dyson who had come for her?"

"There's another possibility," Terry pointed out. "Vic went after the man who threatened her, and the reason she is missing is because she's on the run after shooting him. She doesn't want to be found."

"She didn't go after him," Erin objected. "I saw her go back to the loft after you left to join the search. Ask Officer Stayner. He went to check on her before the bed." She looked at him, eyebrows raised.

Stayner nodded his head slowly. "Yes, she was still there when I checked in on the girls—on the ladies. Both were getting ready for bed."

"Vic was dressed for bed?" Wilmot asked.

Stayner seemed to hesitate for a fraction of a second before nodding his agreement. "Yeah. Lacy nightgown. She said she was on her way to bed. She wanted to be up this morning for… *something*," he finished, eyes on Willie.

"So she didn't come after Potter," Erin said with a nod. "She just went to bed."

"You said you prevented her from shooting Potter in the back after he threatened you," Terry reminded her.

"Yeah. So Vic didn't shoot him. Maybe he had a partner out here. Or a Dyson stalking her ran into Potter. But it wasn't Vic."

"You know she didn't have any qualms about shooting him in the back."

"But she didn't go after him. So that doesn't make any difference."

"He might have called her. Or she might have seen him through the window. You don't know what might have happened after you were in bed and Stayner was gone."

"For that matter," Wilmot rumbled, "we don't know for sure that Vic *didn't* shoot him after the confrontation. You could be covering for her. It's a little suspicious that he was shot in the back with a small caliber weapon like Vic might be carrying. After being shot, he might have kept running for a while, so you thought she had missed him. But eventually, the blood loss or the shock killed him. Here."

Erin rubbed her forehead. "Vic did *not* shoot him," she insisted. "You know me. Why would I lie about it if she did? She was within her rights to do it when he was threatening us with a gun."

"Not when he was fleeing. Not in the back."

Erin folded her arms across her chest. "You really think that matters with an organized crime guy waiting for us in the dark with a gun? Maybe we couldn't see him. He shot at us, and Vic shot back as he turned to hide behind a tree or came after me."

Erin looked around at the foliage and nodded her head.

"You can't prove that's not what happened. So why would I cover it up? It's a lot easier to tell you that Vic was protecting us." She clenched her jaw. "But we need to find her. She isn't just staying below the radar because she shot the guy. She's not hiding. Something happened to her. I know it, and you know it," she pointed at each of them in turn, "and you know it, and so do you."

The men looked back at her without saying anything, but none of them argued it. They knew as well as Erin that if Vic had shot a clan member after being threatened at gunpoint, she would have just told the police, and no one would ever have prosecuted her for it.

"We need to find her," Terry agreed, pressing his lips into a thin line. "I agree. I think—first things first—that someone should call her parents. See whether they have heard anything from her or through Jackson clan channels."

He didn't offer to do it himself. He had met Vic's parents and had a pretty good idea of how they would react. Erin wasn't sure it would do any good for her to call. They didn't have a very good opinion of her either. Willie might be able to make some kind of official inquiry through clan channels, but she didn't think there was any love lost between them now. There wouldn't be any "courtesy" calls.

"What about Jeremy?" she suggested. "He might be able to talk to their ma. I don't think anyone can talk to *him*."

Willie nodded his agreement immediately. Erin raised her brows at Terry and Wilmot to see if they wanted her to go ahead and do it.

"We don't want word to get out to the whole town," Wilmot said slowly. "We are still trying to keep this under wraps. Maintain some control over the situation. If you think you could impress upon Jeremy that he can't talk to anyone else about it and get him to agree to make the call, I'll agree to it."

Erin pulled out her phone immediately.

A group of men and women arrived in a tight cluster. The crime scene techs and maybe someone from the medical examiner's office in the city. Erin was surprised that he had gotten there that quickly.

She withdrew a distance away so that she was not in their way and would not be overheard on the phone. She found Jeremy's number and tapped on it.

CHAPTER 28

"Hey, Erin," Jeremy answered the phone in a casual, friendly tone. "What's up?"

"Jer... Vic is missing."

He didn't immediately go into panic mode. "Well, where did that sister of mine disappear to now?"

"We don't know. This is serious, Jeremy. The police want to know if you'll call your parents to see if they have heard anything."

"Why would they have heard anything? Vic doesn't report to them."

Erin mentally rewound to give him the background. "Last night... the two of us were threatened at gunpoint, told to stay out of things that were none of our business. This morning, the guy who made the threats was found dead. Willie has identified him as Eddie Potter, a member of the Jackson clan."

"Potter?"

"Yeah. Maybe Vic recognized him, even though she didn't say. If she did, she might have called your parents to find out why he was after her. Or if she's been taken hostage, they might have been called to let them know what was going on. Or they might be able to ask who went after her and why."

"Okay, okay," Jeremy interrupted the flow of words. "Okay. You know for sure that it was this Potter guy? That he was the one who threatened you?"

"Yeah. He wore a mask, but his clothes were the same, and I saw a tattoo on his wrist. So yeah, we're pretty sure that this guy who is now lying dead in the woods was the one who came after us."

"And Willie identified him as Potter?"

"Yeah."

"I guess that answers my next question… you're sure Willie isn't hiding Vic somewhere? I mean, that would be the logical thing to do."

"If he's hiding her… he's a good actor. They were supposed to meet this morning, but Vic never showed up. He called me, and I went to find her… but she wasn't in her apartment. Then we were walking the path that she would have taken in case she was hurt somewhere along the way and found Potter's body."

"Did Willie shoot him?"

Erin had been staring off into the woods, trying to mentally separate herself from the crime scene, but at Jeremy's words, she looked back at Willie.

Was Willie that good an actor? Erin wouldn't have said so. A good liar, but not necessarily a good actor. He held his cards close but didn't put on a show.

"What kind of gun does Willie carry?"

"I don't know," Jeremy admitted. "What was Potter shot with?"

"Don't know for sure, yet, Terry thought a small caliber, maybe a .22."

Jeremy grunted. "I've never seen Willie pull a piece, but I would expect him to carry a .45 or something similar. Handgun or rifle?"

"Uh… I don't know. They didn't say. But I guess if they thought that it could have been Vic who shot him, they must be thinking it was a handgun. Do you know if that little one that she carried…"

"I've never played with it, but that size, I would expect it to be a .22. Why would they think that Vic did it? I thought you said that you and Vic were together. You can tell them she didn't."

"They said maybe she went after him later."

Jeremy scoffed. "She's not an idiot." He didn't say anything for a minute. "You reckon something happened to her? Somebody snatched her?"

"I'm really worried," Erin admitted. "If you could please talk to your parents, just to make sure they haven't heard anything. And," she dropped her voice, even though there was a lot of discussion going on between the law enforcement officers and the techs and she didn't think anyone would overhear her, "if you have any other connections to the Jacksons that you could use... I know your brothers are in the pen, so they probably can't help. Still, you might know other people in the organization who would talk to you if they knew it was a personal inquiry about a family member..."

"I burned my bridges when I left the organization," Jeremy said. "No one is gonna talk to me. But I'll make some calls. Maybe an old friend of Vic's would be willing to help. Don't call me back. Let me deal with it."

Erin agreed. "Okay. Let me know when you can, okay? We really want to find her."

Jeremy agreed and disconnected. Erin slid her phone back into her pocket.

"What's going on?" a soft voice inquired. "What happened?"

Even though the voice was quiet, Erin whirled around to see who had spoken, startled.

Her gamekeeper, Adele, stood with a rifle held in the crook of her arm. She patrolled the woods for trespassers in exchange for living in the summer cottage. The woods were sometimes used by teenagers for parties or by squatters looking for a quiet place to live. While Erin had compassion for the squatters in particular, she had come to understand that she could be held liable for anything that happened in the woods if she were not diligent in sending trespassers on their way. So she tried to help the indigent in other ways.

Erin gave a long sigh, trying to slow the beating of her heart after being startled by the tall redhead.

"You scared me!"

"Sorry. I was trying not to interrupt or scare you," Adele continued using a very soft voice that would not attract the policemen's attention. "I heard the voices."

Erin looked around. From where they were standing, she could not see the body. But she nodded in that direction, over where Terry was standing talking to the techs, wearing their protective clothing so they would not contaminate any evidence.

"A dead body," she admitted reluctantly.

Adele looked around. "A body? Who? No one we know, I hope?"

"No. Someone from the Jackson clan. He was at the house last night, threatening me and Vic. We called the police, and there was a search."

"I heard. But you two are okay...?"

"I don't know where Vic is. You haven't seen her today, have you? Or any time last night?"

Adele was sometimes up in the dark to perform her ceremonies. Erin kept the fact that there was a witch living in her woods quiet. Those who bought Adele's herbal sachets and woodcrafts referred to her as a wise woman. Erin didn't enlighten them about Adele's ritual practices.

"No. After the police were gone, it was quiet. I didn't see or hear anything. Except maybe..." Adele looked around, frowning. "The birds were making a racket this morning. But they stopped, so I didn't check it out."

"Yeah, I followed the crows to the body."

"You should stop doing that," Adele suggested with just the hint of an ironic smile. "Perhaps you should leave patrolling the woods and finding stray bodies to me."

"Yeah. Sounds like a plan," Erin agreed. It would be a while before she considered a leisurely walk in the woods again. She would stick with tai chi in her backyard and walk on the paved sidewalks.

"How long will the police be here?"

"A few hours, probably. The crime scene techs just got here."

CHAPTER 29

*A*t that point, Terry noticed Adele talking to Erin and walked toward them with purpose.

"Oops," Adele murmured.

It was too late to escape without being noticed, so she waited for Terry to reach them.

"Missus Windsor," Terry greeted her with a nod. "I don't suppose you know anything about our latest discovery."

Adele looked down her nose at Terry. "I do try to keep the woods clean of any kind of trash."

"You were a little late in getting this cleaned up."

"Apparently."

"Did you happen to hear a shot last night or this morning?"

"I did not. I did hear the birds a while ago, but anything from last night was... too quiet or covered up by other sounds."

Terry nodded toward Adele's rifle. "That a .22?"

"Yes. But it hasn't left my side."

"Mind if I take a look at it?"

She shook her head. "No, I don't think so."

"Has it been fired recently?"

"I'm not required to answer your questions."

"If you happened to fire at a trespasser or accidentally wing someone when you were firing at someone else, that would not be a criminal matter," he coaxed.

But Adele was too wily to fall for his assurances. She shook her head.

"I know my job, and so do you. But I did not fire at that man."

"I would just like to be reassured that the gun hasn't been fired recently."

She again shook her head and refused. Terry's cheeks reddened. He did not like being denied when he made a perfectly reasonable request.

"I may have to ask you to come in for questioning."

"I may have to refuse."

Erin smothered a grin. She felt guilty for being amused when Vic was missing. She should be absolutely focused on finding Vic and not being distracted by Adele's antipathy toward the police.

Terry didn't have anything to suggest that Adele was the one who had killed Potter other than that she had a gun that might be the same caliber as the one that had killed him. As were millions of other guns. And, of course, she had opportunity, being free to wander the woods at will. But what reason would she have to kill Potter? Especially shooting him in the back?

Adele gave Terry a half smile and retreated into the woods. He could not hold her, and she had no desire to be around the police.

"Was Vic's gun in the apartment?" Erin asked Terry.

Terry looked at her for a moment before answering. She expected a patient reminder that he couldn't share details of an active investigation with her. She could usually get him to spill the beans by reminding him that the information would be public, so he wasn't breaking any confidences by sharing it. But there wasn't always public information to leverage.

"Her gun was there," he admitted. "And so was her nightgown."

Erin blinked in surprise. She tried to reconcile these two pieces of information and to figure out why Terry would tell her that. Not just the piece of information she had asked for, but an extra bit as well. It was intriguing, and she tried to puzzle out what it meant.

"Vic always wore her holster," she said slowly. "I can't be sure she wore it to bed; you'll have to try broaching that one with Willie! But if she took it off for bed and just left the gun within reach on the bedside table… then she should have been in the nightgown, like Stayner said. If she was dressed, why wasn't she wearing the gun? If she decided to get up again after Stayner had left, the first thing she would have done is get dressed and put on her holster."

Terry nodded his agreement.

"Unless someone was there who let her get dressed but wouldn't let her put on the gun and holster," Erin said slowly.

Terry gave an infinitesimal nod.

Erin felt relieved and sick with worry at the same time. Relieved that Terry was putting it together and believed that something had happened to Vic, that she hadn't just wandered off on her own. She hadn't gone out to kill Potter and then gone to ground so that the police wouldn't be able to arrest her for it.

Somebody had been in the apartment with her and had prevented her from putting on the gun and taking it with her.

And that meant Vic was in the hands of someone who controlled her movements, didn't want her armed, and might intend to do her harm. If it was someone from one of the clans, then Vic had undoubtedly been taken so that they could force Willie to do whatever they demanded.

If she had been a believer, Erin would have sent up a prayer at that moment. And maybe she still should, because Vic believed in prayer, and if Erin could do anything to help her friend be safe, she would. But she had no idea how to pray, other than to hope that some force in the universe would ensure that nothing awful happened to Vic and she would return to them unharmed.

When Terry had been kidnapped, crazy Theresa had nearly killed him and Jack Ward. When Erin herself had been kidnapped, she had been left for dead in one of the natural tunnels that ran through the mountain like Swiss cheese. Hit over the head, bound, and left for dead. That had not been the only time Erin had been abducted. But it had been the scariest, and the one that had brought her closest to death.

She couldn't bear to think of Vic injured and restrained, waiting for them to find her.

"What are we going to do?" she asked Terry softly.

"Everything we can," Terry promised. "Did you talk to Jeremy?"

"Yes. He's going to make some calls. Do you think they'll tell him anything?"

"It's a long shot. But they are more likely to tell him something than they are to tell me."

Erin nodded her agreement. "Is there anyone else who might have killed Potter?"

"Too many people to be sure of anything. It could have been another Jackson or a Dyson. More likely a Dyson, because they were actually enemies. But you never know what might have been going on with internal politics. There are plenty of resentments and conflicts within the clans, too, sometimes more than the outside conflicts. Willie himself, of course, especially if he heard that Potter had just held his girlfriend at gunpoint."

"Is there anyone else working with the clans who might be able to tell you something about internal politics? Like an undercover FBI agent or something like that? Or DEA or whoever. There are so many agencies, I get dizzy trying to figure out what they all do and how they work together."

"I will ask over those channels. But they will stonewall me. Or they won't have the answers, and I won't know whether that is because they are not close enough, or because they know but don't want to tell me because I might get in the way of their investigation."

"What about Beaver? She might know something."

"I'll reach out to her," Terry agreed.

"Have you talked to her the last few days? She was in town on Wednesday. Is she still?"

"I couldn't tell you. She comes and goes like a ghost. She doesn't tell me where she is going to be."

Erin chuckled. She remembered the first time that Terry had met Beaver and had tried to arrest her without knowing who she was. The number of weapons she had been carrying had been impressive, as was Beaver's physique when Terry had commanded her to take off her jacket. Erin was continually surprised and impressed by Beaver. The woman was like a real-life comic book hero.

CHAPTER 30

There wasn't anything else for Erin to do. The police were continuing with the investigation. They would comb the woods for any sign of Vic or the person who had kidnapped her. But that didn't mean they would be able to find anything. There was no guarantee that they had even gone in that direction.

It might just be a coincidence that Potter had been killed. Maybe Adele had seen him out there and fired a shot in his direction to scare him off and had accidentally killed him. Maybe a group of teens out snipe hunting had taken things too far. Vic's kidnapper might just as easily have led her out to a waiting car on the parking pad in the back or the street in front of the house. There was no evidence they had gone through the woods.

Erin returned home, anxious about Vic's disappearance and frustrated with the lack of police leads. They needed to find Vic before something happened to her. Erin had already been worried about Mary Lou's disappearance, but she was even more worried about Vic.

She knew that Vic had not taken off on her own. They talked about everything, and Vic knew better than to do something like that. And Vic had not decided to go after Potter because she had seen him outside in the yard again.

More than that, there were a number of reasons that Vic was in more danger than Mary Lou. Mary Lou was calm and cool and thought things through carefully before acting. She would be watching for a way to get away or for an opportunity to develop a relationship with the kidnapper or one of his people to help improve her odds of survival or escape.

On the other hand, Vic was more likely to react without thinking, to be angry or hot-headed, and to try something inadvisable. Vic was more likely to earn a violent response from her kidnapper or to make him decide that she was too dangerous to hold. Not only that, but being Willie's girlfriend made Vic a target, not just as a means to put pressure on Willie, but to actually hurt him by hurting or killing someone he had strong feelings for. Someone, either Dyson or Jackson, who wanted Willie out of the clan leadership, might use Vic to distract or disable him with grief.

And if those weren't enough reasons to be worried about Vic, there was also the way she was hated and targeted by people for being transgender. Even the nonviolent church ladies in Bald Eagle Falls had targeted her with hate speech. Others, particularly clan men, viewed her as a thing or a nonhuman. And if she was a thing or nonhuman, then they had no problem treating her violently.

People who didn't see their target as human were far more likely to commit violence against her. Erin could easily see a clan member holding her captive, but then deciding she was too much trouble to allow her to live.

Erin shuddered at the thought.

Was she overreacting? Or was she just being practical and seeing things as they really were?

She had to get Vic back before anything could happen to her.

As Erin approached the house, she could hear Nilla barking. She looked at the sky. It had been longer than the hour that Terry had promised, and Nilla had been out in the dog run the whole time.

It wasn't cruel to leave the dog outside for a few hours in nice weather. It was good for him to have the fresh air and sunshine to work off his energy so that he would be quiet when she returned him to his crate.

Erin had decided to go to Auntie Clem's to keep herself busy, but she couldn't leave Nilla in the house. He was like the Tasmanian Devil from cartoons, ready to tear the house apart if left alone for even a few hours.

"I'm coming, Nilla," Erin called out, hoping Nilla would stop barking and not aggravate the neighbors before she could get there and get him settled in his crate. They would complain to the police or call Erin to tell her to take care of it, even though Nilla wasn't hers. They had no idea what was happening with Vic; they would think she was neglecting her animal and ignoring the noise.

Calling out to Nilla seemed to only make him louder and more frantic, and Erin was irritated with herself for making it worse. She should have known Nilla would just get more excited.

She hurried to the dog run once she reached the yard and lifted the latch to open the door and let Nilla out.

Nilla jumped excitedly at her legs but didn't pause for ear scratches; instead, he circled around her energetically, begging for a game of chase or fetch.

"Come on, crazy!" Erin told him, laughing. "I have work to do. I don't have the time to stop and play right now. Come on, you need to go back in your crate."

He barked at her and crouched down, waiting for her to chase him. She should have had his leash waiting and not allowed him out of the run until she had it clipped on securely.

"Nilla! Come on, silly pup. Let's go home. Do you want a treat? A treat?" Erin coaxed. "Come with me. Let's go inside and get a treat."

He knew she just wanted to lock him in his crate, and he was much faster than Erin was. He kept coming closer to play with her, then running away before she could catch him. Erin looked around and found a much-chewed ball.

"Okay, you want to play? Huh? Are you going to get the ball? Here... are you ready..." She wound Nilla up, getting him super excited, then threw the ball for him. He raced after it like greased lightning, then brought it back to her. Erin threw it for him a few times, even though she felt like she was wasting time.

After a few throws, Erin grabbed Nilla's collar at the same time as she reached to take the ball from his mouth.

Nilla yipped and objected, but he didn't pull away from her, and Erin was able to lead him up to the stairs, bent over to reach his collar. Erin managed to juggle her keys so that she could unlock the door and hold on to Nilla's collar at the same time.

Once they were in the apartment, she let Nilla go. She would at least be able to catch him again inside.

She filled his food and water bowls and put them in the crate. It was a big crate, larger than most people would probably have recommended for a small dog like Nilla. But Erin thought it was nice for him to have a little more room to move around.

"Come on, Nilla. Bet you're mighty thirsty after all that running around. Come on."

She pulled his blanket out and gave it a little shake to release any grit and fluff it up. Something fell out of the folds and pinged on the floor. Erin shook the blanket and returned it to the crate before picking up an errant brass button. She polished it on her shirt. A button from Terry's uniform. He must have snagged it when he had taken Nilla out that morning. She hadn't noticed he'd had any loose buttons. He was usually very diligent about the upkeep of his uniforms. But they had been in a hurry that morning, distracted by Vic's disappearance. Erin slipped it into her pocket.

When she called Nilla over to the kennel, he was obedient, for once, and didn't make Erin chase him all over the apartment. Erin latched the door, and he whined.

"It's okay, Nilla," she soothed. "You just relax now. Take it easy for a while and I'll be back later to take you for a walk."

Nilla walked over to his bowls to sniff them, acting uninterested. But Erin knew as soon as she was out of sight, he would eat, drink, and curl up in his blanket for a nap. He'd gotten plenty of sun and exercise and would be tired.

Maybe by the time she returned, they would know more about what had happened to Vic. Maybe Vic would even be back.

Erin sighed. She knew it was unlikely, but she couldn't let go of the possibility. She had to believe that they would be able to get Vic back quickly.

CHAPTER 31

*E*rin had not been scheduled to work at the bakery, but she
knew she would be at loose ends at the house, wandering
from one room to another, lonely and unable to focus on anything.
At the bakery, at least there were other people, and they could keep
her company. She could lose herself in the routine of baking.

If it were quiet, it might even be a good day to take her first run
at the mock apple pie. She was curious to see how close she could
get to a pie that would convince the taste tester that it was made
with real apples.

So she worked at the bakery, helping to keep the display case
stocked and a few extra goods waiting in the kitchen for when they
ran out of the pizza pretzels the Cox brothers loved or the Morning
Sunrise muffins the pilgrims kept showing up for. There were
always more of them on a weekend.

"Erin?"

Erin wrested herself back from her solemn thoughts of Vic and
what might have happened to her to focus on Bella, standing in the
doorway to the front of the bakery, looking inquiring.

"Oh, sorry, Bella. What's up?"

"Customer here to see you."

She didn't ask Erin if she had time to talk to the customer, like she normally would. Erin raised her brows, waiting for more details, such as who was there and if they were looking for particular allergy information.

Bella didn't tell her what it was all about.

"Okay," Erin agreed. She put aside the pastry crust she was working on and followed Bella out to the front of the store. She looked around, and Bella nodded toward a boy standing on the other side of the display case. Young Peter Foster, one of Erin's favorite customers. She smiled, happy to see him.

"Hi, Peter. How are you doing?"

He turned his face toward her, and Erin saw that he was not smiling cheerily as usual, but his round cheeks were streaked with tears. He tried manfully to smile and show her a brave front, but it was clear that something was wrong.

Erin hurried to the hinged portion of the counter that she folded back so she could walk through to the front to see Peter close up. "Come over here," she told him, motioning to one of the small cafe tables. He joined her and climbed up onto one of the chairs.

"What's wrong?" Erin asked softly. "What's going on?"

"I don't know. Nobody will talk to me about it. They all think I'm a little kid and won't understand."

It was a warning flag to Erin. The Fosters were a very devout family and had strict ideas about how they should behave and what their children could be told. If they had refused to tell him something, she had better not be the one to enlighten him. She didn't want to get on their bad side and not be allowed to talk to Peter and the other children.

"Well... I'm sure there's a good reason they don't want to talk to you about it."

"I'm grown up enough," he told her. "I help take care of the little kids. I can help. I'm like a grown-up."

"I know. You're very mature and have a lot of responsibility."

He nodded his agreement. He picked up a napkin and wiped the tears in his eyes and cheeks. He blotted his eyes again and, calmer, continued.

"It's my dad." A big sniffle. "He didn't come home. Mom says he is just working, but he isn't. I know all the places he works; he isn't at any of them. Mom says not to lie, but she's lying to me about it."

Erin swallowed. Mr. Foster was missing now?

"Sometimes parents think that their kids need to be protected. Or that they will say something that they shouldn't. It's not always fair. I know you're a responsible boy and wouldn't do anything your parents told you not to. But parents are still… cautious. They want to protect you."

"I want to know where my dad is!"

She put her hand over his. "I don't know where he is or what might have happened. You'll just have to wait until your mom is ready to tell you that. Help her with the girls and Allan, and don't pester her. Maybe she'll feel better about talking about it."

Peter wiped his eyes with the heels of his hands. "You think she'll tell me?"

"I don't know. I can't tell you that." She swallowed and tried to keep her question casual. "Do you know if your mom talked to the police about it?"

Peter shook his head. "She said he was at work."

So Terry didn't even know. Was that because Mr. Foster was working with one of the clans? Mrs. Foster didn't want to tell Peter where he really was because she didn't want him to know about the details?

But Erin didn't think Mr. Foster would work for one of the clans. He was very outspoken about his moral beliefs, and she couldn't see him doing the devil's work with one of the clans.

"Well, you'll have to trust your mom for now. If you argue with her, it won't help, but if you listen and try to help her, she might decide you're old enough to know the truth."

"Okay." He sniffled. "I can do that, you know."

"I know." She squeezed his hand. "You help take care of your mom. And tell me if she needs anything. Do you want something to take home to her? Some muffins or cinnamon rolls?"

"Yeah. She really likes the cinnamon rolls."

"Okay, let's get her some of those. They are from my day-old freezer, so there is no charge, okay? I don't want her to think that you stole the rolls or the money to buy the rolls."

"She wouldn't think that," he scoffed. "She knows I wouldn't do that."

"They're just a present for her, because if your dad is away working, she probably has a lot of extra work to do, and she could use a nice treat for her and the little ones."

"And me!" Peter insisted, indignant.

"And you," Erin agreed. "Let's go get them for her."

CHAPTER 32

"*I*s everything okay?" Harold asked after Erin saw Peter on his way with a sack of cinnamon rolls and a plastic bowl full of cream cheese frosting. "Is he all right?"

Erin didn't want to gossip about the Foster family, but she was sure people would figure it out sooner or later. The way people talked in Bald Eagle Falls, it was probably already being discussed in the Fosters' social circle.

"Peter is worried about his dad." Bella stopped to listen to Erin's answer as well, looking concerned. "According to Mrs. Foster, he's just out on a job..." She didn't want to say much more than that.

"Out on a job?" Bella repeated. "He works at the Book Nook."

"He might have a couple of side gigs too. People need more than just one job to get along these days, especially raising a big family like that with Mrs. Foster at home. I don't know if she has some kind of home-based job. I don't think so. She's got all of those kids to take care of, and they think that providing is the man's responsibility."

"The Book Nook is still closed. I thought they would try to keep it open, even if Naomi was away, but..." Bella trailed off.

"They probably can't," Erin said. "If they don't have the

authority to act for her or the business, or don't have access to all of the accounts and vendors…"

Bella nodded slowly, frowning.

"When I was sick, you guys could keep the bakery running because you had your own keys and access to the schedules and checklists," Erin pointed out. "And if anyone questioned whether you were allowed to run things and put in orders from our suppliers, I would have told them you did. But something like this… if Naomi was the only one running things and everybody else just stocked shelves or ran the till… it would be hard to keep the business running."

She thought about how long her employees would be able to keep the business running if something happened to her. What about payroll or the bills Erin paid monthly? Would Vic know where to find everything and enter it into the computer?

She was assuming Vic would be back. What if something happened to Erin and Vic was not around? Would the other employees have enough information to keep things running? Would people believe they had the authority to do so? Or would they insist they had to wait for Erin's return?

She could see that Bella was thinking these things as well, adding them to the things she would need to learn before running her own business. Things that maybe Erin should have thought about prior to this.

"Do you think Mr. Foster is okay?" Harold asked.

"Well… I hope so. A lot of people have… dropped out of sight recently. I hope that he's just at another job. If Mrs. Foster hasn't reported him as missing, then you have to trust that she knows where he is."

"Do you think Uncle Nelson would know?"

Erin opened her mouth and closed it again, trying to find the words.

There could be more than one person named Nelson around. It might be a family name repeated several times throughout each generation as a way to honor their progenitors. It was not a common first name, but sometimes, it was those distinctive names that were most celebrated.

"Who is your Uncle Nelson?" Erin managed eventually.

Harold didn't look at her like she was crazy for not knowing. He was from out of town, so he didn't treat her like many of the long-time Bald Eagle Falls residents, who thought she should have absorbed all of the culture and history by now, or somehow have inherited it genetically.

"Nelson Dyson," Harold offered.

"Is he... does he know Willie? Is he Dwight Dyson's son?"

Harold wrinkled his brow and thought about it for a moment. "Yes."

Dwight was the previous leader—or at least figurehead—of the Dyson clan.

"And he's your uncle?"

"Yeah. I don't know; he might actually be a cousin, but when your cousin is like your parents' age, then you call him uncle. It's for respect. Like you don't have to call him mister, but you can't just call him by the first name like the cousins you play with."

Erin nodded her understanding.

"I imagine... you probably don't see him very often."

"No, not a lot," Harold admitted. "But sometimes he takes the other cousins out on a fishing trip or somewhere else. And Mom says you don't say no to Nelson Dyson. We're going on another trip tomorrow."

"You're going to see him tomorrow?"

Harold nodded. "Supposed to be up early to go with him. Not earlier than the early baking shift. But earlier than for school."

"Well..." Erin pondered. "You could ask him if he knows where Mr. Foster is if you want to. But you have to judge that for yourself. I don't know much about what he's like. And if your mom says you're not supposed to ask him questions, you should listen to her."

"No. She says I should always ask questions if I want to know how things work."

Erin felt a little queasy at the thought of Harold asking Nelson questions about how the clan worked. Was he being groomed to be a soldier for the Dyson clan? Or maybe a position higher up in the clan? If he was being encouraged to ask questions, that didn't sound like just an entry-level street soldier.

She thought Harold wanted to become a baker, but she might have misjudged him. Maybe he just saw the need to get some experience and enjoyed the perk of being able to take home whatever day-old baking he liked. Like most celiacs, Harold hadn't grown up with much choice for baked goods. There were a lot more gluten-free options available now, but not the variety and quality of what Erin produced at Auntie Clem's Bakery. She was not too humble to admit that her baking was head and shoulders above anything that could be found prepackaged on the shelves of a grocery store in the city.

"Well, maybe you can ask your mom whether it is something you should ask. I don't want to encourage you to ask something that might make Nelson upset or that your mom would think was too intrusive. I don't know what kinds of questions she wants you to ask."

Harold considered this, then nodded. "Okay. I think it is okay, but I'll ask my mom."

"Do you have any older brothers?"

Harold pushed his glasses up. "Yeah, two of 'em."

"Do they live with you? Could you ask them about it? They might be able to tell you whether it is something you could ask your uncle about."

"We're all going fishing; I might have a lot of questions about the people who are missing."

"Be careful," Erin cautioned. "Really, I don't want you to get in trouble for asking too many questions. Especially about something like that. Maybe your mom meant a different kind of question."

He gave her a puzzled look, but agreed he would talk to his brothers about it before talking to Nelson. Erin blew out her breath in relief. She did *not* want to be responsible for Harold getting hurt because he had asked Nelson Dyson the wrong questions.

"You're friends with Willie, aren't you?" he asked Erin.

"Well… yes, I think I can say we're friends. At least, we were before he became the leader of the clan."

"Then you should be friends with him now. You could ask *him* about Mr. Foster."

"I guess I could. But we're already trying to figure out what happened to Miss Victoria. I don't think I should complicate it by bringing other people into it."

Erin didn't want to distract anyone from Vic's disappearance. She wanted Mr. Foster to be okay and to return healthy and strong to his family, but first, she wanted Vic home.

CHAPTER 33

CAN U MEET?

*J*eremy texted Erin while she was at the bakery. She normally would have stayed to help with the closing and ensure they had everything prepped for the ladies tea Sunday morning.

But Bella was very familiar with everything that needed to be done and capable of supervising the others and getting it done. And the faster they could figure out what had happened to Vic, the better. Every hour seemed to weigh more heavily on Erin's shoulders. She couldn't believe that Vic was missing. When she got into her work, it felt like Vic was just off to the city like she was many Saturdays, and would be back any time. But as soon as she let her mind drift to other things, she started to worry again.

She texted back to Jeremy.

Sure, where and when?

Any time am home now

Ok will head over

She let Bella know she was leaving. Bella nodded, unconcerned. "You're not supposed to be on today, anyway. I don't need you here."

Erin laughed. "Way to make me feel welcome."

"Go home, girl. Have a long hot bath and relax."

The last thing Erin needed was to be home alone with her thoughts. But she smiled and agreed, not telling Bella her actual plans.

Jeremy lived in a basement suite not far from Erin's house, so she parked her bug in the garage and walked over. She went around to the back door and rang the bell as indicated on a piece of paper taped to the door. When Jeremy came to the door, she handed him a bag of muffins. "I thought you might like a little something. You can just throw them in the freezer and defrost one when you want it for breakfast or a snack."

Jeremy pushed back his shaggy blond hair and smiled his trade-mark grin. "Those are great. You know I ain't ever gonna turn down your baking."

Erin smiled. "Figured as much."

He stepped back and motioned her inside. They went down the stairs to his apartment, and he invited her to sit.

Not much had changed since the last time Erin had been there. It was a bachelor's suite, with little thought put into the furniture and decor. A functional space. Erin knew that Beaver stayed over sometimes when she was in Bald Eagle Falls. She glanced around to see if Beaver was there, but she did not appear to be, unless she was sleeping or working behind the closed bedroom door. There weren't any extra bags or clothes in evidence.

Erin sat down on the saggy couch. "So… did you find anything out in your inquiries…?"

Jeremy sighed and spread his hands in a helpless gesture. "I wish I could say that everyone was concerned and helpful and helped out the best they could."

Erin nodded sympathetically.

But Jeremy had asked her to come over, so she had to assume he'd found something out. He hadn't just wanted the company.

"There is a lot of disruption right now," Jeremy offered. "With Willie taking over with the Dysons, a lot of the Dysons want to either take him out or jump ship. So there's this back and forth between the clans right now, with Dysons wanting to defect over to Jacksons, or else just leave completely."

"So that accounts for some of the 'missing' people," Erin anticipated.

"Yeah. It's a good time to just disappear. And with so many people doing that, there's just so much that the leadership can do to keep track of everyone."

"So the Jackson clan must be getting bigger and stronger. That's good for them." Erin pretended this didn't matter to her, when in reality, it made her feel sick. She didn't want either clan to get stronger. They had been fairly balanced in their powers, and that had kept either of them from being able to overrun Bald Eagle Falls or the other small towns nearby. In the city, of course, there were other urban gangs and organized crime groups to compete with.

"I didn't get that feeling," Jeremy said slowly. "I don't know what else is going on, but it doesn't feel like the balance of power has shifted."

"Is there a third group? There's rumor of an underground cartel."

"I heard that... don't know if it is true. No one I talked to could say who was in this third gang..." He frowned, shaking his head. "I don't know who is running this other group. No one can say. Do you think it is just a fake? Something made up?"

"No... I don't see how it could be. If there is no third cartel, then... where are people going?"

Jeremy nodded his head but didn't look convinced.

"Did anyone have any suggestions as to where Vic had gone?" Erin asked. "Who has taken her?"

"Some people are leaving, too. Leaving and not coming back. Maybe people who have supposedly gone to this third cartel are just people who have... left."

"Yeah. But Vic didn't just leave." Erin fixed Jeremy with a hard stare to emphasize her point. "I know she didn't. And you do, too."

Jeremy scratched his head and raked his fingers through his long, thick locks.

"Yeah, I know," he agreed. "But no one seems to know anything. And I'm not getting a lot of cooperation. Everyone knows I'm a traitor, and they don't want to talk to me. I can't expect them to answer my questions; it just reminds people that... I've never been dealt with. I don't usually worry about anyone coming after me... but I can't keep reminding people who I am and expecting them to ignore the fact that I left the clan and am happy living my own life."

"I don't want you to get kidnapped or killed either. You'd better not ask any more questions. I'm sorry I got you involved."

"I put myself in this position. It's not your fault. I just think I need to be careful."

Erin nodded. She scratched at a line of what she assumed was dog drool on her pant leg. Had she really gone to the bakery looking like that?

"But there is one thing," Jeremy offered.

"Yes?"

"They are saying that there are people who have disappeared who are *not* with either clan."

"The ones who have left on their own."

"But there are people who have not left on their own. People like Mary Lou or Naomi who are not associated with a clan, so they don't have any reason to run away."

"So... you think it is the third cartel?"

"If the third cartel exists... why would they take people with no clan affiliation and no... special skills. Why would they take someone like Mary Lou?"

Erin shook her head. It didn't make any sense. None of the gangs would want them. As far as Erin could tell, they were not related or close to anyone in the clans.

They kept going right back to the beginning. Who had reason to take those people? If it wasn't the clans, who was it?

"What about Beaver?" Erin asked. "Does she have any ideas?"

"Well, if she was around, I could ask, but she's incommunicado."

"She was here Wednesday. Was she just passing through?"

Jeremy raised his brows. "Was she?" he asked innocently. "I don't know; she didn't say anything to me." He shrugged. "You know Ro. She comes and goes. Sometimes we get a chance to meet, and sometimes we don't."

"I thought you guys were a little more... *serious* than that," Erin said carefully. "Doesn't she... stay here when she's around?"

"Sure, if she's staying over for a night or two. But if she's just passing through, or if she is doing something undercover, then obviously she doesn't. We see each other when we can, but she's busy."

"Are you... exclusive?" Erin's cheeks got hot. "Never mind, that's none of my business, and I'm not here to talk to you about your private life. I just wondered whether Beaver might be able to help... I mean, she knows Vic... she's helped us out before when we needed her..."

Jeremy laughed comfortably. He didn't answer the question of whether he and Beaver were exclusive, and Erin assumed that the answer was "No," and did not want to get into it.

Then his expression sobered. Like Erin, he appeared awkward laughing or discussing anything else with Vic missing. She could be in danger, or worse, she might already be dead. Erin couldn't bear to think of that and pushed it out of her mind.

"I don't know if Ro would be able to do anything... or maybe suggest someone who could or an avenue to take." Jeremy pulled out his phone, and Erin could tell by his taps that he was typing a text message. A swoosh sounded as he sent it out, and then he put his phone down on the coffee table. "I don't know if she'll be able to answer right now. But you never know."

Erin looked down at the phone lying on the table and tried to think of what else to say to Jeremy. It was difficult to carry on with small talk under the circumstances. Vic was always the one who saved Erin from difficult social situations where she didn't know what to say or do, and Erin felt her absence keenly.

"I could really use her to save this conversation right now," Erin laughed weakly.

"Beaver?"

"No." She laughed harder at that, feeling a little giddy. Beaver was the complete opposite of Vic. She was blunt and didn't care whether what she said was socially appropriate. She would say what she thought and if anyone didn't like it, that was too bad. "I meant Vic. She's better at this kind of thing than me."

"This kind of thing? I'm not sure anyone is good at dealing with a situation like this."

Erin nodded her agreement. "I know. I just thought… she always knows what to say."

"Well, we'll have to ask her when she gets back."

"Yeah." Erin swallowed, a lump in her throat.

CHAPTER 34

*J*eremy's phone lit up and played "Secret Agent Man." He grabbed it and hit the answer and speaker buttons, then held it between them.

"Ro. Hey, I've got Erin with me. I guess you heard…"

"Yeah, I just heard about Vic. Sorry I didn't call earlier."

Erin could hear Beaver chewing her wad of gum over the phone and felt physically ill. Jeremy looked at her to let her take over and talk to Beaver, but she shook her head. Motioning for him to continue.

"We don't know how to find her," Jeremy said. "The police are on it, I guess, but you know the Bald Eagle Falls police department." He looked at Erin and backtracked. "I mean, I know they are good, and they try hard, but they don't have the resources that the FBI or staties have. And you might know what to do or who to contact to get someone to take a look at it. Someone who has a chance of figuring out what happened to Vic."

"Bald Eagle Falls has already looped them in," Beaver said. "They've got a number of cases, and they are aware that there is a big organized crime problem that has blown up."

Erin was glad to hear they weren't just trying to figure everything out on their own. It seemed like the situation was way too big to be handled by just one small-town police force.

"I always thought there was a little more to your friend Willie than there appeared to be on the surface," Beaver observed with a chuckle. "I would think he would have a pretty good idea of where Vic is or who was involved in her disappearance."

"If he knew, he would have her back," Erin objected. "Or he would have told the police where to find her."

"You think he would leave that up to law enforcement?" Beaver's tone was skeptical. "I doubt that. He'll be trying to figure out a way to get her back without police involvement. If he knows who's got her, the police will be the last to find out."

Erin didn't think Beaver was wrong. Willie and law enforcement did not get along with each other. She knew from experience that Terry did not trust Willie, and Willie did not trust Terry or any other authorities. They had seen each other as the enemy since Erin had first arrived in Bald Eagle Falls. Other than the few times that Terry had called upon Willie to help him with a search and rescue or something else that called for Willie's experience. The two of them cooperated with each other when necessary, but there was no love lost between them.

"You think Willie knows who has Vic?" Jeremy asked. "And he's just... trying to figure out how to get her back by himself?"

"He has lots of people on his side now," Beaver pointed out. "He's not just a loner anymore."

"But how many of those people are actually on his side and how many want just as badly as the Jacksons to get him out of the clan?" Erin asked. "He didn't know where Vic was this morning, I can tell you that. I was there."

"He's had several hours to find out." Beaver continued to chew her gum too close to the mic.

"Do you think he has found out?" Jeremy leaned closer to the phone. "Do you know anything about it?"

"He is not taking me into his confidence, and I don't have any independent information."

Jeremy sighed. He rubbed the center of his forehead. "I've reached out to anyone I can think of on the Jackson side who might be willing to help me, and no one seems to know anything. Some people have gone to the clans for protection, some have run away, but there is another group who... there just doesn't seem to be any explanation for it. The clans don't know where they've gone, and it doesn't make sense that they've just run. People with families. Stable people who don't have any association with the clans, and yet... they're gone. I'm not putting Vic into that category. I know she's being used to leverage Willie somehow. But there's a suggestion of some shadow cartel..."

Beaver grunted. "No such thing."

"What?"

"No. Just people making up boogeymen. If there was an underground or shadow cartel, we would know about it. It isn't that easy to keep a whole organized crime cartel a secret."

"You don't think so? Or you know?"

"Look, Jer," Beaver chewed her gum in their ears. "You just can't keep something like that a secret. If there was an organization that was big enough to be a challenge to the Jackson and Dyson clans, they wouldn't be able to cover their tracks."

"So it's all just, what... a red herring?" Erin asked. "There is no third gang?"

"That's right," Beaver agreed. "Any action attributed to a shadow cartel... is not. It's a false trail."

Erin thought about that. She had believed that there was another gang trying to insert themselves into the fray, taking advantage of the increased fighting between the clans and within the Dyson clan. She wasn't sure they could believe Beaver's declaration that there wasn't.

She suspected Beaver would have no trouble lying to them about something she didn't want them to inquire into too closely. She would do whatever it took to get the results she wanted.

Beaver had shown Erin in the past that she would cross lines if she felt it was necessary to get what she wanted. And it was obvious that she didn't care what other people thought of her and was prepared to break with social norms, and possibly the law, however she liked.

Jeremy and Erin looked at each other, Jeremy's gaze asking whether there was anything else Erin wanted to ask Beaver while they had her on the line. Erin shook her head. Talking to Beaver hadn't exactly been enlightening, but it had made a few things clear.

"Are you going to be around, Ro?" Jeremy asked, dropping his voice to a more intimate tone. "If you're in the area, you know you can stop by. Stay over. Whatever you want."

Erin shifted uncomfortably. She wasn't a prude, but she didn't want to infringe on their private conversation. She stood up and motioned to Jeremy. "Just going to use your restroom..." she mouthed, and headed toward it. She could give the two of them a couple of minutes of privacy to finish their discussion.

Jeremy grinned at her and picked up the phone, toggling the speakerphone off.

CHAPTER 35

*I*t was almost physically painful for Erin to go home, have supper, and spend the evening with Terry and the animals, knowing that Vic was not there and that they were not any closer to finding out where she was.

Was Vic okay? Was she being held somewhere against her will but being cared for, fed, and given the necessities of life, even though she was being used as a tool against Willie?

Or had she been mistreated or killed by someone who resented Willie and wanted him to suffer for some perceived slight? For being the direct descendant of Hannah Dyson and displacing anyone else out of the position. Maybe it was Mona, the matriarch of the clan before Willie admitted his identity and agreed to take his rightful place at the head of the clan. Maybe one of her children or followers who had believed that they would step in to take her place. Maybe Nelson or one of his friends or followers, who thought that Dwight Dyson was the leader of the clan rather than just the figurehead, and had imagined himself to be the next in line.

Or maybe it was someone with a personal grudge against Willie. Or one of the Jackson clan, hoping to bring the whole organization toppling down by getting control over its leader.

Why had Erin ever encouraged Vic in her interest in and relationship with Willie? When they had all found out that he had a clan background, why hadn't Vic just stayed away from him?

Erin shifted her position, her movements restricted by Terry and the animals cuddled up to her from every side. Terry released his arm around her shoulder to allow her to find a new, more comfortable position. Orange Blossom glared at Erin, licked his back fur, and shook his head briskly. The sound of his ears flapping did not bring the smile to Erin's face it usually did.

"Are you okay?" Terry asked.

Erin sat forward on the couch and tried to get to her feet. K9 groaned and didn't get up, but Nilla jumped to his feet, his whole body wagging and wriggling with enthusiasm.

"Shh," Erin told him. "It's quiet time, not playtime."

"I don't think that one understands anything but playtime and feeding time," Terry observed.

"He's such a whirlwind. I think it's time to put him down for the night. I'll take him outside. Do you need to go outside?" Erin asked K9. He looked up at her but didn't appear to need a trip to the backyard. He put his head back down and sighed, sounding very tired at the end of his arduous day.

"Do you think I should bring the crate over here or put him to sleep in the apartment?" Erin asked Terry.

"I don't want you trying to get that huge crate down the stairs. Just put him to bed over there. He'll be fine."

"You don't think he'll cry, being alone?"

"Maybe for a while. But Vic and Willie have a variable schedule. Sometimes they're out for the nightlife. They must put him to bed by himself those nights."

Erin felt a bit better about that. Terry was right; trying to wrestle the bulky crate down the stairs would not be an easy job. It would take at least two people. Maybe a small crane.

"Okay. I'll just be a few minutes while I take care of him; then, I think I'm going to bed." She looked at the TV. "I don't even know what we're watching. That tells you how well I've been able to concentrate tonight."

"You're tired," Terry agreed, rather than saying she had every reason to be distracted. They avoided the topic of Vic's disappearance during the evening, both of them thinking their own long thoughts, knowing that they were no closer to bringing her home.

Erin escorted Nilla out to the yard and waited while he did his business, then called for him to go home when he headed back toward her back door. "Come on, Nilla. Time to go home. Time for sleep."

He raced around the yard, trying to entice her to chase after him, but Erin coaxed him to go back to the loft apartment.

"Come on, Nilla. Be a good boy. Time for bed."

"Do you want some help?"

Erin startled at the voice out of the darkness and turned to see who it was. She had hoped it would be Willie, but knew by the time she focused on the figure in the darkness that it wasn't him. It was Stayner, taller and slimmer than Willie. Younger. On the other side of the law.

"You startled me!"

She had known that he would be there. Terry had told her that he had asked Officer Stayner to patrol the street, backyard, and woods behind the house to ensure no one was lurking around. They didn't want any more trouble.

It felt to Erin like locking the barn after the horse was gone. What was there to protect? Vic was already gone. It was silly to reject Stayner's presence because Vic was no longer there, and yet to fear for her own life, worried that even with Terry and Stayner close at hand, something catastrophic could happen. Look at what had happened to Mary Lou, disappearing even with three men in the house.

Maybe it would be good if Erin got kidnapped. Maybe they would take her to where Vic was being held, and they could comfort and help each other. Maybe Erin could convince the kidnapper to let them go or she and Vic could work together to devise an escape.

Of course that would never happen. It was pure fantasy, and Erin knew it.

Nilla ran toward Stayner, yapping and growling at him. Erin bent down to grab him.

"Sorry," she apologized, "he doesn't like men. Except for Willie."

"Blasted dog. Fat lot of good he did in protecting Miss Webster."

"Well, he's little, but he does his best." Erin managed to grab Nilla and tucked him under her arm. "Come on, you fierce little devil. I know. You'd tear him to bits if you could."

Stayner laughed at the little dog's menacing growls. "I can take him up to the apartment and put him in the crate if you like. You can go back to Terry and your critters and get to bed."

"It's okay. I'll take him up. I don't think he'll settle for you; it would be a fight every step of the way. He doesn't like men," she repeated.

"I could handle him."

"Yeah, but I don't just want him handled. I want him to be calm for the night and not make noise barking and howling, or the neighbors will complain."

"Fine," Stayner walked away from her, heading toward the woods. "Whatever you like."

Erin watched after him for a minute, then mounted the stairs and took Nilla up to the apartment. She unlocked the door and got him settled in, giving him a treat for being a good boy. She left on a lamp in the bedroom and turned the TV on quietly, hoping it would help Nilla not to feel alone.

She looked around the apartment once, hoping to find some clue that would leap out at her and tell her where to find Vic or who had taken her. Vic's nightgown still lay on the floor where it had been dropped. Whoever had taken her had not wanted her to be obviously out of place. He had not marched her through the woods or shoved her into his car in her nightgown.

She turned off the rest of the lights, said goodnight to Nilla, and returned to the house.

"All tucked in?" Terry asked.

Erin nodded. "Yeah." She looked at the TV. "Are you going to stay up and watch the rest of this?"

He studied her. "No. I'll come to bed with you."

"Good. I don't want to be alone."

"It's been a hard week. Hopefully... next week will be better."

"You're going to find them, aren't you? All of the missing people? Everyone who has been kidnapped, who didn't run away or defect to the other clan?"

"Yes," Terry said firmly, though Erin doubted he really felt that certain about it. "We're going to find them. We're going to bring them home."

Erin tried to keep the tears from leaking from her eyes. "We are," she agreed, even though she would have nothing to do with it. "We are going to bring them home."

Terry stood up from the couch. He put his arm around her shoulders and squeezed. Just a brief little comfort, then he let her go. Maybe he sensed that if he pulled her into him and wrapped both arms around her, holding her close and tight, she would lose it. She wanted to retain some semblance of control.

"I'll see you in there," Terry said lightly, and headed for the bedroom.

Erin just needed to brush her teeth, wash her face, and use the bathroom before sliding into bed for the night. Tomorrow was Sunday, and Auntie Clem's Bakery only opened for the ladies tea, which only lasted an hour. Two hours of work, including the brief setup and cleanup. Well-worn checklists ensured that everything was already prepared and would go smoothly.

"Oh, I should go to Charley's tomorrow," Erin told Terry as she snuggled against him. "Someone has to check on Iggy and make sure he has food and water."

"I forgot about her iguana."

"Chameleon," Erin corrected.

"Iggy the iguana."

"Nope. Iggy the chameleon."

He pulled her in close. "Your sister is weird."

Erin chuckled. "Yeah, I'm afraid I agree with you on that one."

She closed her eyes and quivered, trying to keep her body under control, trying not to let herself succumb to emotion.

"It's going to be okay," Terry told her.

"I feel like I'm caught in the middle of some horror movie. People keep disappearing. My friends, my sister, the people I care about." She leaned into him. "You'd better not disappear on me."

"I won't. We are going to get everything sorted out. The clan unrest will not last forever. Everything will settle down to normal again. It's just a matter of time."

"But we don't know how much time anyone has. We don't know how long they will hold on to anyone. It is more dangerous the longer they wait, and they know it. They don't want to be discovered, so they won't let it go on forever. A few days... they're going to want to end it. To make sure that they are not discovered."

"We will figure it out before then," Terry promised. "The problem is that there is so much confusion with the clan unrest and so many people... in flux. It's a bit chaotic. But we will find them and sort it out. We will get everyone home safely."

Erin closed her eyes and mentally repeated his words like a mantra, trying to envision it, trying to convince her brain that it was true.

We will get everyone home safely.

We will get everyone home safely.

CHAPTER 36

*E*rin tried to sleep in, but as usual, she wasn't able to sleep much past her normal wake-up time, and when she forced herself to stay in bed and go back to sleep, she started having nightmares.

The real world was enough of a nightmare without adding more into it. She slid out of bed, taking care not to disturb Terry, who, after the week he had been through and the hours he had worked, needed all the sleep he could get.

The animals greeted her as she got up, Orange Blossom immediately launching into a loud complaint about how long it had been since Erin had put anything into his food dish. As far as he was concerned, a cat needed to be fed a dozen times a day, and she never lived up to his expectations. It was a sad life for a cat.

"Shh, shh. You're just fine," Erin murmured to him. "Breakfast will be in your dish before you know it. You'll be such a happy kitty…"

Marshmallow was already waiting in the kitchen. K9 had followed Erin from his crate in the bedroom. She had to remember to take care of Nilla as well. She would see to him when she let K9 out and let the two of them play together.

And then there was Iggy. She didn't really want to have to look at the bulb-eyed critter in the reptarium in Charley's house or the jumpy creepy crawly crickets that were his repast. She couldn't believe that Charley kept those things in her house. Even in the fridge. It was disgusting. Who wanted to open a container in the refrigerator and find it full of skittery brown vermin? Ugh.

But she would have to force herself to anyway. Charley would never forgive Erin if she let something happen to Iggy.

That was a lot of animals. At least she didn't have to take care of Adele's companions too. But her critters were expected to take care of themselves most of the time and only came to Adele for occasional companionship.

What kind of animal would Mary Lou have, if she wanted a pet? A parrot? What animal would be the least messy and creepy? Maybe a pet rock. Erin smiled at the thought, even though she was still shattered about the missing women.

Erin didn't know how she got through the ladies tea with so many faces missing. Those who remained had done their best to keep up a pleasant front. It was forced, Erin knew, but she appreciated their trying to keep things normal. She had wondered if she should cancel the ladies tea until the trouble with the clans was over. But the church ladies who remained still wanted to act as if everything was fine and perfectly normal, so Erin would continue with the ladies tea for as long as she could stand it.

Bella and Cheyenne promised to get everything cleaned up and sent Erin on her way. "Go take care of that slimy lizard, and I'll make sure everything is ready for tomorrow," Bella promised.

"Iggy isn't slimy," Erin told her, though she wasn't sure why. It wasn't like the critter needed defending. "He's dry. I wouldn't ever touch him, but he isn't mucusy."

Bella grimaced. "Ugh. Gross. I don't know what people see in them."

"Me either," Erin admitted. "But I can't let him die while Charley is away."

"You're a better woman than me. If I were you, I would send Terry over to take care of it."

Erin hadn't even considered the option. Terry and Charley didn't exactly get along, and Charley wasn't Terry's sister. She was Erin's. Erin had a responsibility to take care of things for Charley. For as long as she could.

She hoped it wouldn't be a long time. For Iggy's sake as well as Charley's. And Erin's.

She left the bakery and drove over to Charley's house.

She didn't knock and call out this time. She didn't want to do anything to attract the attention of the neighbors or anyone else watching her or the house. She took out her keychain and quickly let herself into the house.

The house had a musty, stale smell. It had been shut up for too long without anyone taking care of it. She remembered the milk that she had left in the fridge the first time she had been around looking for Charley. She would have to dump it out now. Hopefully, it wouldn't be so sour that it would make her gag. With her keen sense of smell, Erin could tell the instant milk started to turn, but other people waited until it was so rancid she could smell it a block away.

Just the thought made her gag, and she couldn't afford to be sick before she even opened the fridge. Maybe she would have to send Terry back over to deal with the milk later.

Erin decided to see to Iggy before worrying about the fridge. He would distract her from her thoughts, and even if he was creepy, the smell of his reptarium was less offensive than a cat litter box or other pet smells. Maybe that was why Charley liked him.

She quickly looked through the house to see whether anything had been touched since she had last walked through the house with Vic.

Erin took a quick look into the bedroom. It was funny how much the mussed-up blankets made it look like Charley was lying in the bed.

It even smelled like Charley. The stale, alcohol-laden sweat that clung to her skin when she had been out on a bender.

Erin stopped in the doorway and stared at the mound of blankets. Were they really rising and falling, or was it just her active imagination? She longed so much for everyone to come back that she was seeing what she wanted to.

"Charley?"

There was a moan. A real, audible moan. Erin shoved the bedroom door open so hard it banged against the bedroom wall.

"Charley!"

She rushed to the bed and jerked back the blankets. Charley lay tangled in the messy blankets, her face pale and wan. She barely stirred as Erin shook her shoulder, trying to rouse her.

"Wake up. Charley. Charley!"

She tried to tamp down the rising tide of panic. There was nothing to be afraid of. Charley was right there in front of her, not lost, not kidnapped, not killed and buried in a shallow grave somewhere or weighted down in one of the many ponds or rivers nearby with a pair of concrete boots.

She backed off, trying to catch her breath and look at the situation logically and calmly.

Charley had returned home. So she must have been gone voluntarily. She had just been away on a trip. A bender, judging by the smell and how soundly she was sleeping. She had been worried or upset about how things were going with the clans. Maybe she had been threatened. Maybe she was trying to decide whether to go to one side or the other for protection.

But neither wanted to claim Charley. She had started out with the Dysons, but when everyone had found out her biological parents were part of the Jackson clan, they had ejected her and didn't want to have anything else to do with her. And, of course, the Jacksons hadn't wanted a Dyson soldier in their midst. Two years later, nothing had changed.

Maybe Charley had just been hiding out on her own. Traveling far from the clans or staying with a friend in another city. She hadn't told Erin because… she hadn't wanted a lecture. Or because, as Terry had said, she didn't want Erin to know anything if someone came looking for her.

"Charley." Erin sat on the side of the bed and pushed tendrils of Charley's hair out of her face.

Charley was back. She was safe and sound.

Erin watched Charley's face and listened to her breathing. Her breath came in long and slow. *Very* slow, with long pauses between each breath. Alcohol was a depressant. Charley had apparently had enough that it had depressed her breathing. That was dangerous. People could die from too much alcohol.

Erin hesitated, then pulled out her phone and called Terry. The phone only rang a couple of times before the call was picked up.

"Erin. Finishing up at Auntie Clem's?"

"No, I left early. Came over to Charley's to take care of Iggy."

"You should have let me know; I could have helped you. Are you okay?"

"Charley is back."

"What?" Terry's tone told her that he was as shocked as she was. "She's back? That's great, Erin. Did she tell you where she's been? That girl has some explaining to do."

"She's... asleep. Unconscious. I can't wake her up. She's had a lot to drink."

"Well, she'll sleep it off, then. And she'll have a good reminder of why it is best not to drink that much!"

"I'm afraid she's had too much to just sleep it off. What if... she could have alcohol poisoning."

"Well, that is possible," Terry admitted. "How is her breathing and pulse?"

"Really slow. Long breaks in between breaths. She's pale. I'm worried."

"Okay, let's get an ambulance over there, then. I'll come over, too."

"Okay," Erin agreed. "That would be really good. I know some first aid, but... I'd rather have a medical expert or at least a first responder keep an eye on her and ensure she will be okay."

"I'll get the dispatcher to send someone over. I'll see you in a few minutes."

CHAPTER 37

*E*rin sat on the side of the bed, listening to Charley breathe. She really was afraid that it might stop before the ambulance could get there. If there weren't any ambulances in Bald Eagle Falls, they would have to wait for one to arrive from the city, and that could take an hour or more.

A few minutes later, she heard the door open and Terry's call. "Erin?"

"In here."

He followed her voice and entered the bedroom.

"I can't believe she's back," he said, reaching out to take Charley's pulse. He watched her chest and listened to her breathing. "You're right; it is very slow. She must have had a heck of a wild night."

Erin looked around. "By herself? It doesn't look like there has been anyone here since I was by last. She drank that much alone?"

"We've seen her do it before."

"When she lost Bobby. But that was different. And she didn't pass out. She was just… overwhelmed and grieving." Erin looked around the room. "There aren't even any open containers in here."

There was no sign of alcohol. Just the smell that was seeping out of Charley's pores. There were no bottles, no cans, no glasses.

Not even a flask. Charley was fully dressed under the blankets, so it didn't look like she had planned to drink herself to sleep.

"You're right," Terry agreed. "You mind watching her for a minute while I look around?"

"Uh..." Erin knew that Charley would not want a cop wandering around her house, even if he had the best of intentions. "Maybe you'd better not. You don't have permission or a warrant."

"Don't need a warrant to see what is in plain sight. I am here lawfully, under exigent circumstances, to check on her welfare."

Erin didn't say anything else. He was determined to have a look around, so look around he would.

"Come on, Charley," she coaxed. "Can't you wake up? Come on, I need to talk to you. You need to tell me what's going on, what you know."

Maybe Charley hadn't been kidnapped, but she clearly knew some of what was going on in the clans, or she would not have run away. She must have believed she was in danger, or she wouldn't have disappeared without even letting Erin know where she was going.

Charley stirred slightly and made a faint noise but remained unresponsive.

"Charley," Erin pressed harder. "Wakey wakey, eggs and bakey." That was just the kind of thing that would drive Charley crazy. Erin being motherly to her. She had a mother, the one who had raised her. She'd been in a rebellious phase, running with Bobby Dyson— who was definitely the wrong crowd—when Erin had started looking for her. When Charley had discovered that her biological parents were not who she had thought they were, she had not been very happy about it.

It had not been the long-lost sister reunion that Erin had fantasized about. Her half-sister had been a very different person from what Erin had hoped.

But Erin liked Charley now. She had smoothed away some of her rough edges, and they had found some compatibility in the ownership of the bakery, love of animals, and a few other areas that they could agree upon. Charley and Erin would never be alike in personality, and Erin didn't know if Charley would lose her hard-partying bent with maturity, but there was enough between them now that she was sure of a long-lasting relationship.

"Rise 'n shine, Charley. Come on."

Charley turned on her side, coughing and gagging, and Erin was afraid she was going to throw up, but in the end, she settled again, her breathing still very slow. Louder, now, like she was pretending to be Darth Vader to make Erin laugh. Erin smoothed back her hair, studying her face, looking for any sign that Charley was playing possum.

"Charley, are you okay? Come on, don't you think it's time to wake up now? You don't want to sleep the day away. It's already afternoon, and you're usually up by now."

There was no response from Charley.

A few minutes later, Terry returned to the bedroom. He stood near the doorway, watching them. "You're right. I don't see any open liquor around. I didn't go opening the cupboards to check the garbage or recycling bins," he sighed that he had not been able to do so, "but there isn't anything obvious, and it isn't like Charley is meticulous about cleaning up after herself."

"No," Erin murmured. She frowned at Terry. "So she was out somewhere drinking, and came back like this? How did she even get home?"

"Somebody must have dropped her off. I don't imagine she was in any condition to drive any time in the last eight hours. Somebody drove her, walked her in, dumped her in bed." His eyes were on Charley. "She hasn't undressed or changed for bed. They just left her there."

Erin shook her head. "Who? She must have drinking buddies that she goes out with, I guess. I don't run with the same crowd. But I've never seen her this bad, so it's unusual. I know you arrested her once for being drunk in public. But she wasn't like this, was she?"

"No. Nothing like this, and she and her companions had been drinking quite a bit for quite a while. Her tolerance is very high.

Somebody would have had to pour the booze down her throat to get her this blotto."

Was that what had happened? Somebody had wanted to make sure that Charley was really drunk? Or had they been trying to get information from her? To find out what she knew? Had the person or people she had been running from caught up with her and plied her with liquor to try to find out her secrets?

Charley gagged and coughed again. Terry frowned, looking at her. He listened to her breathing. "She wasn't breathing like that before."

"No. She just started. I thought she was joking around, to begin with, but I'm worried. Maybe she's got something stuck in her throat."

"Let me have a look at her. Why don't you feed the iguana so that is done by the time the ambulance arrives and we don't have to wait. We can follow her to the hospital."

Erin stood up. "Chameleon."

"Whatever."

They brushed past each other, Erin leaving and Terry getting closer to Charley to examine her. Erin tried to blank her mind as she went to the fridge and looked for a bowl of crickets. It wasn't hard to find the pet store container with the vented lid. Erin dumped the milk down the drain as well. It was definitely going bad, several days past its peak.

She looked through the cupboards for the garbage and recycling bins and folded the milk carton to go in with the beverage containers. There were a few other milk cartons and juice boxes or bottles. No booze that Erin could see. She opened the garbage briefly, but knew the bottles wouldn't be there. Not unless someone else had put them there. Why would Charley put some recyclable bottles into the bin and others into the garbage? There were no bottles in the garbage either.

Charley had not come home after several days on the run and decided to drink herself into oblivion. She had been drinking with someone else, and they had brought her home, as Terry had said. If she had been drinking alone at a bar, they would have called the police. Charley had to have been with a companion who had promised to look after her. Or she had not been in a bar.

Erin looked at the pet store container and gave it a little shake. The crickets did not move. She had expected them to be jumping around, but they were not. Were they dead because they had been stored too long or just too cold to move? Insects were cold-blooded. They just slowed down and slept when they were cold.

She looked in the reptarium for Iggy and spotted him on a branch after a few minutes looking for him. Right in front of her eyes, and she had not been able to differentiate him from the tree he lay on. Once she was sure he wasn't waiting by the door to dart out when she opened it, she unhooked the latch and reached in with the open bowl of crickets. She shook them out onto the floor and waited for them to start moving, but they didn't. Hopefully, they would be more active once they warmed up and Iggy would eat them. She didn't think he would eat them if they were dead. She didn't know very much about chameleons, but had absorbed some of what Charley had told her.

A siren was getting closer to the house. Erin carefully closed and latched the reptarium access door and pulled on it to make sure it was fast. Charley would kill her if she let Iggy escape.

Then she went to the door to wait for the paramedics.

"What seems to be the problem?" A tall paramedic with sandy hair mounted the steps.

"My sister… it looks like she had too much to drink. She won't wake up, and we're worried about her breathing."

"Ah. I'm sure she's probably okay, but it is best to get these things checked out."

Erin rolled her eyes at this. She hated being patronized by medical professionals. Or anyone else, for that matter, but medical professionals were one of the worst groups for "there-thereing" and acting as if she couldn't possibly have enough brain cells to under-stand anything medical. Never mind that she had been a caregiver. Even the doctors that had dealt with the people she cared for tended to disbelieve anything she told them, sure that she didn't know what she was talking about.

CHAPTER 38

*E*rin pointed the paramedics toward the bedroom, standing back so that they could get in to see her. She saw Terry leaning close to Charley, his attitude one of concern. She couldn't make out what he said to the paramedics, but she understood his serious tone.

Maybe now the paramedics would believe that Charley's condition was serious.

They examined her, taking her pulse, looking at her eyes, talking to her loudly to wake her up, and listening to her breathing with their stethoscopes. They eventually agreed that there was reason for concern, and the woman returned to the ambulance to retrieve the gurney to transport her. Erin waited as they lifted Charley onto the gurney, then retreated to the living room to give them plenty of room to maneuver and watched them take her out. Terry came to her side.

"Are you okay?"

"Worried, that's all. I know they didn't think it was anything to worry about to start with, but she's not in very good shape, is she? People can die from being that drunk."

"They'll make sure she's okay now. I think it's good to have her at the hospital for monitoring until she is sober. Especially with the change in her breathing. She might have aspirated fluids. That could be very dangerous. You were right to get help. A lot of people might think it was safe to just let her sleep it off, but I don't think it is. I think she needs medical care." He nodded to the paramedics loading Charley into the ambulance. "And they are in agreement. We're all on the same page with this."

Erin nodded. There was a lump in her throat. She had been so relieved to find Charley there, but now she was worried again. Worried that they might not have reached her in time and that whoever had gotten her drunk might succeed in killing her.

"Come in my car?" Terry suggested. "I can use the light and keep up with the ambulance."

Erin glanced at the bug and decided it would be fine parked by the curb until they returned to Bald Eagle Falls. Terry could bring her over to pick it up when they were back.

"Okay," she agreed. They locked up Charley's house and got into the car. "She'll be okay, though, right?"

Terry nodded. "I'm sure she will be."

"Okay."

She was tense when they started on their way, but pretty soon, the adrenaline was wearing off, and Erin was bored with the drive, wishing that they were there already. She pulled out her phone and started to type a text message to Vic before remembering that Vic was missing. Who else should she notify? She was at a loss. Eventually, she put her phone back in her pocket, shaking her head.

"Sorry," Terry said, glancing over at her.

"Maybe Vic will come back on her own," Erin said hopefully, her voice breaking, "maybe the same thing will happen, and she'll just be back in her loft where she's supposed to be."

Terry nodded and didn't say how much he doubted that was a possibility.

～

Erin was quiet on the way to the hospital. She hoped that Charley coming home was the first sign that everything was going to get back to normal. She had been the first of Erin's friends to disappear, and now she was the first to come back. Was it a good omen? Or was it a bad one because she still wasn't out of the woods? Bad things could still happen.

"She'll be okay," Terry assured her. "I'm sure she'll be fine. They'll get an IV going to rehydrate her. Intubate her for breathing support. And then it will just be a matter of time before she's awake with the biggest hangover she's ever had in her life."

Erin nodded. "Yeah. She'll be okay. It will all work out."

And maybe tomorrow, Mary Lou will be back. She wouldn't be drunk. She would have to have a more believable reason for having been away. Maybe… she had hit her head on the wall when bending over to tie her shoes—it could happen, Erin could testify to that—Mary Lou could say she had knocked herself out, given herself amnesia so that she didn't know who she was or where she was going until she had woken up a few days later and it had all come back to her. Willie had once been bashed on the head, and the concussion had prevented him from being able to tell anyone who he was and what had happened to him.

And then Vic… Erin tried to think of a third believable situation. Vic had a lot of friends outside of Bald Eagle Falls. Maybe one of the folks she had met on the Alaskan cruise, or someone near Moose River from her old life, or a cousin that she had never thought to mention before had shown up and insisted that Vic go out with them for a party. Vic had lost track of time… maybe come down with a virus that had kept her feverish and drowsy for a couple of days, and then she would return home when she felt better.

She knew neither of these fantasies was going to come true. Still, Charley's return gave her one ray of hope that it was at least possible that one of the others would return as well.

CHAPTER 39

Once they reached the hospital, Erin did her best to provide admitting with the personal information they needed about Charley, including her name, birthdate, and address. She wasn't very helpful with any of the medical history stuff. She didn't know her own family medical history or any of the childhood diseases that Charley had contracted. They had never really talked about medical stuff, and maybe they should. They might share several medical conditions or predispositions.

"I'm sorry I don't know more," she told the nurse taking the information down. She shook her head, her cheeks warm. "I haven't actually known her for very long. I should know more of this stuff."

"Don't worry about it," the nurse told her with a sunny smile. "Thank you for what you have been able to provide. It's better than admitting her as a Jane Doe!"

Erin shrugged, still embarrassed. "Can you tell me how she is?"

"The team is evaluating her now. I can assure you that we will do everything necessary for her. It didn't sound like she was in serious condition. Just in need of supervision until she starts feeling better. But that's not official. We'll wait to see what the team has to say."

It was a few hours before Charley was settled in a room, and Erin and Terry were escorted to her side.

Late afternoon sun streamed in the window, and Charley was actually awake. Not the most clear-headed. She still spoke with a slur and her eyes occasionally closed and then flew open in surprise. She did not have a tube down her throat, for which Erin was grateful.

"Charley! You scared the heck out of me!" Erin told her, finally able to unleash her feelings and let Charley know how foolish she had been. "First, you disappear, don't show up for your shift, don't even call me to say that you're not going to be at the bakery and have left town. I was really worried about you. People have been kidnapped, and I thought... I didn't know what to think. Whether to believe that you had been taken too! Or whether you had just taken off or had someone chasing you..."

Erin shook her head, pausing for breath and to gather her thoughts.

"Why am I here?" Charley asked, blinking.

Erin adjusted the blinds so that the sun was not shining in Charley's eyes. Her wince became less pronounced.

"You had too much to drink. I went to the house today to feed Iggy, and there you were, passed out cold. Your breathing was really bad, and we were afraid..."

Erin swallowed a lump in her throat and couldn't put it into words.

"Who were you drinking with? Who brought you home?" she demanded. "They should know better than to just drop you like that when you were in such bad shape. You could have died. And they just dropped you there and left, didn't care if you were okay or not."

Charley raised her left hand and looked at the IV. She rubbed her forehead, trying to understand what Erin was saying.

"I was drinking?" She frowned, shaking her head. "I'm drunk? Why was I drinking?"

"I guess you don't need a reason," Erin said, which was probably unfair. "You were worried about the clans, maybe? Or maybe your friend was trying to find out information about the clans by getting you to drink?" She shrugged. "Whatever it was... you had way too much."

"I wasn't drinking."

"Oh, no?" Erin challenged. "You were pretty full of alcohol for someone who wasn't drinking. I can still smell it on you. It's coming out your pores."

Charley sniffed her arm and made a face. "I don't understand how I got here," she said.

Erin looked at Terry and rolled her eyes. He looked sympathetic.

"What do you remember?" Erin demanded. "You must remember something from the last four or five days."

Charley shook her head. There were frown lines in the middle of her forehead. "It's all a blank."

"What's the last thing you remember?"

"I remember... I was going to go to the bakery."

Trust Charley to use that as her reference point. *I was on my way to the bakery, I swear.*

"Okay," Terry said in a perfectly reasonable voice. "And what do you remember about going to the bakery?"

"I... nothing. I just... I woke up here. I thought... I must have been sick or something."

"You must remember something that has happened in the last four days. You were out with someone, drinking. Who came to see you and convinced you to go with them? Or did you just decide on your own that things were getting too risky with all of the clan activity, and you would take a little impromptu vacation? Where did you go? It must have been out of town, because someone would have seen you if you had stayed in Bald Eagle Falls."

Charley stared at Erin with wide eyes. "Erin... I don't remember. I swear it. It's all so foggy, and I want to go back to sleep..."

Erin sighed. Hopefully, Charley would be more clear the next time she awoke. If she couldn't really remember right now because of the amount of alcohol she had consumed, it would eventually come back to her. Wouldn't it?

Alcoholic blackouts didn't always work that way. She would just have to wait patiently and hope that Charley remembered.

Or maybe she shouldn't push at all. After all, it wasn't her responsibility to find out what had happened with Charley. There was no law against going out and drinking, or against going home absolutely blotto. Charley hadn't done anything against the law, and it wasn't Erin's right to know what was going on with her.

Maybe she should just let it go.

Erin shook her head, finding it difficult. She wanted answers. But maybe there weren't any. Maybe she would never find out exactly what had driven Charley away, or why she had come back in the condition she had.

"You don't even know who drove you home?" she asked.

Charley shook her head and winced, face very pale. "Sorry, Erin," she mumbled. "I just don't know. I feel mighty rough. My head is killing me. My throat hurts. My head..." she pressed her hand against it, "My head's pounding like a marching band." She swore. "Do you think they could give me a handful of Tylenol?"

"I'll ask them about a painkiller," Terry offered, and left to talk to the nurses. Erin suspected that he had gone out to give her a chance to talk to Charley alone, in case Charley was holding back because she didn't want to speak in front of him. Erin waited until he was out of the room for a few seconds before trying again.

"Did something happen that you don't want the police or Terry to know about?" she suggested.

Charley leaned back against the pillow, eyes closed. "No, Erin. I don't know what happened or how long I've been away. It's all just one big fog. I can't believe it's actually Sunday. That doesn't make any sense, I'm missing like... four days. How could I have been gone for so long, and no one knows what happened? How could I not remember?"

"I don't know. I guess you had a lot to drink."

"The doctor said that he would run a drug panel," Charley said, "In case someone roofied me."

"Do you think they did?" Erin felt like a hand was squeezing her gut. "Oh, I'm sorry, Charley, here I am getting after you, and you're trying to figure out whether... someone did something to you."

"I don't know," Charley said. "I don't feel like... you know. But I mean... there are some weirdos out there who have fetishes. But I'm not *hurt* or anything. Just... kind of freaked out. I can't believe I was gone and can't remember anything that happened."

CHAPTER 40

When Erin woke up the next day, she had difficulty remembering what had happened in the last twenty-four hours. Things had been so disrupted over the past few days, and having Charley back had changed everything... or maybe it had changed nothing.

When her alarm sounded, she got up and got ready for work in a fog. She had set up all the bakery shifts and done some of her planning, though she wasn't on top of things like she should be. She couldn't remember who was on the morning shift with her. She was so used to it being Vic that she kept forgetting, and then remembering, about Vic being missing.

Terry insisted on driving her to Auntie Clem's. "I'm not keen on you walking in the dark," he told her.

As if anything ever happened that early in the morning.

"I'll pick up the bug and drop it off in the bakery parking lot during the day, so it will be there waiting for you when you're ready to go home. You're not working the full day, are you? Have you got someone to cover the closing shift for you?"

"I honestly don't remember."

"You haven't had near enough sleep. I don't think you should

223

work straight through. You need to take a break for your own health."

"Yeah. I'll make sure I get someone to cover the afternoon. I probably set up one of the students. I just don't remember."

Terry nodded understandingly. "It will be okay, I'm sure. Just be sure to take care of yourself."

"You think Charley will be back today?"

"I think she'll need to be picked up. But yes, I imagine she will be released today. Once all of the alcohol has cleared her system and they make sure she doesn't have any fluid on her lungs, she'll be fine."

He dropped her off at the back door and gave her a kiss good-bye. He stayed there until Erin had opened the door, turned on the lights, and disarmed the burglar alarm. Everything was fine, so she waved at him and shut the door.

Other days, there had been surprises at the bakery. She was glad this was not one of them. She didn't think she could have faced a burglary on top of everything else.

No one else was there yet. Erin started in on her morning checklists. She knew them all off by heart. It was a relief to just follow the checklist and do all the things she knew she needed to do. It was her zen place, like a meditation.

After a while, there was a knock at the back door, and Erin went over to it to let her employee in. She took a routine glance through the peephole before opening the door. Always best, especially when she was there by herself, to make sure she knew who she was opening the door to.

But it wasn't one of her employees or a deliveryman. It was Willie. Erin quickly opened the door and allowed him in. He wouldn't want to stand around outside where people could see him.

"Willie!" Erin's heart was pounding, and she wanted to ask him if he had found Vic, but she was afraid to. "Is everything okay?"

"Sure. Everything is fine," he agreed, voice low and calm. "I wanted to make sure Charley had gotten home safely since I hadn't heard anything."

Erin stared at him. "To make sure that Charley got home

safely? Yes... she did. She was... she's in the hospital, but she should be back today."

"In the hospital," he frowned. "What is she in the hospital for?"

"Alcohol poisoning. Her blood alcohol levels were off the scale. She can't remember anything from the time she was gone. How did you know she was coming back?"

Willie scratched a whiskery cheek, thinking about it. "I... heard rumors. Applied pressure in certain areas... for her to be returned."

Erin's jaw dropped. "You mean... that she really was kidnapped? She wasn't just out partying with her friends?"

He nodded, looking amused. "I thought it was strange that I didn't hear anything back. But I guess if she couldn't remember what happened to her, that would explain why you weren't calling me, demanding answers."

"Consider them demanded. What happened to her? They thought maybe she was given a date rape drug too. They cause amnesia."

Willie nodded. "Neat trick. Well, I'm sorry that she had to go through that. But maybe it's better if she doesn't remember anything anyway."

"What do you know?"

"Not a lot. Just heard she was being... held. Questioned about her knowledge of certain things in the clan. It's not that long since she was part of the clan, serving and dating Bobby Dyson. She could still have information that might be helpful to those who... want to dismantle the organization."

"Dismantling sounds like the police. Do you mean that the police took her and were asking her about how to... disrupt the organization?" She thought about Beaver. She could see Beaver doing something like that.

"No. Not the police. Others would like to be able to take control, and to do that, a certain amount of disruption is necessary."

"Someone who didn't want you to lead the clan."

Willie nodded.

"But you weren't there when Charley was. How could she tell anyone anything that would affect you?"

"It is complicated… but the bottom line is… Charley didn't know anything. She couldn't tell them anything about the actual power structure of the Dysons, because she had only been aware of the figurehead. That doesn't get anyone anywhere."

"And you heard that… *someone* had Charley?"

"Yes. So I asked nicely for her to be returned unharmed."

Erin could just imagine how *nice* Willie had been about it. He was, generally speaking, a pretty calm and friendly guy. But she doubted that demeanor extended to traitors within the clan who kidnapped people to try to take down the power structure of the organization.

"Okay… wow. I didn't see that. I just… went to Charley's house to feed Iggy, and found her at home. I thought she'd gotten there by herself. But then we figured out how drunk she was, and thought that she must have been dropped off by whoever she was out drinking with. I never thought… that she actually *had* been kidnapped and returned."

Willie nodded. "Well… as long as she is unharmed and is released from the hospital today, then that will be the end of it. But if she was injured or permanently harmed… I want to hear about it."

Erin nodded slowly. "Okay. Of course. I'll tell you… but I'm sure she's fine. She was talking to us yesterday."

"Okay. I'd better be on the move."

"Do you want a muffin?"

He smiled. "Of course I do. But you don't have anything made yet, do you?"

Erin reached for a timer just as it started to ring and pulled the first batch of muffins out of the oven. "Let it cool for a few minutes. You don't want to burn yourself."

She put a muffin into a wrapper for him. As she handed it to him, she took a deep breath.

"And… Vic…?"

CHAPTER 41

*W*illie shook his head. "I don't know yet. I'm working on it."

"No one has threatened you with her? Tried to use her to get you to do something... to step aside?"

"I can't tell you anything about it."

Erin swallowed. That didn't sound like a "no."

"Can't you... do what they want? For Vic?"

Willie eyed her. "Ever since I accepted this role, I've been looking for a way to unwind it and step down. You don't think that I would do anything for Vic?"

Erin nodded. "I'm sorry... I know that. I'm just so worried about her. I thought when Charley came back, she would be able to tell us something. She would say that Vic was okay and tell us who they were all being held by, and we would be able to tell the police, and they would be okay." She wiped a tear that leaked out of her eye. "I hoped..."

"That's what we all want," Willie assured her. "We're all looking for a way to help Vic and the others to get home. The trouble is that with so much going on and so many other factions fighting each other, even figuring out which one of them took her is... nearly impossible." He reached over and gently wiped the tear with his thumb. "Nearly," he repeated. "But I am going to find out. I managed to get Charley freed, didn't I? Though she might not be thanking me with the headache she has today."

Erin chuckled. "Maybe it will convince her never to drink again. Poor Charley." She wiped the corners of her eyes, trying to keep them dry. She swallowed, trying to clear the lump in her throat. "You're going to find Vic. And you're going to bring her home," she said in an unemotional, clear voice. Telling her brain how it was going to be. Trying to make her unconscious mind believe it.

"Whatever it takes," Willie promised her. "Just trust me. No matter what you see or hear about me... trust that I will find a way."

"Okay," Erin agreed. "You'd better get on your way, then. Enjoy the muffin."

"That I will. Thanks, Erin."

Then, he was gone as quickly as he had come. The scent of cinnamon and sugar lingered as Erin worked through her checklists. In another half hour, she heard a knock on the door. This one was far more tentative. She put down the batter she was pouring and went to the door. Looking out, she saw that this time, it was her employee. She opened the door.

"Harold." She looked him over. "Are you okay?"

"Yeah. Sorry I'm late. I actually... just got back from my fishing trip this morning. I couldn't come in all stinking like fish and sweat, so I had to go home and clean up first." He looked at her anxiously. "Is that okay? I'm sorry."

Erin nodded. "That was probably the right choice," she agreed. "Even if you don't have much contact with the customers, you don't want to be all smelly and gross back here. Working around hot ovens is sweaty enough work without a weekend's worth of fish and body odor."

She gagged just at the thought. She had never been able to eat fish. It always smelled rotten to her, and even just being in the same room as cooking fish was enough to set her off.

"Next time, maybe just shoot me a text," she suggested, getting herself a glass of water.

"I did. Didn't it go through?"

Erin reached for her phone. "I didn't notice, but I've been pretty busy, and I was talking to…" She saw the alert on the screen. "Yes, it did. Sorry about that. Thanks for being responsible. Why don't you get started on the chocolate chip cookies?" She motioned him to the binder, which was open on the prep list.

Harold nodded and grabbed his apron, looking relieved to be jumping into a routine job.

"Did you get any sleep?" Erin asked him. "You must be worn out. Why didn't you get back until this morning?"

"Uncle Nelson said he wanted to stay for longer." Harold shrugged. "I didn't exactly have any choice. We all went together. I'm just a teenager and he's the boss, so…" He sighed. "I didn't have a say."

"Well, make sure you do jobs that don't require knives, and don't go poking your spatula into any bowls with the mixers running. I don't need an accident because you're too tired. What about school? You have classes after you finish your shift here."

"I did sleep last night. And I've been napping in the afternoons, after fishing. So I'm not sleep-deprived. I might be ready for a nap during History, but…" He yawned at the thought of it and laughed. "At least I can catch up by reading the textbook."

"Okay, well, you take care of yourself and don't take any chances. I don't know what Nelson was thinking, keeping you so long. I guess he just didn't want the weekend of fun to end."

Harold started measuring dry ingredients into a large bowl.

"It was a lot of fun," he admitted. "We all had a good time."

"That's good."

Erin didn't ask Harold whether he had gotten any of his questions answered about the feud and Willie's appointment and what it meant for the rest of the Dyson clan. And whether he had any idea who had taken Vic.

"I know you were hoping Uncle Nelson would be able to tell us something about Miss Victoria," Harold said after a while, bringing it up himself. It wasn't a promising beginning. Erin thought about the hollow look in Willie's eyes. The way he had been asking questions and trying to find the answers to what had happened to his girlfriend. If he had failed, what were the chances that Nelson had succeeded?

But Nelson had been in the organization a lot longer than Willie. He had a lot more connections inside the clan.

"He said it is someone outside of the clan," Harold said. "It has to be someone who isn't a Dyson, and maybe not even a Jackson." Harold concentrated while measuring out ingredients, and then stirred them together. "Even though he's a Dyson, he still has a lot of contacts in the Jackson clan, people he talks to when he has to negotiate business. Even though the clans are enemies, that doesn't mean they never talk to each other. They have to talk sometimes."

"I guess they would," Erin agreed. "Just like during war... the leaders still talk to each other, even though the soldiers don't."

"Yeah!" Harold agreed enthusiastically. "That's what he said."

"And the Jacksons said it wasn't anyone in their organization either?"

"He didn't know. He said it wasn't, but sometimes... people do their own things. Even though they aren't supposed to do anything like that without directions from their bosses, sometimes people go rogue."

"Like Crazy Theresa."

Harold looked at Erin, his eyes wide. "I heard about her and some of the stuff she did. Did you really know her?"

"We crossed paths a few times. I wouldn't say *know* her. Because we never had any real conversations... just her bragging or threatening. But yes. I met her a few times. And she was..." Erin searched for a way to describe Theresa. "Aptly named."

Harold snorted with laughter. "Got it," he said. "So sometimes, people like her go and do their own thing without being told to, and maybe the leaders of the clan don't even know about it until later on. So Uncle Nelson said he would still try to find out who took her, but he wouldn't know... until he knew."

"Right. Well... we'll hope that he can find something out. And

Willie is trying to find out, too. But I don't know if either of them will be able to find anything. If it is someone who isn't associated with either clan…" She shook her head and took a deep breath, forcing herself to continue in a calm voice and not let the tears collect in her eyes again.

"But why would someone outside the clans want to take her?" Harold asked. "People don't just get kidnapped randomly."

"Well… sometimes they do, but I don't think this was random. Not with the timing. Not with the fact that Vic is Willie's girlfriend."

She thought of the look in Willie's eye when she had asked him whether someone had tried to use Vic to leverage him, to force him to leave the clan. He had received a message through some channel. Accompanied with proof that they had Vic.

Erin was sure of that.

CHAPTER 42

*T*he question hit Erin as she poured batter into loaf pans for the white sandwich bread.

Where was Vic?

Not "Who had her?" but "Where was she?"

They had to be holding her somewhere. There were too many parties involved to know which one had taken her, but what if Erin could find the *place* Vic was being held?

It was a ridiculous prospect. The mountain was riddled with caves and mines. There were houses and shacks on lands that had been abandoned long ago. There were hundreds of other places for a criminal to hide a hostage.

But Erin could narrow it down. It couldn't be a place frequented by either of the clans. It had to be close enough to town for the kidnapper to go back and forth to Bald Eagle Falls for supplies or to do his job without anyone noticing the change in routine.

It could be any house in town. But with so many people on the alert for kidnappers or clan activities, worried about the disappearances, knowing that Willie's girlfriend had been taken, people would be far more alert and watchful of their neighbors. Erin would work on the assumption that Vic was not being held in someone's house. She just couldn't search all of the homes in Bald Eagle Falls.

She looked at the time on the clock on the wall. It wouldn't be long before Bella was out of school and could come by for the dinnertime rush. Until then, things would be quiet. It was not easy keeping the bakery staffed with Vic and Charley both out of circulation. They were the ones who put in the most hours, other than Erin herself.

But Cheyenne, a single mom who came in to help a few hours a week, had stepped up to help, significantly increasing her hours until the others could get back or Erin could sign on a couple more part-timers. She could stay on until closing and help Bella through the rush.

Erin wiped her hands on a dishtowel and went to the front of the bakery to talk to her.

"I need to run a couple of errands. Can you mind things here until Bella gets off?"

Cheyenne, her auburn hair pulled back into a practical ponytail, turned a sunny smile on her. "Of course, ain't no problem. Go get those errands done before everything closes."

Erin nodded her thanks. "Great. And you'll be on again tomorrow, right?"

"Until Charley is up to working again. Then she and I can split until..." Cheyenne hesitated, then went on, "until Vic is back."

"I'll see you tomorrow, then."

Erin didn't stay to explain where she was going or end the conversation more gracefully.

Vic didn't need her to make small talk. She needed Erin to find her.

And Erin was going to.

She whipped off her apron, hung it up, grabbed her things, and left the kitchen in a mess for the others to clean.

The first place to check was the basement of the bakery. A long time ago, tunnels had connected a number of the businesses on Main Street. They had been walled over since then, and walled over *again* when they had discovered that the tunnels were being used for drug trafficking and distribution.

Had they been opened up again? Erin didn't know how many businesses might have access to the old tunnels. If she couldn't find anything, she could at least suggest that the police do a thorough search to make sure they were not being used again.

She made a quick trip down the stairs to her storage room. It was K9 who had found the entrance the last time. This time, Erin did not have his sensitive ears and nose to her advantage. But she knew where the tunnel was and where the opening had been. They couldn't exactly move the tunnel. She examined the wall closely. She couldn't find any breaks in the cement between the cinder blocks that made up the sturdy wall. They had built the wall strong, so if someone opened up a tunnel from another business, they would still be unable to access the bakery.

Erin ran her fingers along the cracks. She looked for any unevenness in coloring, any sign of a release mechanism that would allow the entire wall to swing out. Using her phone LED for oblique lighting, she looked for shadows indicating a ridge or break in the wall. She used it to look for fingerprints or disturbances in the dust.

Nothing.

She hadn't thought that the tunnel had been opened up again. With the burglar alarm and locks in the bakery, it wouldn't be an easy access point like before. But people had skills. Getting past alarm systems and locked doors was easier for some people.

Eventually, she gave up on the wall covering the tunnel. She was pretty sure there was no way into the tunnels from Auntie Clem's Bakery anymore, or vice versa. She could get Terry to come by later with K9, just to be sure.

She climbed the stairs back into the kitchen, startling Cheyenne.

"Oh! I thought you were already gone!"

"Sorry," Erin apologized. "I'm heading out right now."

Her next stop was the Book Nook.

She didn't think that she would actually find anything there.

The Book Nook did not, as far as she knew, have access to the tunnels, but she couldn't help thinking that she might find a clue in the Book Nook's basement.

First, Naomi had disappeared, and then Mr. Foster. Without the two of them, the Book Nook could not remain open. Had they been taken because someone had wanted to use the Book Nook's large storage room for something? Or they already were, and needed to make sure they were not discovered? The Book Nook got a lot of big, heavy deliveries. One of the part-time employees could be shipping drugs through there, and Naomi had stumbled onto what was going on, and they'd had to silence her.

Erin went to the loading dock of the Book Nook behind the store rather than trying to access it from the front door on Main Street, where people might notice her. She had noticed previously the front door of the Book Nook was not very secure, and in her experience, back doors, especially loading dock doors, tended to be less secure than the obvious front doors.

She was right, and the lock on the door that pulled down over the loading bay was so flimsy Naomi might as well not even have taken the time to lock it. Erin could almost pry the door up without unlocking it. A few shakes or a pry bar would have popped it easily. But Erin wanted to stay quiet and unobtrusive, and did not want to take the chance of breaking the lock, so she pulled a narrow nail file from her purse and inserted it into the keyhole. It took a few seconds of play before the lock clicked open, and the door opened its wide maw to welcome her. Hardly any more secure than those little locking diaries.

Erin stepped in and pulled the door shut again, pushing it down into place with a click so that no one would be able to tell there was an intruder. She didn't turn on any lights. It wasn't dark enough yet that anyone would notice from the street outside, but if she stayed for too long, she might give herself away.

CHAPTER 43

*E*rin took a minute to look around the door and the loading dock to make sure that there was no burglar alarm she might have tripped before going on to explore the rest of the store.

She didn't want to take too long there. There were other places she wanted to explore before the day was done. She was prioritizing the list in her head. Places that were close enough to town for a kidnapper to find convenient. The list was getting too long, and she was starting to panic.

She couldn't afford to let herself be overwhelmed by the job. She would do what she could, suggest places to the police, maybe get some of the townspeople to help her check out the outlying abandoned properties and buildings. Bald Eagle Falls was a small town. People would band together and help out if she asked them to. Just like they had when Roger had been missing.

Willie had organized that search. Erin wished he was back to his old position, running his own businesses, helping out with search and rescue when his skills were needed, wiring networks and security alarms. Why did he have to be leading the clan?

She hurried down the stairs, turning on the light on her phone to use as a flashlight and shining it ahead of her. At the bottom of the stairs, she flicked on all the lights in the basement and looked around.

She ignored the feeling of vertigo from being down there again. The last time she had been down there, she had found a body, and it had not been a pleasant experience. Just being down there made her stomach tighten, and brought back all of the resentments of the man dying and Erin falling under suspicion because of her past. Even with everything they had been through together, Terry had still not been one hundred percent sure of her innocence.

Pushing the feelings aside, she walked briskly through the aisle, looking at the piles of books and boxes. Was there anything out of place? Was she being ridiculous, thinking that someone could have been trafficking drugs or something else through the Book Nook?

Why else would both Naomi and Mr. Foster have been taken?

She opened the flaps of boxes to gaze inside and found nothing but books. A few times, she picked up heavier hardcover books and opened the cover to make sure nothing was hidden inside. How often had she seen TV movies where a book had been hollowed out to hide a secret?

But there was nothing. No matter how many boxes she went through or books she opened, she couldn't find anything that seemed even the least bit out of place.

Erin looked for an entrance to the tunnels but found nothing. The walls appeared to be seamless and intact. Admitting to herself that there was nothing to find, she finally went back upstairs.

If not trafficking or smuggling, then what was going on at the Book Nook that warranted kidnapping the proprietor and one of the employees? Something had prompted the kidnapper to take them. Erin entered Naomi's office and started going through everything on her desk. Her in basket, her file drawers, everything on the desk. She had no idea what she was looking for, but she kept looking. She hoped that something would jump out at her. She clicked the mouse on Naomi's computer and was confronted with the lock screen.

Erin was no hacker. She tried a few passwords, hoping that Naomi had used something easy. She found that a lot of people in rural areas used their phone numbers, but trying Naomi's business phone forward and backward had no effect. Erin lifted the keyboard and flipped it over to see if there was a sticky note on the bottom with the password. A small photograph had been stuck underneath and fell on the floor. Erin bent down and picked it up to put it back on the desk. Who used actual printed photos anymore? She flipped it over as she slapped it down on the desk. She stared at the photo for a moment. Officer Rodney Stayner. Out of uniform. Not naked, just in casual clothes. She hadn't often seen him dressed casually. Usually, when she saw him, he was either on duty or talking to Terry before going on or coming off.

He'd come a long way since he had first come to Bald Eagle Falls a year before when Terry had been suffering from a severe concussion and unable to work. Stayner had been an outsider, young and untested, brash, quick to jump to conclusions, judgmental, sometimes unsure of proper procedure, even though he was determined to do everything the right way and enforce the law with exactness.

He had, since then, shown a great deal of growth, becoming a part of their community, learning how to connect with people. Doing extra little things that surprised Erin with his thoughtfulness, showing that he had been well brought up. His parents had taught him how to take care of himself and others.

She still didn't like him, but he was growing on her. She could stand him. She could see how much he had grown and matured in just that time. One day, he would be a fine, seasoned officer, a family man, and a real part of the community.

And that personal growth had apparently begun as well, Stayner integrating well and establishing relationships with the locals. Erin had not suspected anything was going on between Naomi and Stayner. Had she been blind, or had they just been doing a good job at keeping it a secret?

Naomi was older than the young law enforcement officer, which was probably one reason they kept it quiet. But there wasn't a shockingly large age difference between them. And there were certainly precedents in the community, including Beaver's relationship with Jeremy. And Willie's with Vic, for that matter.

Erin carefully tucked the photo back under the keyboard and tried a few variations on Stayner's name in the password field on the screen. No luck.

She was vaguely surprised that the police hadn't taken the computer away as part of their investigation into Naomi's disappearance. But she supposed they couldn't just take every computer of anyone reported missing. They might have looked at it after Naomi had disappeared. Mr. Foster might have had the password. If there wasn't anything relevant on it, there was no need for the police to take it away and store it in their evidence warehouse.

Eventually, she gave up on the computer. She had other places to check out. The bakery and the bookstore were just the first two, and she'd known that neither of them was likely to magically reveal the location of the missing persons.

She let herself back out of the Book Nook, carefully re-closing the loading bay door.

CHAPTER 44

*E*rin decided she'd better go home before heading out to any of the more isolated farms or caves. She needed to fortify herself for that job. Especially if she were going to search the natural caves and tunnels that ran throughout the mountain.

She hated caves and tunnels.

She had not liked them before being knocked out and left tied up in one to die. After that experience—waking up in the darkness and trying to drag herself through the tunnels, with no real hope of escape—such spaces caused a level of panic that was difficult to describe. But she had been able to go into one or two again briefly.

And it had not killed her.

If it meant saving Vic and her other friends, she would force herself. She could do it.

But first, a meal and a break. Assuming Terry was working late again, she would return after supper and search some of the closer locations. She figured she could check out two or three before she needed to go to bed.

It was a good thing she had recovered from her concussion. She couldn't see herself being able to go into a cave while she was still wobbly and sick.

Maybe she would only check out abandoned buildings today and put off caves until the next day.

Erin parked her bug in the garage. When she stepped out of the garage, she looked around for any threats. Unlike that night when she and Vic had been confronted by Potter, daylight offered some comfort. And she knew that Potter was no longer a threat. But he certainly wasn't the only one with an agenda.

There was movement deeper in the trees, and Erin stood still, watching closely. It was probably Adele. Doing her job and watching for trespassers.

But as Erin focused on the figure, she could see it wasn't Adele, tall and spare with red hair. But it did look like a woman.

Whoever it was, she blended into the trees, and before Erin could get a good look at her, she had faded back into the woods and disappeared from sight.

Erin took a few steps after her. "Beaver?"

Beaver, if that was who it was, did not come back into view. Erin followed, though she knew it probably wasn't the wisest thing to do. She knew the woods now. Mostly. She wanted to know whether that figure had been Beaver or someone else.

Was Beaver still in Bald Eagle Falls? If so, what was she doing there? Not staying with Jeremy; at least not before he had called her. Maybe he had convinced her to stay with him for a few nights while she conducted her investigation.

Erin didn't get too far into the woods. It was quiet and still, with no sign that anyone had been there. If it had been Beaver, she had disappeared, leaving no sign of her passage.

She retreated to the backyard and considered whether to try calling Beaver to see if it had been her, and if so, what she was doing there.

But what was the point? If it had been Beaver, she probably wouldn't answer her phone, and if she did, she would not tell Erin what she had been doing there.

When she let herself into the house, Erin was surprised to find Terry home.

"Oh! I wasn't expecting you to be off yet. You've been putting in so many hours lately…"

Terry yawned and scratched his jaw. "It has been a lot of hours," he agreed. "And we can't keep going at this pace. Reckon I could stand a quiet night home."

Erin nodded and tried not to show her disappointment that she could not conduct any of the searches she had been planning. It would do her good to have a nice quiet evening at home reconnecting with Terry. Refreshed and reenergized, she could recommence her searches tomorrow. Not at nightfall when visibility was low and she was more easily spooked.

"Are you okay?" Terry asked, frowning at her.

"Yes. Of course, I'm just fine." Erin pulled on an apron to start working on supper. Maybe instead of thawing frozen baked goods to go with the meal, she would make some fresh biscuits.

Her hand brushed against her pocket, and she noticed a pebble or some other small, hard object in it. She reached her fingers in and pulled it out.

Not a pebble, a button. She looked at it for a moment before offering it to Terry. He looked down at the brass button in her palm.

"What's that?"

"A button from your uniform."

He frowned. "When did I lose that?" He started running his fingers over his uniform, searching for the spot it was missing from. Erin ran her eyes over him. Everything seemed to be in place. She walked around him, looking at his sleeves, and shook her head.

"It must be from one of your other shirts. Not this one."

"I would know if I was missing a button," he insisted.

"It must be from one of your other uniforms," she repeated.

He shook his head. "Where did you find it?"

"In Vic's apartment."

They both just stared at each other. Erin thought back to the day Vic had disappeared and everything that had happened that day.

"I didn't see it at Vic's apartment," Terry objected.

"Well, it must have come off when you went in there to look for her. I found it when I took Nilla back to his crate that night." She frowned, concentrating on it, trying to remember everything clearly. "It was... in his crate. In the blanket. It fell out when I shook his blanket out. I guess it might have been there for longer. But why would it be? You hadn't been there any other time recently. You just went in when Vic didn't answer the door. And took Nilla out of his kennel. It must have come off then."

Vic was a private person, and despite her friendship with Erin and Terry, she did not want the police in her apartment. She had made that fact abundantly clear in the past. Erin thought she had gotten over the sentiment as she had gotten more used to Terry. But Vic had never invited Terry over for anything. She was handy and took care of any maintenance or repair work herself. If there was something she couldn't handle or needed a second pair of hands for, she had Willie, who was very good with all things mechanical and electrical.

"You hadn't been there any other time," she said.

"No. But you know, she could have something with gold buttons on it. A gold button isn't automatically from my police uniforms." He took the button from Erin's hand and held it up to one of the decorative buttons on his uniform. They were identical.

Terry's forehead creased.

"It could still be someone else's. Someone else on the force might have been over there."

"You would know if someone else had been called over there."

"It wouldn't have to be on an official call. Someone could have been there to check in on her, talk to Willie, or for some kind of social call. Just because she doesn't want me in her apartment, it doesn't mean that no one in a police uniform has ever crossed the threshold."

Erin shook her head slowly. "It's *Stayner.*"

CHAPTER 45

"Rodney?" Terry shook his head. "What would make you think that? It could be, of course, I'm not saying it wasn't. But what makes you jump straight to him?"

"He was here that night. He told me he would check out the backyard and ensure everything was good with Vic. We were both so worried about everything that had happened. Mary Lou and Naomi disappearing. Potter getting the drop on us and threatening us with the gun."

Terry nodded. "So he stopped in to check on Vic. You know he was over there. That makes sense."

"But it doesn't make sense that his button would be in the blanket in Nilla's crate. How did it get in there?" Erin rubbed her forehead. She paced back and forth across the kitchen, trying to work it out in her head. "Vic wouldn't have let him into the apartment. She didn't know him as well as she knew you. And didn't really like him, either." She met Terry's eyes. "He was the last one to see her."

"What are you saying?"

"Just what you're thinking. He was *inside* her apartment. The next morning, she was gone. Her bed wasn't slept in. Her nightgown was on the floor. She disappeared between getting changed and actually going to bed. It had to be Officer Stayner."

"You don't know that. She could have made the bed and gotten dressed in the morning. She could have made the bed and gotten dressed in the middle of the night when she was taken or left to meet Willie. All we have is Willie's word that they planned to get together in the morning. That could have been a cover story. He could have met with her in the night."

"She didn't get up and get dressed in the morning and then get taken. I was watching the loft for when she turned the light on. The light never went on. She was already gone before I got up."

"Like I say, they could have met during the night."

"You don't really believe that," Erin countered.

"I can't jump to the conclusion that Rodney Stayner kidnapped Vic! He's an officer of the law. What reason would he have to take her? It doesn't make any sense."

"What reason did anyone have to take her? As leverage for Willie. Trying to get Willie to do what he wanted. To use Vic as leverage to make him quit the Dyson clan. Willie as much as said so!"

"Yeah? When did Willie say that?"

Erin opened her mouth. Had she told Terry about Willie coming to the bakery or what had been said during that conversation? She might have neglected to say anything about it to him. After all, Willie hadn't told her who it was who had Vic. He didn't seem to know himself. But he knew that she was being used as a weapon, that he was being told to do something that he didn't think he could do.

"Uh… it was just this morning. He swung by Auntie Clem's for a muffin."

"For a muffin?" Terry repeated skeptically.

"Well, I gave him a muffin. He didn't say that was what he came for."

"And you talked to him about who might have taken Vic?"

"Not about who it was. He didn't know. But about why she was

246

taken. Because someone was using her to leverage him to do… something."

"To get out of the clan," Terry suggested.

"He didn't say, exactly. But yeah, I guess that would be what it was. He wants to get out of the clan, but he promised to take his position as the heir and there are a lot of expectations that prevent him just quitting."

Terry rolled his eyes at this. Erin should have known. He didn't have much sympathy for Willie and figured he should have been able to unwind his commitment to the clan more easily than that.

"And Willie told you that. That someone was pressuring him, using Vic to get him to leave the clan."

"More or less…" Erin tried to remember Willie's exact words. "He was pretty vague, but I understood what he meant."

"But Rodney?" Terry asked in a strained voice. "He couldn't do something like that. How could he? It's his job to uphold the law, not to take things into his own hands to threaten and coerce the criminals."

Erin refrained from insisting that Terry was falsely accusing Willie of being a criminal. He hadn't done anything, as far as they could prove. He had been forced into the position he was in. He had never wanted to be the leader of the clan. It was his birth, not something that he had any control over.

But it didn't matter whether he really was or not. That was how Terry saw him, and that was how Stayner saw him, and that was the point. Stayner thought he was justified in taking Vic because he was doing it for a good reason. He wanted to get Vic's boyfriend out of the clan, so he was doing her a favor by kidnapping her.

"You think Rodney was the one who killed Potter?" Terry asked.

Erin swallowed, thinking about it. She reluctantly nodded. "Yeah… I think it must have been. He was back there, watching us, watching for his chance to get in and take Vic. He and Potter, both lurking around back there… Stayner was quicker on the draw."

"I don't know. It doesn't all fit together as easily as I would like. I can't… I don't know if I believe he could have done that."

"Then where did the button come from? If it isn't from one of your uniforms, where did it come from?"

"He went over there to check on Vic. We already know that. He lost it while he was talking to her. Maybe he went in to check on window security or some other hazard he saw. Maybe Nilla attacked him. You know he doesn't like men. Maybe he ripped it off of Rodney's uniform. Carried it back to his crate."

"Yeah… maybe," Erin had to admit that was at least possible. "So… how are we going to find out? Are you going to ask him?"

"You know he won't admit anything just because I ask. He'll have a plan. He'll have a story ready."

"But we know it isn't true. Why didn't you know that he had been over to check on us?"

Terry hesitated. "What?"

"When I told you that he'd been over that night. You didn't know that he had been. Why didn't you know?"

Terry was silent for several very long seconds. "Because he didn't call it in," Terry said eventually.

Erin nodded. Why wouldn't he call in that he was going to check on Erin and Vic? If something happened to him, the police would need to know where to look for him. Every cop knew that. They knew they had to check in to make sure someone knew where they were. In a situation like Terry had once been in with Crazy Theresa, that was the one thing that had saved him. They had known that was the last place he had been. Without that, both he and Jack Ward would have died.

"Why didn't he call it in? He just forgot the proper radio procedure?"

"No. He knows proper procedure." Terry's voice was very calm and measured. No emotion. Erin struggled to keep the anger and dismay out of her voice, but Terry had mastered himself. She didn't know how he could be so calm.

"Where is he holding her?" Erin mused. "Where is she?"

"We don't know—"

"Did you know he was seeing Naomi?"

"No… he doesn't talk about his personal life. That's nice, I didn't know he was seeing anyone."

Erin just stood there staring at him.

"You think he had something to do with Naomi's disappearance too?" Terry challenged. "Why would he kidnap the woman he was dating?"

"Because she knew something. Maybe he had said he was in one place, and she knew he hadn't been. Maybe he had tried to use her as an alibi. Or she found something… a note, a text on his phone, a paper that fell out of his wallet. Something that tipped her off that he was involved in something he shouldn't have been."

Terry was silent.

"And then Mr. Foster. Because he knew that Stayner and Naomi had been seeing each other and didn't want it to leak out. Didn't want anyone to know there was any connection between them."

"This is all speculation," Terry said finally. "We don't know any of this for sure. It is an awful lot to be hanging on the discovery of a button."

"I *know* he was seeing Naomi."

"How did you find out that little tidbit?"

"She has a picture of him on her desk."

Terry's brows drew together. "We checked out the Book Nook after Naomi disappeared. There was no picture of Stayner on her desk."

"Do you think he would have let you see it if there was? But it wasn't displayed in a picture frame. It was under her keyboard."

"And you knew this because…"

Erin couldn't exactly confess to breaking into the Book Nook. "I saw it there once. She didn't know that I had seen it."

"You just happened to see it?"

"I went over there to—"

"Don't tell me you went over there to pick up some trays. You've used that one before."

Erin cleared her throat. It angered her that he automatically assumed she was lying and trying to make up a reason she had been there. She *could* have gone into Naomi's office to ask her a question or pick something up and have seen the picture. Terry didn't know that she hadn't.

"What about Charley?" Terry asked. "If Stayner was the one helping people to disappear, then wouldn't she have known that's who had been holding her? She never said anything to indicate that it might have been Rodney."

"She can't remember anything because she was drunk and drugged. That's what they give you those date rape drugs for. Not just so that you are easier to control, but so that you won't remember what happened or who you were with."

"You can't assume it was Rodney when she doesn't remember."

"I don't think it *was* Stayner who took Charley," Erin contradicted.

Terry looked taken aback. "You don't?"

"Willie said it was someone within the clan."

"How did Willie know that? This was from your conversation today?"

"Yeah. He said he wanted to make sure she was okay. That she was returned safely. He was the one who put pressure on this guy to return her. That was why she suddenly reappeared. So we can thank Willie for that."

Terry's skepticism about this story was evident, but he didn't argue. "And why was she being held?"

"For her knowledge of the organization. Her time inside the clan and dating Bobby. She knew things about the way the organization worked. Maybe things that would help them to dismantle the organization. But not Stayner. I actually asked him whether it was the police that wanted to dismantle the clan leadership, and he said it wasn't the police. So it couldn't have been Stayner."

"Two kidnappers?"

Erin nodded. "Well… considering how many people have been disappearing, it's not surprising. If Stayner took Naomi, Mr. Foster, and Vic, that's a lot of people to keep track of and control. He wouldn't want to have Charley on top of that."

"I'd think Charley would be enough of a handful all by herself," Terry observed.

"Yeah," Erin gave a little laugh. "She would. Whoever it was, he was probably ready to return her, even without Willie putting any pressure on. Just to get some peace and quiet and be able to think."

"I don't imagine Vic is much easier. She might not be as wild as Charley, but she has an attitude. I doubt she has been easy to push around."

"Naomi is quiet, at least. She wouldn't cause anyone any trouble. But Mr. Foster..."

"Seems like a quiet, unassuming guy until you get him riled up about his religious beliefs," Terry finished.

"Yeah. Poor Officer Stayner." Erin couldn't help laughing. She felt such a huge relief as they unwound the kidnappings and the motives behind them. It almost seemed like they were in the clear.

But they weren't. If they were right, at least three people were still in Stayner's hands.

And it wouldn't be easy to get them home safely.

They were both startled by the sound of the doorbell. Erin looked at Terry to see if he had been expecting a visitor. He looked back at her with the same expression, obviously thinking that it was for her.

The doorbell rang insistently a couple more times. K9 barked in protest. Terry and Erin both moved at once, heading to the door. Terry motioned Erin back and looked out through the peephole.

His shoulders relaxed, and he looked back at Erin and then opened the door.

Melissa stumbled into the room. Her curly hair was even wilder than usual, as if she had been running her fingers through it to make it stand out as far as possible. Melissa loved to make a splash, and being the bearer of dramatic news was one of her favorite things. She looked at both of them, holding her hands up in a "wait" gesture and breathing heavily, trying to catch her breath.

She was acting as if she had run all the way from the police department offices, which Erin doubted. She looked out the window but did not see a car parked against the curb. So maybe

Melissa *had* run over, or did a combination of walking and running. It was too hot to run. Erin went into the kitchen to fill a cup with cold water while they waited for Melissa to catch her breath.

"Okay, sorry," Melissa said, blowing out a puff of air and valiantly trying to catch her breath. "Whew. I don't know the last time I ran like that."

She accepted the glass of water that Erin handed her and took a few swallows.

"Thanks." She looked at Terry and took a deep breath before her announcement. "Willie Andrews... is dead."

CHAPTER 46

*E*rin gasped and put her hand over her heart. "What?" she asked in disbelief.

Terry scowled and shook his head and looked at Melissa. "What is going on? How could Willie be dead, and why are you here? Why didn't this go out over the radio?"

"Don't know why, but radio communications are out. Nothing is going through."

Terry pulled out his radio and keyed the mic, but the system was silent. There was no response, no static or buzz of activity.

"Well, there is no need to rely on radio communications with cellular technology. They may not be the best choice for outside of town, but within Bald Eagle Falls, the signal is always pretty good…"

He looked down at his screen and scowled. Erin took out her phone and looked at it. No bars.

"How can there be no bars inside town? The cell tower is right here!"

Melissa gave a shrug. "We don't know what's going on, but the quickest way to get to you was… to come over here in person."

"Well, thank you for your initiative," Terry acknowledged.

"Now, tell me what you can about Willie. What did you hear? Where did the report come from?"

"The call came in about fifteen minutes ago." Melissa looked at a jeweled watch on her wrist, pausing to make sure they both saw it. "It came from Detective Ward in Moose River. He said that Willie had been assassinated, but they didn't have much information yet, and more would be transmitted as it came in."

"Jack Ward," Erin repeated, still having a hard time accepting the news. A good man who should not have survived the injuries he had received from Crazy Theresa Franklin, yet he had recovered quickly and been back on duty within weeks. He was a reliable source.

She couldn't believe that Willie could be dead. She had just seen him that morning; it was incomprehensible that he was dead after being so hale and hearty. But of course, his health first thing in the morning had no correlation with the bullet—or whatever weapon—had put an end to his life.

How was she going to tell Vic? It was bad enough that Vic was not there, held hostage by some cop who hoped to engineer Willie's removal from the leadership of the clan. But for Willie to be killed while Vic was gone and to have to tell her when she got back… Erin didn't know how she could handle that.

Vic would be crushed. Willie was the first man to accept her as a woman, to be able to see past all of the ugly words and judgment condemning her and accept her for who she was. How could she lose him now? She had been so upset when she had found out about his connection with the clan. The fact that they came from feuding clans had been difficult for her to get over. Now, clan life had taken him from her.

"Then what happened?" Terry asked Melissa.

"We tried to put it out on the radio, but couldn't raise a reply. So I tried calling everyone. The landline at the police department is working, but everybody is on cellphones, and those are down too. I don't understand how the cell tower and radios can both be out, but they are. We need to call Wil— someone to look at the system and see if he can tell us what is wrong. Someone who can troubleshoot that kind of thing."

Terry nodded but didn't stay focused on that. "For both the radio and the cell signal to be down... I've never seen anything like that happen before. It has to be sabotage."

Melissa shook her head, wild curls bouncing. "I don't know. I guess so, but I don't know how these things work. Radios always worked for my dad. I don't know what to do when the system quits working."

"Did you try rotating through channels? If one band is not working, we can try another..."

"Dispatch is doing that now."

"We need to find Officer Stayner. There is reason to suspect that... he has been mixed up in some of the disappearances in town. We need to keep that from leaking out... and yet to be able to coordinate our actions. Do you know where Rod is supposed to be?"

Melissa's eyes flashed. "You think he has something to do with the disappearances? You mean Mary Lou? Vic? The others?"

Terry nodded. He gave her a stern look. "You cannot spread that around. We need to be very careful here. Extremely careful. We need to get word to Sheriff Wilmot and Tom Banks without tipping off Rodney. Maybe we can use this communications blackout to our advantage."

They looked at each other blankly. It made sense to take advantage of the radio silence to trap Stayner, but how could they do that without a communications system?

"You said that the police department landline was still working," Erin said. "Who else in town has a landline? Can we... use a phone tree to find out where everyone is?"

"How would that work?" Terry asked.

"We write down everybody we can think of who has a landline." Erin thought about the disaster communication plan she had seen or heard of being used before. "We split the list into three. We call the first one-third of the numbers, giving each person two other people to call. Each of those people calls two other people they know of who have landlines and tells them to call two other people, and so on. The message to each person is to locate Sheriff Wilmot, Tom Banks, and Rodney Stayner, and call the police department landline with their locations."

Terry nodded slowly. "Okay. We can split up the list of first-level calls to get word out as quickly as possible. We don't want the clans or other criminals taking advantage of the blackout before we track everybody down."

"Mrs. Peach next door still has a landline," Erin said, "I can make some calls from there."

"Melissa and I can go back to the police department and make calls from there. Is Clara still in?"

"She was when I left," Melissa confirmed. "She wouldn't go home in the middle of an emergency."

"Okay, that's four of us, at least. Let's brainstorm a list. The Moose River police department has a landline, too; we need to call them and get more information from Jack Ward and let him know how to get ahold of us."

"He didn't call from the police department number," Melissa said. "He was on his cell, I think. It wasn't very clear. Maybe what-ever it is… affected him at some level as well. Maybe Moose River is on the edge of the affected area."

"Well, we know we can reach the police department, so we'll start with them, and they can find a way to talk to Ward and communicate further details to us."

CHAPTER 47

$\mathcal{E}$rin was energized by their plan. For the first time in a week, she felt like she could breathe. They were going to find Vic and the other missing people. They knew who the culprit was. By sticking to their plan, they could take advantage of the communications blackout to locate Stayner without his being aware of it.

She hoped that Terry really believed Stayner was their man. It was the only theory that made sense.

She passed out gluten-free protein bars for everyone to sustain them while they made their phone calls, since it was suppertime and none of them were stopping for a meal. And she thawed out a plate of cookies to take to Mrs. Peach's house. She couldn't just go over there empty-handed asking for a favor. Mrs. Peach would be up, but she usually had her dinner early, and in the evening, used her new hot tub and atrium to relax before bed. Erin would be intruding on her wind-down routine.

Terry and Melissa headed to the police department offices. Erin lingered to ensure the doors were locked and the burglar alarm armed, then walked next door to knock on Mrs. Peach's door.

It always took Mrs. Peach a while to get to the door, so Erin waited patiently, feasting her eyes on the pretty spring flowers in the borders and picturing Mrs. Peach making slow progress through the house using her walker. Hopefully, she wasn't already in the hot tub. She wouldn't want to get out of the tub to answer the door or to answer in her bathing suit or cover-up.

In a few minutes, the door opened and Mrs. Peach peeked through the crack before shutting it to slide off the chain and let Erin in.

"It's so nice to see you again, Erin!" Mrs. Peach greeted her with a big smile. "It has been so long since we had a nice chat."

"It has," Erin agreed. She had been neglecting her elderly neighbor. Mrs. Peach didn't get a lot of visitors, and Erin needed to make an effort to visit more often and ensure everything was okay with Mrs. Peach. She showed off the plate of cookies. "I brought you some cookies and a sad story."

"Oh, you don't say!" The old woman looked intrigued. She motioned toward the living room for Erin to go ahead of her to sit down. Erin sat on the couch and put the plate of cookies down on the coffee table.

She remembered Mr. Peach's last hours lying on the couch and shifted uncomfortably. But she was going to have to get used to it. It wasn't like the couch had been soaked in blood or other bodily fluids. Erin waited for Mrs. Peach to settle into a comfortable chair and then held the plate of cookies close so she could select one.

"Oh dear, I should not eat these in the living room," Mrs. Peach said with a chuckle. "I will have to vacuum."

"Do you want me to get you a small plate?" Erin offered.

"Oh, no. This is fine. I like to cut loose every now and then. So, what is this sad story? I have heard about people disappearing ever since that Willie Andrews joined the clan again." She shook her head. "You would think he would have learned the first time. Alienated himself from his fiancée, his parents, everyone. For what? He thought he was going to make a lot of money? Be a big, powerful gangster, and everybody would respect him?"

"I don't think so," Erin said, thinking about what Willie had told her about that time. "He did want to make some money... was rebelling against his parents too, I think. I would say he *did* learn his lesson, though. It wasn't actually his choice this time."

"Everybody has a choice," Mrs. Peach said firmly, shaking her head.

"Well, he accepted his place in the clan because he was trying to protect Terry and me. I wish he hadn't, but I also didn't want to be dead."

"Oh, no," Mrs. Peach agreed, her eyes and mouth round O's of surprise. "I'm glad you and that handsome officer came through it okay. But the clans... I wish the police could find a way to shut them down."

"I know. Me too. And they are trying, especially now with everything being disrupted. The problem is that everyone is trying to take advantage of the disruption for their own reasons. Those people who are missing... did you hear that Vic was one of them?"

Mrs. Peach nodded solemnly. "A terrible thing. She is such a nice girl. So pretty. Have the police made any progress in figuring out who took her? I don't know what to think of all of the missing people..."

"We have a theory," Erin said carefully. She didn't want to be accused of slandering Stayner if they could not get enough evidence to arrest and convict him. "But in order to catch him and get Vic and the others back, I need your help."

"My help?" Mrs. Peach tittered. "What help can an old lady be?"

"Well, like many other wise women of your age, you have kept your landline, haven't you?"

"My landline? The phone? Yes." Mrs. Peach nodded vigorously. "People my age understand the value of having a hardwired phone. And not just because it means we always know where the phone is!" Mrs. Peach looked at the side table, where an old beige 80's phone sat.

Erin nodded. "It's an important lesson for us today," she admitted. "The police radio channel is down, and so is the cell network."

"Well, I'll be!" Mrs. Peach nodded wisely. "So now it is down to us oldsters to show you how the old technology is best!"

"I'm hoping I can use your phone for a few calls. Quite a few, actually. We need to get some emergency messages out, and land-lines are the only way right now."

"Of course. Certainly. You go ahead and use it for however long you need."

"Thanks, I really appreciate it. If you want me to do it in another room, or if you want to go ahead and do your usual nightly routine, I don't want to be in the way. I'll just take care of these calls and not disturb you."

"You go ahead," Mrs. Peach motioned to the phone. "I'll just sit here for a bit. Have a couple of cookies."

Erin felt a little awkward making her calls with an audience. Still, she could understand that it was something unique and enter-taining. Even though she was repeating the same short script to each person on the list as she worked her way through it, it was still a spectacle Mrs. Peach did not see every day.

Some people immediately grasped what Erin needed to be done and agreed, taking down the second-level phone numbers she gave them and promising to call them and give them the message right away. Others seemed to think she was a salesperson or crank caller or were hard of hearing and could not comprehend the emergency and how they were expected to help.

Erin had a headache by the time she got through the calls. She sat back, shaking her head, after taking one of the cookies from the plate. She dialed the last number on her list, the police department.

"Bald Eagle Falls police," Clara's voice snapped in her ear.

"Hi, Clara. It's Erin. Is Terry available?"

"Let me see if I can get him for you. He's on the phone."

Erin was put on hold and waited for Clara to pass Terry a note or send him an email letting him know Erin was waiting. It was a couple of minutes before the line was picked up, and Terry was there.

"Erin. How did it go?"

"Easier and harder than I thought it would be."

He chuckled. "Yep. I can understand that. We have had success, though. We were only halfway through the list before we started getting incoming calls. We have the sheriff and Tom onside now, patrolling and calling in on landlines every five or ten minutes. But… so far, no sign of Rod."

"That's strange. I mean, he's supposed to be on shift, isn't he?"

Terry sighed. "He is. But the fact that no one has called in to say they have seen him is not evidence that he isn't where he should be. Just that no one we reached with our phone tree has eyes on him at the moment. He could be outside town in a more remote area, or a place like a bar that has lots of cellphones but just one landline in the back, not in sight of the restaurant area."

"I suppose." Erin had thought that once they got the word out, it would be pretty easy to locate Stayner and the others. But it was going to take time. "How about Jack Ward? Have you been able to talk to him?"

"Not yet. I have a call out to him. Don't know if they are having problems with communications in Moose River like we are. If they are intermittent, they might not realize they have a problem. But his office said they would have him call me once they got in touch."

"Okay. Do you have anyone else you need me to call? Or do we just sit and wait now?"

"I can give you a few that didn't answer the phone, and you can see whether you can reach them. It might be easier with a private citizen's caller ID. People tend not to take calls from the police or 'unknown caller.'"

"True," Erin admitted. "I know I tend to let those go to voicemail. The unknown callers, that is. I usually take the ones from the police department." She smiled.

She didn't usually get calls from Terry on the police landline number. Usually, they came in from his cell phone. But she wanted to make him smile.

"Yeah," Terry agreed, his voice flat, obviously thinking of other things rather than what she had said. "Here are the numbers you can try…"

Erin wrote them down in her planner as he read them off. "Okay, will do," she acknowledged. "Talk to you later."

After hanging up with Terry, Erin paused, listening. She heard a dog barking nearby and tried to identify whether it was Nilla. It might be. She looked at the time on her phone. She should probably head home in half an hour to take him outside.

"Is that Vic's dog?" Mrs. Peach asked.

"I think so. He's inside, and you shouldn't be able to hear him, but… I guess if he's loud enough, you can. He should be fine for a little longer."

Mrs. Peach nodded. "I do hear him sometimes, but he's usually pretty good. Maybe someone is walking down the back alley."

Erin made a mental note. Maybe they needed to install some sound-absorbing tiles or seal the door and windows better. She would ask Terry what he thought needed to be done. Her mind immediately went to Willie since he and Vic would normally do the work themselves, and Willie would probably have some ideas about what else could be done.

But Willie was gone. She couldn't believe that it was possible. He had always been larger than life, such a strong personality and person. But being plunged into the position he had been, with two clashing clans and a lot of internal dissension, was more than one man could handle. If he didn't have enough of the clan on his side… something was bound to happen sooner or later.

As she reached for the phone to make the next series of calls, the doorbell rang. Erin looked toward the door.

"Is that one of your friends?" Mrs. Peach asked.

"I wasn't expecting anyone… you weren't…?"

"Lands, no. My friends all go to bed early. And they know my routine. Would you mind…?"

"Sure." Erin jumped up to answer the door. She opened it a couple of inches to peer out and saw Officer Rodney Stayner on the doorstep.

CHAPTER 48

*E*rin stared, her mind whirling as she tried to figure out what to do. No one had been able to find Stayner, and there he was.

She didn't know what to say to him. She didn't want to give away that they knew anything, and slamming the door in his face might give it away. She could try to talk to him on the doorstep and hope he went on his way. Then she could call Terry back and let him know where to find Stayner, and he and Sheriff Wilmot could decide how they would approach him.

"Ah, Erin," Stayner nodded. "I was looking for you. Could we talk for a minute?" He jerked his head, indicating he wanted her to go back to her house.

Erin shook her head and started to shut the door, but Stayner put his shoulder to it and pushed it in, hitting Erin and making her step back out of the way.

"Hey!"

"I just want to talk," Stayner repeated. He closed the door behind him and looked at Mrs. Peach. "Privately," he told her.

"Oh, hello, young man." Mrs. Peach smiled vaguely. "Would you like a cookie?"

She reached for the plate and held it out to him. Stayner shook his head, but ended up taking one anyway, maybe figuring he could deal with her better if he smiled and accepted one.

"Well, okay. Are these yours, or…?"

"From Auntie Clem's," Erin said. "I thought I would just come over for a visit before Mrs. Peach goes to bed."

Stayner stood there awkwardly, waiting for Mrs. Peach to leave. But she did not withdraw to another room. She picked up another cookie and looked at it, humming. Stayner, deciding she had dementia, turned to Erin.

"I thought I'd better check in and see how you were doing. I know you have Terry to look after you, but it never hurts to have someone else keeping an eye on things. I don't know if you're aware, but we're having some communication issues…"

"Yes. I found that out."

"So everyone needs to be on alert right now. We don't know why everything has gone wonky or who might have sabotaged those systems." He looked around. "Seeing as you are friends with Willie Andrews and Victoria Webster, I thought it was a good idea to make sure that you hadn't been targeted by one of the clans."

"That was very thoughtful of you," Erin told him. She kept her voice as calm and even as she could, but she was sweating bullets and afraid he would notice the fact. She knew Stayner hadn't come to Mrs. Peach's house just to check on her welfare. She tried to smile normally so that Stayner would not know that she had any suspicions about him.

"When you weren't at home, I was a little worried. Someone could have come and snatched you, too. Bald Eagle Falls isn't the safest place to live right now."

And maybe she should leave? Was that what he was trying to tell her?

"Just visiting a neighbor and friend." she kept her tone light and pleasant.

"I could walk you home, if you like. I'm sure Mrs. Peach wants to get to her bed."

"It's very kind of you to offer. But I'm fine. It's just next door. No one is going to attack me between here and there. I'm sure there are people who need your assistance far more than I do right now. And they can't call out the usual way. Have you checked in with the police department?"

"Of course," he lied smoothly. "They're working on it."

Nothing about having to check in every five or ten minutes to let them know where he was and pick up any emergency calls.

"Great." Erin sat back down on the couch. "I'll see you later."

He didn't leave. After a moment, he sat on the couch beside her, turned toward her to continue the conversation. Up close and personal.

Mrs. Peach continued to hum and eat her cookie.

"Have you made any progress in your investigation into what happened to Vic?" Stayner asked.

"Uh… I'm not investigating it. That's a police investigation, and I'm not privy to it. I hope you are making progress. I would really like to see her home soon."

"Erin Price not investigating?" Stayner smiled indulgently. "That's like saying the sun won't rise in the morning. It may be cloudy, but the sun still comes up. Sometimes, it is just obscured." He stared into her eyes, waiting for her to break down and tell him what she knew. Was she supposed to take his inquiries as being kind and attentive? Believing in her when the rest of the police department didn't? She was not going to fall for it.

"Time for the hot tub," Mrs. Peach declared, getting up. She wiggled her fingers at Erin. "Toodle-oo! I will see you tomorrow."

"Okay," Erin agreed. "Thanks. I'll see Officer Stayner off and lock up."

Mrs. Peach shuffled away, completely ignoring Erin.

"Getting batty, that one," Stayner said with disgust. "She's cooked her brain in that hot tub."

"It's just mild dementia. It won't get better, but she's still managing on her own." Erin hoped that her words would reassure him of Mrs. Peach's incompetence so he wouldn't consider her a threat. And she hoped that Mrs. Peach would lock herself in her room where it was safe and wait until Erin and Stayner were gone.

She looked toward the door. Had she given herself away to

Stayner? Or did he believe that she was still looking to the clans for Vic's kidnapper?

"I'll walk you back to your door now," Stayner suggested.

"I should go check on Nilla. I heard him barking a little while ago. I think he needs to be taken out."

She saw a flash of anger cross his face, then it was gone.

"That's Vic's dog?"

"Yeah. Were you over there? Checking to make sure it was locked up?"

He looked at her, not answering. It seemed obvious to Erin from his expression that he knew she was on to him. She didn't know what he planned to do about it, but now he had her alone. What would he do? Take her like he had taken Vic? Or would he opt for a more permanent solution, like he had with Potter, left lying in the woods dead and alone?

"I guess you must have heard about Willie?" she asked.

He was startled. "Willie? What about him? I haven't heard anything new."

"Right before the communications went down. We heard from Moose River that he had been killed." Erin's eyes burned. She tried not to let them well up with tears. Her throat was tight, and she hated to use Willie's death as a stall, but Willie would have understood. He would want Erin to do whatever was necessary to keep Stayner at bay until she could figure out how to get away from him safely. She hoped that Terry would call her back with a few more numbers to call, or to get an update on the people she had talked to.

But she feared he wouldn't. He had too much other work to do to keep calling her for no reason.

"Killed?" Stayner demanded. "How? By who?"

"We don't know yet. Communications went down and Terry was still trying to get more information. You could call him and see whether he has managed to find anything else out."

Stayner shook his head. "I don't want to bother him. What did he tell you?"

"Jack Ward called. He's a detective with the Moose River police department."

"I know him."

Erin nodded. "He said Willie was assassinated. He didn't know all of the details yet, but he was going to follow up and find out. You could try calling him." She motioned to Mrs. Peach's beige phone. "Landlines are still working."

His eyes fastened on the phone. "Landlines," he said with realization.

"Ancient technology, right?" Erin asked with a laugh. "But still a popular choice, especially in a rural area like this, where cell phone coverage can come and go. But I'd say… fifteen or twenty percent of homes still have a landline."

He looked angry at the thought. Had Stayner himself had something to do with the communications malfunction? He seemed personally affronted that so many people still had landlines and he hadn't thought of a way to keep them from being used. Maybe there was a substation nearby where he could have disrupted the hard lines as well.

He looked torn between whether to try Mrs. Peach's phone or not. Maybe he was afraid of what he would find, or that by doing so, he would reveal his location when he wanted it to remain a secret. But he wanted to know what had happened to Willie.

"I could call," she suggested. "Do you want me to check for you?"

He shook his head immediately. Didn't want her using the phone. Didn't want to give her the opportunity to call for help. He was being very careful, trying to figure out what to do with Erin. Her going to Mrs. Peach's house and their ability to communicate over the landlines were two complications he hadn't foreseen.

Erin took another cookie, needing some natural movement to disguise her anxiety. She would have to bring more cookies for Mrs. Peach if she and Stayner ate half of them. She knew that Mrs. Peach was partial to ginger cookies. Maybe she would make a batch of fresh ginger cookies rather than defrosting more baking from the freezer. Mrs. Peach deserved fresh.

"So Willie is gone," Stayner said meditatively. "What does that mean for the clan now? If they had pinned all of their hopes on the heir someday taking the throne, and now he is gone and hasn't left any children of his own…"

"I don't know," Erin shook her head. "I guess they'll have to figure something out. But maybe it will eliminate the dissatisfaction of Willie being 'promoted' over everyone else, and everything will settle down." She chewed and swallowed a bite of chocolate chip cookie. "I guess there is no more reason to hold Vic or any of the others… If the kidnapper was trying to leverage Willie, to make him step down… then he's achieved his goal."

Stayner looked sharply at Erin. She turned her eyes away, avoiding his gaze. Pretending that she didn't know the kidnapper was sitting right there talking to her. Would he release anyone? Or would he decide he had another reason to keep holding them? Or was it too late, and they had never been held at all, merely disposed of?

"If Willie is dead… all of this work…"

Erin finished with, "was a success," at the same time as Stayner said, "was for nothing."

She held her breath. She nibbled at the edge of the cookie, willing him to consider her words. He had what he wanted. Willie was out of the picture. He could just let everyone go, having achieved what he set out to do.

Of course, if any of them had seen Stayner's face or knew what he had done, his career as a law enforcement officer in Bald Eagle Falls—or anywhere—was over. No matter how he tried to explain that it had been for the greater good, a conviction, or even whispered rumors of kidnapping would be the end of everything he had worked for.

Maybe he should have thought about that before he had done what he had.

CHAPTER 49

*W*atching Stayner, Erin caught a movement in her peripheral vision. Something out the window. She reached for the plate of cookies, drawing Stayner's eye.

"You want another one?" she suggested.

He shook his head in irritation. "No. No more cookies. I need to know—"

"You don't like them?" Erin asked earnestly, blinking at him as if her eyes were welling with tears.

"Yes, they're delicious. They are always good. But I need to focus on—"

"Did you notice that there are two different kinds?" Erin asked, still holding the plate in front of him, leaning her face closer to it. "If you look really carefully, you can see that these ones are made with buckwheat flour," she pointed, "and these ones..." Erin pointed at one of the other cookies.

Despite himself, Stayner looked closely at the cookies that Erin was pointing at.

"You see the slight difference in color..."

The front door swung open with a resounding bang. Erin pushed the plate of cookies toward Stayner's face, making him strike out defensively to block it rather than reach for his gun and turn to see who was coming in the door. In a split second, Terry's hand was on Stayner's shoulder.

"Hold it right there, Rod," he said in a low, threatening voice. "Keep your hands up. Don't move."

"What is this?" Stayner protested, starting to lower his hands. Terry's hand tightened.

"I said to stay there and not move your hands."

"What do you think you're doing? I'm a cop! We've worked together for months! What is this?"

Sheriff Wilmot moved in from the back hall and Tom Baker trailed Terry into the house and held his service weapon pointed squarely at Stayner's chest. Erin moved back slowly. There were cookies all over the carpet. More vacuuming for Mrs. Peach.

"Mrs. Peach, is she okay?" she asked Wilmot since he was the one who had come from that direction.

"The old gal is just fine," Wilmot said, smiling. "She knew exactly what she was doing."

"You might think that I'm just a crazy old lady," Mrs. Peach told Stayner, coming slowly into the room with her walker, her movements much slower than the sheriff's. "People always underestimate old people. It's time you learned that not all of us seniors have old-timer's disease." She gave Erin a broad, toothy smile. "And do young people not know about extensions?"

"Hair extensions?" Erin teased.

"Phone extensions! I do have phones in other rooms, young man," she lectured Stayner. "You thought I was just a crazy old lady and wouldn't call the police." She shook her head. "Like I didn't know what was going on right in front of my own eyes!"

"We do appreciate it, ma'am," Terry told Mrs. Peach, smiling his approval. He took Stayner's gun and other equipment, and handed his handcuffs back to him. "Put those bracelets on."

Stayner obeyed, scowling. Once they were ratcheted shut, Terry bent down and also removed Stayner's ankle holster.

"You don't work with a guy for months without knowing he's got a throw-down."

Stayner started to rise from the couch, but Terry pushed him back down. He leaned toward Stayner, eye to eye, his expression stern.

"Where are Vic and the others?"

Stayner looked around at everyone watching him. "How would I know that? We've been investigating for days, but I don't—"

"I've been investigating while you've been blocking and misdirecting," Terry corrected. "It surprised me when Erin said you had been by to check on her and Vic the other night, but I thought it was just a nice gesture. One cop looking out for another cop's family. You hadn't reported that you were coming over, but you had already clocked out. A little off-duty protection for a fellow officer. I appreciated it, especially when Vic was kidnapped, but Erin was still safe. But you didn't need Erin; you needed someone to use as leverage against Willie."

Stayner sat back, eyeing Terry and not answering.

"Willie is gone," Terry told him. "Did Erin tell you? Killed by his own soldiers. Big coup. He should have seen it coming. He's been dealing with the infighting ever since he stepped in." Terry cleared his throat and avoided looking at Erin, as if he knew any eye contact would start her crying, and he knew she wouldn't want to break down in front of everyone else. "The man was always a thorn in my side, but I'm sorry it had to happen that way."

Stayner dropped his eyes and stared down at the carpet as if fascinated by it.

"If you want to be dealt with kindly by the courts, you'd better not let anything happen to those hostages," Wilmot told Stayner. "The first thing to do is ensure everybody is safe and well. If the authorities see that you have cooperated fully and that you never intended to hurt anyone with this scheme, you will be given more leniency."

"I was trying to stop the violence and killing," Stayner said, his jaw set. "I was trying to stop the feuding between the clans. It's been going on for generations, and I saw an opportunity to make a real difference. To disable them. To stop it and have the chance to wipe these organizations out. I don't know why law enforcement has let these activities go on for years. They should have gotten tough about it years ago. They could have stopped it."

Sheriff Wilmot nodded slowly. "It's not as easy as it sounds. You have to use a balanced approach. You don't need someone gunning for all of your law enforcement. Someone like Crazy Theresa gets it in her head to start taking out officers, and in a little place like this... then what do you think happens? No one else is going to step forward and volunteer to take their places. And you can't just go around arresting people without knowing that you'll be able to get convictions. Young pups like you always think you can just march in and clean up the town like some TV Western. But it's not that easy."

"Well, I don't think I did too badly," Stayner said. "I succeeded, didn't I?"

"Assassinating Willie was your doing? I don't think so. That would have happened with or without your interference."

"No one would have dared to do it if it wasn't for me. And Willie himself wouldn't have let it happen. I told him that if he wanted things to go back to normal in Bald Eagle Falls, he'd better throw himself on his sword. If he didn't... he would have to deal with the fallout."

"And you think Willie's death will make a difference? That this will change anything?"

"If the clan doesn't have a clear leader, it will break down. You can go in and arrest the others competing for the leadership, and they won't have any direction."

"We need *evidence* to make arrests. And the Jacksons will come in and take up whatever business the Dysons lose," Wilmot pointed out.

"That's when you have to put the pressure on the Jacksons, too," Stayner told him, his voice harsh. "Look, I shouldn't be the only one willing to step forward and deal with this. If you're afraid to do anything, and Moose River is afraid to do anything, you just end up with this feud that goes on and on."

"Right now, I want to see those Bald Eagle Falls citizens returned to their lives," Wilmot told him. "You think you're some kind of avenging angel? You can just come in and mess around with people's lives? Treat them like pawns in this game of yours? That isn't the way life works. You put yourself in that position, and you become one of them. An outlaw. A criminal."

"I never hurt anyone," Stayner assured him. "Those people are just fine. I wouldn't hurt any innocent people. Though..." he frowned, "I'm not sure we can refer to that Jackson girl as an innocent bystander. She was part of the organization. She breaks with the Jacksons to hook up with a Dyson and thinks it won't have any negative effects? The *leader* of the Dysons?"

"He wasn't at the time," Erin pointed out. "He made his break with them years ago. No one knew he would one day be called on as the heir of the family to act as its leader."

"*He* knew. And I'm sure she did, too."

"Well, she isn't going to cause any problems," Wilmot said reasonably. "That's all over. Willie is gone. There is no reason to hold Vic or anyone else."

Stayner scowled. "If he'd just quit and gone back to his life, he would have found them. It was his own stubbornness that kept them hidden."

"They're in one of his mines?" Erin guessed. "That's where I was going to start looking next."

"*You* were going to look in the mines?" Terry repeated in disbelief. He knew better than anyone how much Erin hated the mines and tunnels.

"Yes, I was," she told him firmly, looking him in the eye.

Terry shrugged and shook his head. "Okay. You were," he agreed.

"How did you figure it out?" Stayner demanded. "None of you showed any sign of suspecting what I had done."

All eyes turned toward Erin. She was embarrassed.

"Well, it wasn't me. I mean, it was just by luck, really. You lost a button. When you took Vic. She must have pulled it off in the struggle. I found it when I took Nilla back that night. I didn't realize at first. I thought Terry had lost it when he had gone in to check on Vic. But... he wasn't wearing a uniform when he went in there. He was wearing a T-shirt. He couldn't have lost his uniform button in there."

"That darn dog," Stayner griped. "Yeah, I know—*he doesn't like men.* No excuse for the stupid dog to come after me. There was no 'struggle.' Vic knew better than to fight with a gun on her."

"Nilla was protecting Vic," Erin pointed out. "That's not stupid. Just loyal."

"I wasn't even touching her. She dropped a piece of paper. Trying to leave you some kind of clue or message. I bent down to pick it up, and that dang dog comes after me, biting and scratching, launching himself at me like... one of those dogs that goes after badgers. Didn't have a clue what he was up against, the stupid thing."

Erin supposed they were lucky that Stayner hadn't shot Nilla.

"Which mine are they in? We have to get them now." Erin wiped at tears leaking out the corners of her eyes. "I don't want them to spend another night in a mine. Not another minute."

CHAPTER 50

*E*rin wanted to be the first one into the mine, but of course, the police would not allow that. There was no guarantee that Stayner had been working on his own; he might have guards or co-conspirators inside protecting the hostages.

Erin thought he might have been protecting her from herself as well, ensuring she didn't have to go inside. Instead, she was waiting outside while the police went in to retrieve the hostages. While Erin hated being on the outside, she also suspected that she did not want to see the conditions that the hostages had been held in.

Especially toileting arrangements. If there was a honey bucket in there, Erin would throw up, just as she had on the Alaskan cruise. Not very helpful in the midst of a rescue.

So she waited outside the entrance of the mine, trying to ignore flashbacks to when she had been left for dead in one of the tunnels, and when Vic and the others had been trapped by an explosion when treasure hunting.

Caves and mines were not good places. They just weren't.

They were not safe.

Stayner could have booby-trapped the place, rigged an explosion to collapse the entrance once everyone was inside. Erin could be in the same situation all over again—only this time, there was no police radio or cell phone to call for help. She would have to drive back to town for help.

Nilla wriggled in her arms and licked her face with his fast tongue, distracting her from the flashbacks. Erin wiped at the tears on her face and cuddled Nilla, waiting for disaster to fall.

"I'll bet you just can't wait to see your mommy," she told Nilla in a choked voice.

Nilla licked her again, whining and wriggling.

There was a noise from within the mine. Erin detected Terry's voice. Had they not found the hostages? Had Stayner not told them the correct location? He might have signaled someone that he had been caught by sending them to a monitored location instead of the actual holding site. Erin held her breath, hugging Nilla against her cheek.

Nilla started to bark and wriggle frantically, kicking out and scratching with powerful back legs, and Erin was forced to let him go to avoid having her arms shredded. The little white dog dashed toward the indistinct clump of people emerging from the mine.

Erin heard Vic's voice rise above the others and ran toward them. She wasn't as fast as Nilla and was trying to be careful not to trip over anything in the dark. They should have set up some bright lights instead of just using the headlights of the vehicles.

Vic had scooped Nilla up and was trying to calm down the wriggling, yipping mass of white fur. She saw Erin coming and held her other arm wide for a hug. In an instant, Erin found her place there, hugging Vic and an armful of Nilla to her, laughing with tears running down her face.

"Oh, Vicky! Oh, I've been so scared. I was so afraid of what might have happened to you!"

Vic returned the embrace, holding her tightly.

"It's okay, Erin. Everything is okay. I'm all right. We all are. It wasn't fun, but no one was hurt."

Erin tried to settle her sobs enough to talk clearly and looked at the rest of the group that Terry, Sheriff Wilmot, and Tom Banks had brought out of the mine.

"I'm so glad Nilla is okay," Vic laughed at the dog squirming in her arms. She kissed him on top of the head. "That stupid Stayner kept saying that if I didn't do what he said, or if'n I tried to escape or contact anyone, he would go back and kill him! He was so mad at Nilla that I was afraid he would even if I did everything he said."

Other townspeople were waiting behind Erin, there to provide medical support, food, transportation, and moral support. Whatever was needed. To begin with, Erin saw no one but Vic, her best friend, the person she had been most concerned about. Vic had been the most critical hostage, the one Stayner could be sure that Willie would do anything to protect.

Erin was finally able to pull herself back from Vic to look around, rubbing dog hair into her eyes as she tried to wipe away the tears. She saw Naomi smiling at her, and behind her, Mr. Foster, looking worn and worried. And... no one. Erin tried to blink her eyes clear and looked around the small group.

"But... what about Mary Lou? Where is she?"

Vic shook her head. "She wasn't here, Erin. I don't know... Stayner said he didn't know where she was; he didn't take her. I didn't know whether to believe him or not." She sniffled, trying to keep her composure. "Maybe he did take her, and something went wrong..."

Erin swallowed a couple of times, trying to keep the hot lump in her throat from growing so large that she couldn't breathe.

"Or maybe there's another mine," Vic suggested hoarsely.

Erin didn't say anything, and neither did the others. If something had gone wrong with the abduction of Mary Lou, Stayner would have disposed of the evidence. Maybe down an old well or mine shaft that would never be used again. He hadn't had time to dispose of Potter's body, but it had been several days since Mary Lou's abduction, and her remains had not been discovered.

They walked as a group across the clearing to reach the other waiting volunteers. People handed the hostages bottles of water and offered sandwiches and treats.

Vic looked around at the friendly faces, disappointment in her eyes. She saw Erin watching her.

"I guess... I was hoping he would be here. I know he can't get away from the clan whenever he wants to, but..."

No one had told her yet about Willie. Erin pulled Vic close, bumping their heads close together.

"Oh, Vic..." Her voice broke, and she didn't know how she was going to break it to her. The enormity of what had happened was overwhelming.

"What?" Vic's eyes welled with tears. "No! No, tell me what's happened!"

"I can't... we just got word tonight. I don't know what happened. But..."

"Tell me!" Vic insisted and turned away from Erin to Terry and Sheriff Wilmot. "What happened? Why isn't he here? What happened to Willie?"

Wilmot cleared his throat. "We don't yet have confirmation or any details," he warned. "But we were told that... he'd been killed."

"No!" The cry was torn out of Vic.

Erin looked at her haggard face, pale in the light of the moon and the car headlights, and started crying in earnest. If there was one thing she couldn't block out, it was someone else's pain.

"I'm so sorry," she choked out, squeezing Vic's narrow shoulders as they started to shake. "I'm so, so sorry..."

She didn't know what else to say. She didn't believe all of the platitudes. She didn't believe Willie was gone to a better place or that Vic would see him again.

She didn't believe in angels, ghosts, or spirits.

When life ended, it was over, and Vic would have to learn how to go on with her life without Willie.

Erin would be there for her, would do everything she could to comfort and help her friend, but she knew they would never see Willie again, in this life or another.

CHAPTER 51

$\mathcal{T}$he return home was a blur. Erin wasn't sure of any of the details later, even who she had traveled back with. She had not let herself be separated from Vic, and Vic didn't let go of Nilla. They were a package deal.

Erin's living room was crowded at first. She wanted to hear what had happened to everyone, but their words went right over her head. She stared at their dirt-smudged faces, at Vic's pain-filled eyes, and she couldn't comprehend anything else.

Naomi and Mr. Foster left with Sheriff Wilmot. They would tell him their stories and return to their own families. The helpful townspeople were sent on their way, Terry telling them that Vic needed space and that they would be able to talk and give their condolences later.

Erin caught a glimpse of Campbell Cox's face in one group of onlookers, etched with pain and worry. She wanted to talk to him but had nothing to tell him. No idea of what had happened to Mary Lou, why she wasn't with the others, and whether he would ever get her back. It made no sense. She should have been there with the others.

The house went quiet. It was just Vic's muffled sobs and Erin's sniffles as she held Vic and tried to control her own emotions and be strong for her best friend.

There was a knock on the door. Not the front, but the back. Erin expected a steady stream of visitors to the front door, even though they had sent everyone away. In the morning and throughout the day, they would bring their casseroles and condolences.

Terry stood up and went quietly to the back door to see who it was.

"Erin," he said, calling her attention to him. "Erin."

Erin pulled her attention away from Vic with great effort, getting up and walking to where she had a view of the back door. There, she saw a woman in camo pants and a bulky green jacket, hair in a ponytail, and strong jaws constantly chewing gum.

"Beaver!" Erin was surprised to see the federal agent there. And yet, not surprised, because Beaver did show up at the most unexpected times and places and often knew details of a case the Bald Eagle Falls police were working on before the police did.

Beaver stepped into the kitchen, and behind her was a shorter, older woman. Erin's mouth dropped open at the sight of the gray bob and neat pantsuit. Mary Lou smoothed her suit nervously, venturing an uncertain smile.

"Mary Lou! Where did you come from? Oh, I'm so glad you're safe!"

Despite the fact that Mary Lou was reserved and not very demonstrative, Erin flew to her and gave her a warm, welcoming hug. She was solid and real. In the face of the loss of Willie, Mary Lou's safety was even more poignant.

"Oh! Do the boys know you're safe? I saw Cam earlier, and he was really upset that we didn't find you with Vic and the others."

Erin let go of Mary Lou, shaking her head in amazement. "Where were you? Here we thought everyone had been taken by the same person, but Charley wasn't, and you..." She looked at Mary Lou and Beaver, trying to discern what had happened.

What was the story?

"You were closest," Beaver told Erin. "Geographically speaking. So we thought we would stop here first."

"What happened? How did you find her?" Erin looked at Mary Lou, trying to take in every clue. "Are you okay? You look better than the others." Erin glanced back toward Vic, still sitting in the living room out of sight. She hadn't yet showered, changed, or eaten any food the volunteers had handed out after the rescue.

"I'm just fine," Mary Lou confirmed, looking uncomfortable with all the attention.

"I didn't need to find her," Beaver said, chewing her gum. "I knew where she was all along."

"You knew? How could you know and not tell her family? They've been going crazy trying to find out what happened to her!"

Mary Lou hung her head, looking down at the floor. Erin couldn't understand her attitude. She should have been relieved and excited to return to her family, but she seemed guilty and ashamed. Not like Mary Lou at all. Mary Lou always did the right thing and held her head high. Even when she was beaten down by life's circumstances, she still had her pride. She did the right thing, and she knew it.

"I knew where she was because I was the one who took her," Beaver told Erin with amusement in her eyes.

"What?"

"It sounds like this may be a long story," Terry suggested. "Why don't you come set for a spell. Erin, do you want me to put the kettle on?"

Erin nodded. "Yes, would you? This is unbelievable."

She led Beaver and Mary Lou into the living room. Vic, eyes swollen and face red and blotchy, looked at the two of them in surprise. She wiped her nose. "Mary Lou? You're okay?"

Like Erin, she had nearly given up on Mary Lou being found alive.

They all sat down while Terry started preparing tea in the kitchen. Nilla was cuddled on Vic's lap, and K9 lay on the floor. Because of the presence of the dogs, Orange Blossom was not in sight, probably pouting on the bed in Erin's bedroom.

"*You* had Mary Lou?" Erin asked Beaver. "Why? I don't understand."

"It was clear to me that with Willie Andrews in the position he was, the people closest to him needed to be protected. I had a couple of agents watching Vic because I assumed that was where Willie's enemies would go first."

That had clearly not worked. What had happened to those agents? Erin hadn't even realized any agents had been watching the house. They must have been hiding in the woods, hoping to cut off any approaches.

But she couldn't wrap her mind around why Beaver would think that Mary Lou was a potential victim to those who, like Stayner, were intent on forcing Willie to do what they wanted. She had rarely known Mary Lou to say a kind word toward Willie. She had thanked him politely when he had been instrumental in helping to find Roger when he had wandered off. But she had told her sons to stay away from him, and Erin thought it was clear that she subscribed to the opinion of most of the church ladies that Willie was lazy and shiftless, was taking advantage of Vic's youth, and many of the other things that had been said about him, including the assumption that he had been working with the Dysons when he had not.

Mary Lou could see the confusion in Erin's face and sighed, looking at Beaver and then back at Erin and Vic.

"Willie and I... have a history," she admitted.

"Oh, is that so?" Erin questioned with a laugh that came out unexpectedly. She hadn't intended to laugh when they were talking about the man they were mourning. She quickly composed her expression. But she couldn't help being excited to learn of a secret relationship between Mary Lou and Willie. "Exactly what history do you have?"

Mary Lou looked at Vic, blushing.

"We were both young and foolish," she explained. "Things could never have worked out between us, and I left any thoughts of Willie Andrews behind many years ago."

Vic blew her nose. "It isn't like it matters. It wouldn't have mattered to me anyway. That was before I was even born."

"You already knew?" Erin demanded.

"No. But Cam is about my age, and assuming he is Roger's, Mary Lou 'left any thoughts of Willie behind' before they got married, so…"

"Oh." Erin followed the logic and nodded. "Yeah, I guess so. You guys were an item…" Erin prompted Mary Lou, "back before he did his time with the Dyson clan?"

Mary Lou took a deep breath in and let it out slowly. "At the beginning of his time with them. He said he just needed the money. I was foolish enough to believe he could serve those five years without getting into anything too serious. But then I started to see how it was changing him. And I knew I couldn't stay with him. He couldn't be that close to the Dysons without it changing him… and neither could I. And I wasn't okay with letting that influence into my life."

It was no wonder she believed that having once been in the clan, he could never truly leave its influence behind. And why she would not want her boys to have anything to do with him.

Vic wiped at her tears. They were still flowing freely.

Erin's heart ached for Vic. She remembered Willie's words.

You don't think that I would do anything for Vic?

How would Vic go on without him? Erin knew that it happened. People, even those who had been deeply in love, lost their spouses and remarried and went on to have happy lives. Vic could fall in love again, could find someone else who would accept her for who she was. It had been hard for her and Willie to work things out between them—their roles, their pasts, all the things that could make or break a relationship.

"And how did you know about this?" Vic asked Beaver. "How could you know something that happened twenty years ago that neither told anyone about?"

Beaver looked at Mary Lou. "There were signs. I'm pretty good at reading people. I'd talked to both of them privately a time or two. Things are revealed." She shrugged. "When I saw the writing on the wall with the clan and all of the dissension and talk of insurrection, I knew Vic and Mary Lou needed to be protected."

"But you didn't protect Vic," Erin pointed out resentfully, "You just let her be taken."

"Well… in my defense, I had a couple of agents on her house, and I did *not* expect law enforcement to swoop in and scoop her up. I was expecting action from the Dysons or Jacksons, not Stayner."

Terry brought in a tea tray and put it down. Erin did not feel like tea, but Vic probably needed it, and it was something to keep her hands busy until they stopped shaking. She busied herself with pouring hot water over leaves until everyone had been served. She sipped her tea without tasting it. Usually, she enjoyed detecting all the ingredients in the herbal tea mixtures, but today, she took no pleasure in it.

"What happened to the agents?" she asked Beaver. "They told you that a cop had taken Vic away, and you sent them home?"

Beaver shook her head. Despite her usual casual, carefree demeanor, Erin thought she could see the anger bubbling. "I haven't found them. Since they were not in that mine with the others… I can only assume he disposed of them some other way. And that he will never talk because that would get him the death penalty."

Erin swallowed, sorry she had accused Beaver so quickly. "Maybe he stashed them in another mine."

"You can rest assured that we will be checking every one we can. But there are a lot of mines and tunnels around here, as you know, and if we don't find them quickly and Stayner doesn't talk…" She clenched her jaw tightly before she started chewing her gum again. "That'll be a black mark against my name forever."

Erin envisioned Stayner checking on her, then scouting out the backyard and the woods, and spotting the federal agents watching Vic's apartment. How would they know that the uniformed cop who approached them with an outstretched hand would not blanch at killing a couple of federal agents to kidnap the girlfriend of a crime boss they were guarding?

Maybe he hadn't known at the time that they were federal agents and had thought them members of one of the clans, not discovering his mistake until it was too late. He wouldn't have had a lot of time to kidnap Vic and to take care of a couple of bodies before being called in the morning and pretending he knew nothing about it. He hadn't managed to dispose of Potter's body. But it would have been more vital to dispose of the agents.

"I can't believe it was Stayner," Erin said, shaking her head. "I never liked the guy, but I thought he was a true-blue cop and would enforce the law to his dying breath. He always acted so... righteous."

Beaver nodded, her gaze hooded. "People are not always what they appear to be."

CHAPTER 52

*E*rin's phone buzzed in her pocket. She ignored it at first, but it kept vibrating, and eventually, she pulled it out of her pocket, irritated.

She realized belatedly that the cell tower must be back up again. Maybe the buzzing was all the messages left while the network was down being delivered to her phone.

There was a number on the screen. A phone call from a number she did not know.

But it was not a good time. People needed to exercise some common sense about when to call.

She sent it to voicemail.

In a moment, it vibrated again. She looked down at it as a text message appeared briefly on a banner at the top of the screen.

Erin answer your phone

She mentally cursed the person who continued to harass her even after he should clearly have understood she was not taking any calls.

"Something wrong?" Terry asked.

Erin tried to compose her face. Obviously, she was showing everyone in the room her feelings about the irritating caller.

"Sorry. I just don't know why someone would be so persistent at a time like this."

"Maybe they don't know," Vic pointed out, rubbing tears from her cheeks with the heels of her hands. Already, her nose and the skin around her eyes looked completely raw. Erin wanted to gently put cream on them and give Vic a reassuring hug. And tell her what? That she could find someone else? That the pain would pass?

Erin sighed. She thumbed a message back to the caller.

not a good time

send Vicky to loft

Erin blinked at this message and tried to make sense of it. Who would want Vic to go back to her apartment? Someone who knew she had been rescued from Stayner and hoped to get his hands on her himself? But anyone who had heard of the rescue must also have heard the news of Willie's death.

"What is it?" Vic asked, looking at Erin's grimace.

Frowning, Erin turned the phone so that Vic could see the message. Her brain tried to analyze the words in the message. No one referred to Vic as Vicky but a few intimate friends, and even then, only at the closest moments.

Vic looked at the screen and then back at Erin's face.

"Could it be...?" she started, then shook her head, looking away with a scowl. "No. But..."

She pushed herself to her feet.

"No," Erin warned. "Be careful! It could be—"

Vic was running to the back door. Beaver was on her feet in a flash, hot on her heels. Terry was a bit slower, a few feet behind, his hand grasping his gun and pulling it from the holster before he was out the back door.

Erin felt like an old woman trailing behind them, her brain still trying to make sense of it all. Only Mary Lou was behind her, and she didn't seem inclined to leave the house to find out what was going on. Maybe Erin was too eager to run toward trouble. But she just wanted to help Vic. If it was a trap...

Vic was up the stairs to the loft and wrenching open the door. Beaver, right behind her, had produced a gun from somewhere.

Terry was still half the long flight of stairs behind them. Erin pounded up after everyone was gone, already in the apartment. At least if it was dangerous, the people with weapons had beaten her there.

Erin ran in, puffing embarrassingly hard. Terry and Beaver were standing back, their weapons held down at their sides rather than at a suspect, and they parted slightly so Erin could see past them.

Vic, sobbing, clasped in the arms of… Willie. Erin gasped.

"What?"

Willie looked across the room at her, patting Vic on the back, and raised his brows.

"What?" he asked innocently, "You believe everything you hear? I told you, 'Whatever it takes.'"

The rest of his words came back to her. "Just trust me. No matter what you see or hear about me… trust that I will find a way."

"You're okay? You're not hurt? You're not…"

"Not dead," Willie agreed. "But don't spread that around. You haven't seen me. This has to stay under wraps until I tell you. You breathe a word of it, and you could wreck everything."

Erin looked at Terry. "You said he was dead."

"Melissa said he was dead," he corrected.

"Melissa said Jack Ward said he was dead," Erin remembered.

"It wasn't Jack Ward," Willie said. "It was… somebody who sounded reasonably like Jack Ward. Who happens to be away from the office right now, unreachable."

"And how did you engineer the communications outage?" Erin demanded.

"That wasn't me. That was just… serendipitous."

"It was Stayner," Terry said. "He sabotaged the systems. Not to help Willie." He shook his head. "To give himself cover. So that no one could say where he was—or wasn't—during the blackout."

"And he came after me," Erin stated.

"You were one of his targets, anyway. I can't say if he had any others. But he definitely wanted to put a stop to your investigation." Terry considered this for a moment. "He's never been

289

thrilled about how you stick your nose into some of our investi-gations."

"I don't stick my nose in," Erin protested. "In fact, I try to stay as far away from your investigations as possible."

"Yeah," Terry agreed. "That's the scary part," he said with a chuckle.

Erin looked back at Willie.

Not dead.

Willie was not dead.

"I can't believe you're okay. And that everyone was convinced that you were dead."

"They have to stay convinced," Willie said firmly, as if Erin might not have understood the first time. "You can't say anything to make people think it is a lie."

"So that's how you decided to get out of leading the clan? By faking your own death? What are you going to do, go into hiding for the rest of your life?" A terrible thought struck Erin. "You can't leave here! You can't!"

She couldn't stand to lose Vic. Vic was the one person who had fully accepted her when she had come to Bald Eagle Falls, who had been there for her the whole time and never been judgmental or negative toward her. Of course, there were other people who had been carefully supportive. And Terry. But she'd never had a best friend like Vic and couldn't stand the idea of losing her.

"We're not going to go into hiding permanently," Willie reas-sured her. "We're going to allow the clan to operate without me for a little while. Let them figure out how they are going to manage the leadership of the clan if I'm not there. Then, when they find out that I'm not really dead, they won't care. They'll have the stable leadership they need and won't *want* an heir to the throne hanging around."

CHAPTER 53

"How did you do it?" Vic asked, pulling back from Willie after wiping her damp face and nose on his shirt. Willie wrinkled his nose. "How did you convince them you had been killed?"

"Hold that thought. Sit down. Everybody sit down." When Vic sat down in the small living room area, he tossed a tissue box onto her lap. He disappeared into the bedroom and came out a minute later, buttoning up a clean shirt.

"I had help. We staged an assassination. Filmed it. Started it circulating. It didn't take any time at all to go viral to the entire clan. Nelson will take over. Once he's been in for a few days or a couple of weeks, they'll get used to the idea, and they won't want me back when they figure out it was all a scam."

"But you were this long-hoped-for leader of the clan that is supposed to make everything right," Erin protested, "You're Hannah's promised heir and all of that. You kept saying how hard it was to get out of it once you had accepted the leadership because you were the only one who could actually take the position, and there was no one else if you wanted out."

"So I had to create an heir," Willie explained. He gave Vic an apologetic look, holding up his hand to forestall any protest. "*Not a* blood heir," he told her. "Not another descendant in Hannah's bloodline. I don't want to subject anyone else to that. A legal heir." He looked around at them. "I wrote a will."

"You wrote a will?" Vic looked at him. "That's all it took? You just wrote a will, and everything is hunky-dory?"

"Finer than a frog's hair," Willie teased. "It is very important to get all of your affairs in order. But I didn't just have to write a will. I had to write a will *and die.*"

"So they would look at your will to see who your heir is and appoint him?" Erin asked. "And that was Nelson?"

"Bingo," Willie agreed. "And now we just wait until he is well-entrenched. Then I can exist again, and no one will want me back."

"Mona never did like you," Erin observed.

Willie shook his head, blowing his breath out noisily. "No, she did not," he agreed. "That woman did not like me and did not like anything I did. She and Nelson get along much better. She'll be happy with the succession." He sat down on the arm of the couch beside Vic. "The matriarchal line will like it because I was Hannah's heir, and Nelson is my heir, so the line goes on. Those who approved of Dwight as the figurehead will be happy because Nelson is Dwight's son. And Nelson's network will be happy because that is who they have wanted for years. All three factions will be united, instead of splintered and working against each other."

"Which is great for the clan," Terry said dourly, "not so great for law enforcement."

"Despite what certain officers in the police force think about it being a good idea to break apart the leadership of the clan, Officer Piper," Willie said, glaring at Terry, "a stable clan leadership and balance between the Dysons and Jacksons is better for law enforcement. There will be less violent crime, and things will run much more smoothly without unnecessary civilian casualties."

"Don't think that any of us approve of what Rod Stayner did," Terry warned.

Willie nodded. "I don't," he agreed. "I trust *my* law enforcement officers to uphold the law."

Beaver chuckled. "Well. At any rate, I'm glad to have you home to look after *this* one," she told Willie with a nod at Vic. "She is not particularly cooperative about matters relating to her own safety and security."

Willie looked at Vic affectionately. "Have you been causing Agent Beaven trouble?"

"Talk about hassle!" Beaver exclaimed. "Doesn't want anyone looking in on her. She's fine all by herself. Doesn't care what threats there might be on her personal safety. She's fully capable of looking after herself."

Vic leaned against Willie, her eyes closed. "Okay, maybe I wasn't as capable as I thought," she admitted. "A cop pulling a gun on me was not something I anticipated. And don't expect me to camp in any mines in the near future. Let's go somewhere else on vacation. Florida or Hawaii."

"You think he's actually going to be able to keep quiet and stay under the radar?" Erin asked. "I've seen Willie try to 'rest' before, and… it's not even restful to *watch* him."

Willie sighed. "I'm ready for a break. You have no idea what running an organization like that—or trying to run one—entails. I plan on lots of sleeping in and cultivating an interest in afternoon soaps."

"You'll never do it," Erin predicted.

"Maybe not, but I'm going to have fun trying."

CHAPTER 54

$\mathcal{E}$rin looked back toward her house, remembering Mary Lou.

"So, can Mary Lou go back to her family now?" she asked Beaver. "It's safe?"

Beaver nodded. "That's why I brought her back. I think… she's a little anxious about how she will be received. Having to leave her family that way, with no explanation about what was going on… that was hard for her."

"I would think so!" Erin agreed. "At least she knew that Cam was there to help Josh with Roger, but—" Erin stopped suddenly and looked at Beaver. "Was that the plan, then, that you would leave Cam there to help and take Mary Lou? That was all planned out?"

Beaver shrugged. "I'll leave you to draw what conclusions you will."

"But you knew you were going to take Mary Lou. And Cam didn't."

"I couldn't tell Cam anything. He would not have reacted naturally."

"You let him think that his mother had just walked off or was kidnapped."

"I couldn't tell him where she was. No one could know. It wouldn't have been safe for her."

"That's harsh. I can't believe you could do that to him."

"I wasn't doing it *to* Cam. I was doing it *for* him. And for the rest of his family. How would they have felt if she *was* kidnapped by violent criminals who tortured her to get Willie to do what they wanted him to?"

"Still. That's really... mean."

Beaver shrugged. "My goal wasn't to keep everyone happy. It was to keep them safe."

"Let's take her home."

"You're coming?" Beaver smiled and cracked her gum.

"Yeah, of course I am. You said she was nervous about going back. But I know how her family is going to react. I saw Cam just a couple of hours ago and his face when his mom wasn't in that mine with the others. They need her, and she needs them. Let's take her home."

Beaver gave a nod. She looked at Terry. "You mind me taking them? I'll see that Erin gets home safely."

"With things being resolved with the clans, I'm not nearly as worried about it," Terry admitted. "I'm sure she'll be fine."

Erin and Beaver returned to the house, where Mary Lou was standing in the kitchen drinking her tea and watching out the window to the back yard. Making sure that everything was okay but not comfortable being part of whatever was going on.

"Is he back?" she asked flatly. "He's not really dead?"

"It was a fake," Erin agreed. "We can't tell anyone yet. The clan needs to establish their new leadership before they can find out Willie isn't really dead."

Mary Lou nodded, expressionless. "I won't have anything to say about it."

"Let's get you home," Beaver invited. "Your family needs you."

"Do they?" Mary Lou asked faintly. "Maybe they would be better off without me. What if instead of me trying to control everything and make sure that everyone was doing what they were supposed to, they could just do what they want to?"

"They love you," Erin protested. "Without you... I don't think Roger would be able to be home. And the boys couldn't afford the house."

"But maybe I am holding them back. Maybe it would be better for them if Roger was in a home and they didn't have to worry about the house. Cam has already found a way to live without us. It wouldn't take Joshua long. He has friends who would help him. He would probably flourish, given the opportunity."

"No," Erin told her firmly. "Joshua needs you. If he doesn't have someone to help him and keep him in school, he won't get that job he wants as a reporter. He won't have any safety net and won't have the money to live on to get started. Because he won't earn a steady income to start with, you know."

"No," Mary Lou agreed. "He won't."

"Joshua needs you. And Roger needs you. You might think that Campbell doesn't need you. Cam might think that he doesn't. But he does. I've watched him while you've been away. He needs you, Mary Lou. Even if he doesn't live with you and only makes contact or comes around occasionally, he still needs that stability. He needs somewhere to come home to. And to have a mom and dad and brother there. That's what he lives for, you know."

"Does he?"

Erin nodded. "Come on. You're not going to believe it until you see it for yourself. Let's take my car."

"Are you okay to drive?" Beaver asked. "You were pretty shaky earlier."

"I'm good," Erin told her. "I want to take her. Let's do it."

Erin's heart beat hard in anticipation. She knew that despite Mary Lou's misgivings, her family was desperately hoping for her safe return, and they would not be better off without her guiding hand. Those boys had been without her for long enough. They needed her back.

She pulled to the curb in front of the house and waited for Mary Lou to climb out of her seat and prepare herself to approach the house. Beaver, as smooth and silent as a shadow, slipped out of her seat and waited.

"It's going to be okay," Erin assured Mary Lou. She wanted to take the older woman by the hand or arm and lead her up to the house, but knew that Mary Lou would not want to be touched, so she followed close behind, letting Mary Lou take the lead.

She was wondering what they would do when they got to the door. Would Mary Lou go straight in? Would she ring the doorbell or knock on the door, uncertain about how she would be received. Would she open the door and "yoo-hoo" like she was a neighbor? Or would she just stand there, frozen, unsure what to do?

As it turned out, there was no need to worry about such things. They did not reach the door before it opened, and Cam stood framed in the open doorway, looking out at them.

He stared for a moment, then moved forward.

"Mom!" He hurried to her and grabbed her in a bear hug. "I can't believe it, Mom!" He lifted her off her feet and whirled her around until, laughing, Mary Lou begged to be put down.

Cam set her gently back down. He had a huge grin, but tears ran down his cheeks. He wiped at tears on Mary Lou's face, laughing.

"Come on, come on," he encouraged, pulling her to the door and into the house.

Erin stood outside on the sidewalk for a moment, both she and Beaver holding back, wondering whether they should intrude on the little family reunion, but Cam looked back over his shoulder almost immediately.

"Come on, Miss Erin, Beaver, I want to see everyone."

They followed eagerly. Erin, at least, wanted to see everything and take part in the joy of Mary Lou's reunion. They entered on Mary Lou's heels. In a moment, Joshua looked down from the top of the stairs. His face lit up. Eyes wide, he thundered down the stairs so quickly Erin was afraid he would trip and go flying.

Joshua immediately enveloped Mary Lou in his arms. He hugged her tightly and kissed the top of her head. "Mom! Oh, Mom! I was so scared!"

Mary Lou hugged him back, though she couldn't seem to find

the right words to respond to him. He patted her on the back and didn't seem inclined to let her go anytime soon.

"What is it? What's going on?" Erin heard Roger's voice from upstairs. In a moment, he, too, came to the top of the stairs and looked down at them.

He stood with both hands braced on the railing, looking down. Erin suddenly feared that he would either faint or vault over it, unwilling to wait the time it would take to walk down the stairs. But he stood there, staring down.

"Mary Lou? Where have you *been*?" His voice was choked with emotion. He might be limited by his brain injury and the medications he was on to control his behavior, but he knew his wife, and he knew that she had been gone from his life for the past week.

Mary Lou wriggled from Joshua's grasp to go up to Roger, but he turned and started to descend the stairs to come to her. He kept one hand on the rail to steady himself and did not rush down, so Erin's fears that he would injure himself reaching her were allayed.

When he reached the bottom of the stairs, Roger looked at his wife and took her face gently in both hands, staring down into it. The room was nearly silent, a clock on the mantle ticking away the seconds as Mary Lou and Roger gazed into each other's eyes. All of the years and challenges fell away, and they drank in each other's faces like two young lovers, shy and eager and full of promise.

"There's casserole in the fridge," Roger said finally.

Everyone laughed.

"And those onion rolls you like. You should eat," Roger insisted, "You're too thin."

Mary Lou had, Erin thought, lost weight during her time away. Beaver might not have imprisoned Mary Lou in a mine, and in fact, had probably given her everything she could possibly want or need, but worry and being away from her family had worn on her. Features that had been round and soft were now spare, her eyes hollowed out.

"We should all eat," Josh announced, moving into the kitchen and opening the fridge.

Throughout the ordeal, none of them had felt much like eating despite all the food brought in by friends and neighbors. Now that Mary Lou was back, they could let loose and celebrate. There was no need to order pizza or other dishes from the restaurants. They had everything they needed close at hand.

Mary Lou's head swiveled between Josh and Cam. She looked guilt stricken. She held one hand out to Cam, the other toward Josh as if to stop him.

"Boys, I have to…"

"No," Campbell told her, taking her hand and drawing her in for a hug. "It's okay. We're just glad you're safe. You can't imagine everything we were worried might have happened." He looked over her to Beaver. "Thank you for keeping her safe."

He had apparently understood more than Erin had expected. Maybe it had fallen into place when he saw Beaver bringing Mary Lou back. Maybe he had suspected something before then. Maybe he had started to wonder why Beaver had brought him back to Bald Eagle Falls for a visit the day before his mother disappeared.

Mary Lou looked like she wanted to say more, but he squeezed her again and led her to the table.

"There's so much here. What can you eat? We need to fatten you up."

"I certainly don't need to put on any weight," Mary Lou insisted, smoothing her pantsuit over her hips.

"You must have lost ten pounds," Cam insisted. "Come on. There's no diet tonight."

Erin watched them welcome and nurture Mary Lou, pulling her back into her place in the family. She swallowed a lump in her throat. But this time, it was a good feeling. Not grief and loss, but love and homecoming.

"Come on," Beaver told Erin, chewing her gum and stepping toward the others, "let's get in on this."

CHAPTER 55

"Taste test time!" Bella sang out. She sank the knife into the tender golden crust of the mock apple pie and neatly sliced it into narrow wedges. The warm, welcoming scent of cinnamon mingled with hints of buttery crust.

"Does it really taste like apples?" Harold questioned doubtfully. He took the plate Charley handed him and used his fork to tease away the lattice top and examine the filling. "It *looks* like apples. You didn't use crackers for this, did you?"

Erin shook her head. "Not for this one, no. Like you said, gluten-free crackers just aren't the same as Ritz crackers, and I didn't want to make crackers from scratch just to soak them and cook them in a pie! So I went with another method of making mock apple pie that I found in an old recipe book."

"That's got to be apples," Harold said, examining the filling closely. "Did you just do something like using pears, because they're so close? But they're more expensive than apples, so there's no real advantage to using them in a mock apple pie…"

"No," Erin agreed. "The essence of the mock apple pie lies in using more affordable ingredients that are readily available, either because they are local or shelf-stable. Not everyone has access to apples unless they've been shipped across the country."

She looked around at her taste testers.

"Try it!"

Everyone obediently dug their forks into the pie and took a bite. They chewed thoughtfully and looked at each other. Erin swallowed her bite. She had made the pie and still had difficulty believing it wasn't real apples.

Everyone exchanged glances and nodded. "You're sure that ain't apples?" Harold asked, shaking his head. "You've got to be kidding me!"

"Not apples," Erin confirmed.

"And not pears?"

"Not pears." Erin took another bite. "Sometimes, things are not what they seem!"

"Okay." Bella leaned forward. "What is it, then? You have to tell us now! What's in the filling?"

Erin grinned. "It's zucchini."

Everyone's mouths dropped open.

"Zucchini?" Charley demanded.

Erin nodded, taking another bite. "The most delicious zucchini you ever ate," she said with satisfaction. "Just don't tell anyone the secret!"

Did you enjoy this book? Reviews and recommendations are vital to making a book successful.

Please leave a review at your favorite book store or review site and share it with your friends.

Don't miss the following bonus material:
Sign up for mailing list to get a free ebook
Read a sneak preview chapter
Other books by P.D. Workman
Learn more about the author

Your First Bite – Cozy Mystery Starter Pack

Get Your First Taste of Murder and Muffins at pdworkman.com! Start your cozy escape with a free ebook + audiobook, printable recipe cards, and more.

PREVIEW OF CHOCOLATE ECLAIRVOYANT

In the picturesque town of Bald Eagle Falls, Erin Price runs Auntie Clem's Bakery, where gluten-free delights and charming community vibes create the perfect recipe for happiness. But when a series of puzzling predictions are delivered to the bakery, a chill falls over the town and Erin Price finds herself caught in a web of intrigue and suspense. As whispers of clairvoyance swirl around town like flour in the air, apprehension brews among the locals. With teenage Harold Melville—a new bakery employee tied to an organized crime family—in hot water, Erin, her Officer Handsome, and best friend Vic are determined to uncover the truth.

Join Erin and her friends, as she once again finds herself piecing together clues, sifting through secrets, and trying to prevent a recipe for disaster from unfolding.

PREVIEW CHAPTER 1

$\mathscr{H}$arold watched Erin take the tray of eclairs out of the oven. The tops were golden brown and they had puffed out perfectly. Erin handled the tray gently, hoping they wouldn't collapse the instant she put them down or they started to cool. She was hopeful that she had the balance of ingredients right this time and that they would hold their shape so she could fill and glaze them without making a big mess.

The results were always delicious, even if they didn't look good, but she wanted them to look good. She wanted the gluten-free eclairs to be practically indistinguishable from the traditional eclairs made by the pastry chefs in French patisseries for generations.

She knew how it should work in theory, the way that the moisture content of the choux should make the pastries puff up. And the first few attempts had puffed, but they had not stayed that way for long.

"Do you think it will work?" Harold asked eagerly. "They look great!"

"Fingers crossed," Erin told him. She hoped that if she cooled them slowly, they would have the chance to "set" before the pastry cooled too much and they would maintain their shape.

"At least we know they'll taste good!" Vic, Erin's young baking assistant contributed, as she placed spoonfuls of cookie dough on a baking sheet on the adjacent counter in the kitchen of Auntie Clem's Bakery.

"Yeah," Harold agreed. "I almost hope they don't work because the failures taste so good."

"You're not going to be able to keep up with the failures," Erin said. "Even if you share them with your family and fill your freezer!"

"I can try," Harold declared, thrusting out his stomach and patting it. He had the long, lanky frame of an adolescent, and being a celiac, he was on the skinny side to begin with. At least with Erin moving into Bald Eagle Falls and opening Auntie Clem's Bakery, a bakery devoted exclusively to gluten-free baking, he now had a wide variety of delicious baked goods to choose from.

Before Auntie Clem's, there hadn't been many gluten-free options for celiacs in the county. A few prepackaged breads and cookies on the grocery store shelves. One or two stores in the city that brought in a wider variety of goods at shockingly high prices. Or else what mothers could make at home. Modern moms were busy with a lot of outside commitments. They couldn't all spend time slaving over the oven, trying to learn the baffling array of new ingredients and techniques necessary to master gluten-free baking. Especially if their kids also had to be dairy-free or had other allergens, which, luckily, Harold did not.

"How did the custard taste?" Erin asked, going over to the fridge to ensure it was ready for her once the eclairs had completely cooled.

Harold grinned. "What makes you think I tasted it?"

Erin and Vic both laughed. "Because you always taste it," Erin chuckled. She pushed a few locks of dark hair that had escaped her bobby pins back into place and washed her hands. Her hair was too short to keep pulled back into a sleek ponytail like Vic's fine blond hair, and she suspected that even if it were long enough, it would still refuse to stay corralled by the elastic.

At the jingle of bells from the front of the bakery, Erin and Vic both left the kitchen to enter the storefront area and serve their next customer. Vic stood behind the till and Erin behind the display case, ready for the next sale.

But instead of a customer, it was Frank Grayson, delivering the day's mail.

"Oh, hi, Frank," Erin greeted, giving him a warm smile. "How's it going?"

"A real pretty day out there," Frank told her, using his forearm to wipe a bead of sweat that trickled down from his temple. "Perfect day for a picnic."

He handed over a thick wad of mail, wrapped neatly with a couple of elastics.

"Couple new catalogs in there," he observed, knowing how Erin loved to pore over the baking supplies and equipment catalogs to see what she could pick up for a good price, drooling over the more expensive equipment she could not afford, and fantasizing about how it could transform the bakery.

"Thank you!"

"Y'all have a nice day," he told them, and turned to continue to the next store on his route, the Book Nook. He allowed a group of women to enter the bakery, nodding and holding the door open like a gentleman before going on.

Erin nodded to the group, including Mrs. Peach, her next-door neighbor, and Betty Thompson, two seniors who used walkers. Edna, a woman who worked at the library with Betty, was with them, as well as a couple of younger women Erin didn't know well but who occasionally came for the ladies' tea on Sunday.

"We are going to take a few minutes," Betty warned. Erin knew it was true. Betty always took a long time to look over the offerings in the display case, ask her questions about the ingredients or how they were prepared, and finally decide what to buy.

The other women might make their choices faster, but they would wait for Betty to figure out what she wanted first. There was a sort of "order of seniority" that the customers followed. Erin didn't always follow what gave one person priority over another, she just went with the flow.

Erin took the elastic bands off of the mail and shuffled through it quickly, handing a couple of note cards over to Vic. There had been a lot more mail since word of Willie's death had gotten out. A lot of condolence cards, flower deliveries, casseroles, and a myriad of other sympathies expressed with small-town charm. For once, people seemed to have put aside their judgments about Vic being transgender and were just treating her as they would any other woman.

What was left was primarily bills, flyers, and catalogs. Erin turned to take them to her office to review later. Vic flapped one of the cards at her. "This one is addressed to you."

Erin took it back and looked at it. She had just assumed all the personal notes and cards would be for Vic and hadn't looked at the addressee name. But her name was neatly written on the envelope.

"Oh, sorry. I didn't even notice." Curious, she slid her thumb under the corner of the flap to tear it open.

She unfolded the crisp stationery and looked at the sentences penned inside with a frown.

"What does it say?" Vic asked, reading something in Erin's expression.

Erin read the words aloud slowly as if saying them precisely would make them make sense.

A recipe long forgotten stirs trouble anew— Vengeance and blood will soon ensue. Tread carefully, I see danger brew!

PREVIEW CHAPTER 2

"*W*hat?" Vic's eyes were wide with alarm.

Erin looked back down at the neat loops of the handwritten note.

"What is this?" she demanded.

"I don't know. That's really weird," Vic said, shaking her head. "Where did it come from?"

Erin turned the envelope over, but there was no return address. She looked for a postmark, but of course, everything was machine-processed now, and the bar code meant nothing to her.

"I don't know. Maybe Frank knows."

"Who would send such a thing?" Mrs. Peach asked.

It wasn't until then that Erin realized she had read the letter aloud in front of customers. She had been so stunned by the contents of the letter that she had not even thought about them. She had just fastened onto the little verse and read it to Vic without regard to the other people within earshot.

"Oh!" She folded the letter along the original fold lines. "I'm sure it's just a prank. Someone having a bit of fun."

"That didn't sound like a joke," Betty argued. "It sounded like a threat."

"No, not a threat, Edna disagreed. "It said 'I see,' like it is a prediction or vision. That isn't a threat."

"No one can see the future," Mrs. Peach pointed out. "Someone is trying to make trouble."

"Or it is a prank," Erin repeated. "Sometimes people just make things up, try to get people excited."

"They obviously want to stir things up," Vic agreed. "I mean… it says so right in the verse."

Erin looked back down at it, giving a little laugh. "I guess it does," she agreed. "I don't think this is anything to worry about. Just someone playing a game."

"It's not very funny," Betty said. "It's in very poor taste."

"Yes," Erin agreed. She tucked it into her apron pocket. "And I'm sorry I read it out. I wasn't thinking. Did you decide what you wanted to buy?" She directed her gaze to the food inside the display case, hoping to distract everyone from the letter. "Those chocolate chunk cookies are fresh from the oven."

Betty was still scowling about the letter and did not look at the chocolate chunk cookies. Mrs. Peach tried to help.

"Oh, those look very good," she agreed. "Now, what about these? Butterscotch bars? I don't think I've had those before."

"They are delicious," Erin obliged. "Melt in your mouth. I highly recommend them. They have a shortbread crust, and if there's one thing about gluten-free flours, they make great shortbread."

"They sound wonderful," Mrs. Peach agreed. "Do you want some of those, Betty?"

"I want to know who sent that letter. Sending a letter like that is a dangerous thing!"

"Dangerous?" Erin echoed.

"You could incite a panic. People are very impressionable."

Erin thought that "dangerous" was probably a stretch. It might concern some people, but they would quickly see that it was just a made-up prediction.

"What if it really is a vision?" Edna asked. "You can't deny that there are fortune-tellers who can catch glimpses of the future."

"It is not a vision," Betty told her sharply. She was determined to shut down this suggestion. "There is no such thing as clairvoyance."

Edna drew herself up to her full height, which, due to her age, was not great. She stood as tall as her permanently hunched spine would allow, making herself as imposing and authoritative as she could.

"'There shall not be found among you anyone who … practices divination or tells fortunes,'" she quoted. "Why would that warning be in the Bible if there was no such thing as clairvoyance?"

"It means no one should claim to have clairvoyance," Betty shot back. "Not that seeing the future is a real thing."

"That's not what it says," Edna disagreed. "There *is* real clairvoyance, and we are warned against practicing it or having people among us to practice it."

"I don't think we need to worry that a grievance over an old recipe is going to cause bloodshed," Erin said lightly, putting as much humor into her voice as she could. Never mind the recipe book that had recently caused them so much trouble. Or the muffins that had brought death into her sphere more than once. "Now, what can I get you ladies?"

Edna, Betty, and Mrs. Peach eyed each other, but no one stepped forward to continue the argument. Erin nodded, hoping that would be the end of it. She was kicking herself for having read the note aloud without thinking. After all that had happened in Bald Eagle Falls, she should have known better.

"Those butterscotch bars are mighty tasty," Vic prodded.

"I don't know," Betty said, unwilling to give up the conversation yet. "I think we need to be concerned about this threat. Maybe you should call the police, dear."

Erin smiled. "I will take it up with Officer Piper. I'm sure he'll have some good advice on it."

Betty's scowl softened slightly. "He is a fine young man."

"Yes, he is," Erin agreed. "And I'll be sure to tell him you said so."

Betty giggled at that, sounding more like a teen girl than the mature woman she was.

"Everybody loves Officer Handsome," Vic teased.

"Well, he's my Officer Handsome, so everyone else had better just look and not touch."

Vic and Betty chuckled about this. Erin felt that the tension had broken and things would be okay now. The ladies would forget about the letter and its strange prediction, and her faux pas in reading it aloud in front of the customers would be forgiven.

Sometimes, Erin thought he was doing a pretty good job navigating the Bald Eagle Falls social environment. She was getting better at predicting what things would be acceptable or unacceptable to the church ladies. What things were just "not done" in the South. What people expected from her.

And sometimes, she felt like she was still out of her depth, flailing around and trying to stay afloat while people pelted her with more unhelpful rules rather than helping her find her way safely back to shore.

Betty made her selections, and Erin breathed a sigh of relief as she paid for her order and headed for the door. Edna and Mrs. Peach placed their orders without any further comment on the letter's predictions. Once they were on their way with their baking, Erin felt like she was safely ashore again.

She smiled tentatively at the women still waiting to be served. Both were regulars, but not usually inclined to visit or say anything other than a few comments on the weather or Erin's latest new creations in the display case.

"What can I do for you today?" Erin asked Tara Waldon.

Tara was older than Erin, but not as old as Edna and Mrs. Peach. Erin suspected she was around sixty. She had long dark hair and a penchant for bold, bright colors. She looked into the display case, a frown on her face. She glanced at Vic at the cash register, and spoke to Erin in a low voice.

"I really don't think it is appropriate for you to joke around and act so silly, especially about your boyfriend, when *she* has just lost hers."

Erin caught her breath and tried to figure out what to say to this. As far as the rest of Bald Eagle Falls was concerned, Vic's partner, Willie Andrews, who had recently taken up leadership of a local crime family, the Dyson clan, had been assassinated by factions within the clan.

What they didn't know was that the so-called assassination had just been a sham, set up by Willie and a few loyal friends, as a way for Willie to get out of the clan. Willie would remain dead in the eyes of the Bald Eagle Falls residents until Willie felt that Nelson Dyson's leadership of the syndicate was secure and he could afford for it to be known that he had actually left the clan.

So, for the time being, Erin and her best friend and employee had to continue the act that Willie was dead and Vic was deep in mourning.

"Oh…" Erin swallowed. "I'm sorry, Vic. I didn't mean to… make you feel bad."

"You are a nice girl. You should be more careful," Tara told her firmly. "Be more sensitive to her feelings."

Erin nodded her agreement. Vic tried to find a way to move Tara past the topic. "I was joking around too," she said, "It wasn't Erin being insensitive. Sometimes… you just have to laugh. You need something to pull you out of your funk. When my maw-maw died, we went home and put on the silliest, most slapstick movie we could find. It was just the only way to move on."

Tara shook her head, but didn't tell Vic that there was something wrong with her if she was able to laugh about things after her romantic partner was killed. But Erin had the distinct feeling she was thinking it.

"Everyone mourns differently," Vic declared. "I just… want to go on as normal. Sitting around at home isn't going to do anything for me. I need to work. To keep my hands and mind busy with other things. I don't want to just sit at home thinking about Willie all the time."

Especially since Willie was hiding out at Vic's place, and if Vic spent all day there, they got on each other's nerves. It was easier to just follow their regular routine and leave Willie to entertain himself as he had while he'd been going through chelation therapy.

Tara sniffed and turned her attention to the display case. "Well, I do think you are not being very sensitive to your friend's needs," she told Erin. "She shouldn't have to feel like she has to come to work and put on a brave face for everyone."

Erin opened her mouth to object, then changed her mind. She nodded solemnly. "Yes, you're right," she agreed. "We'll need to sit down and have a talk about this. I hadn't thought about it that way."

Tara looked at her for a moment longer, then nodded. "Good," she pronounced. "Now, then... I think I will go with a loaf of multigrain, six dinner rolls, and a pizza shell. And maybe... a half dozen of the butterscotch bars."

"Great." Erin gathered the items and put them into boxes or bags. "And thank you for your advice."

When both women had been served and left the bakery, Erin turned to Vic, shaking her head.

"Am I ever glad that you are *not* mourning Willie. I don't know if I could handle it."

"You did pretty good while we both thought he was dead."

But Erin had been a wreck before Willie had shown up, revealing that he was, in fact, still alive. She couldn't stop crying, set off by seeing her best friend in such pain. She had wanted to hold her, to make her feel better when there was nothing she could do to take away the pain or make it better.

"Don't worry about Tara," Vic said. "Mary Lou said she used to do family dispute mediation. So she is always meddling in other people's relationships, thinking she needs to fix them."

"Really? That would be a tough job."

Vic nodded. "No kidding. I like helping other people out, but couples or family counseling... I don't think I could handle that."

"Was that true about when your Maw Maw died?"

Vic nodded. "Yeah, sure. Sometimes, the only way to stop crying is by laughing. She wouldn't have wanted us sitting around weeping over her. She would have been drinking, cracking jokes, and getting the grandkids together for a game of poker."

Erin laughed. "She must have been some woman."

"She was!" Vic agreed. "And I want to grow up to be just like her."

〜

Chocolate Eclairvoyant, Book #26 of the *Auntie Clem's Bakery Cozy Mystery* series by P.D. Workman can be purchased at pdworkman.com

〜

ABOUT THE AUTHOR

P.D. Workman is a USA Today Bestselling author and multi-award winner, renowned for her prolific output of over 100 published works that span various genres. With a knack for crafting page-turners, Workman captivates readers with everything from cozy mysteries like the Auntie Clem's Bakery series to gripping young adult and suspense novels.

A prolific reader and writer since childhood, P.D. Workman crafts emotionally powerful stories that don't shy away from hard topics. Her books tackle mental illness, addiction, abuse, and trauma with raw honesty and compassion, giving voice to the often unheard. If you crave authentic, character-driven page-turners that hit deep and stay with you long after the final page, you're in the right place.

With each new release, fans eagerly anticipate another thrilling blend of thought-provoking storytelling and relatable characters that define P.D. Workman's brand as an author of unforgettable page-turners—gripping tales that leave a lasting impact long after the last page is turned.

> P. D. Workman, does not shy from probing the deep psychological scars of childhood trauma, mental illness, and addiction. Also characteristic of this author, these extremely sensitive issues are explored with extensive empathy, described with incredible clarity, and portrayed with profound insight.
>
> — —KIM, GOODREADS REVIEWER

Some of Workman's titles have been translated into Spanish, French, Portuguese, German, and Italian.

Workman began writing at an early age and is a prolific reader as well as writer. She is also passionate about teaching and learning, expresses her creativity through art and cooking, and loves exploring the Calgary parks and green spaces where the Parks Pat Mysteries are set. She was a legal assistant for many years and has done extensive charitable work.

Workman was born and raised in Alberta, Canada, and is married with one adult son.

~

Please visit P.D. Workman at pdworkman.com to see what else she is working on, to join her mailing list, and to link to her social networks.

~

If you enjoyed this book, please take the time to recommend it to other purchasers with a review or star rating and share it with your friends!

tiktok.com/@pdworkmanauthor

facebook.com/pdworkmanauthor

x.com/pdworkmanauthor

instagram.com/pdworkmanauthor

amazon.com/author/pdworkman

bookbub.com/authors/p-d-workman

goodreads.com/pdworkman

linkedin.com/in/pdworkman

pinterest.com/pdworkmanauthor

youtube.com/pdworkman

Find P.D. Workman's books at

PDWORKMAN.COM

Scan the QR code below

www.ingramcontent.com/pod-product-compliance
Lightning Source LLC
Chambersburg PA
CBHW030925260626
47169CB00002B/379